DISCARDED
SCONE COLD DEAD

"We can't let this go, Liss," Sandy said.

"What do you suggest we do?"

"Find out who really killed Victor."

"We aren't detectives, Sandy. Let the pros do their job."

"What if Zara's right? What if they decide she did it?"

"Zara?" She spoke sharply to the other woman, hoping to startle her into answering. "Why would they?"

But Zara still wasn't talking. Although the sobs had diminished, tears continued to stream down her pale cheeks.

When Sandy had taken Zara into the guest room to try and get her to rest, Liss went back downstairs. She didn't want anyone in *Strathspey* to be guilty, but even less palatable was her knowledge that, until the killer was caught, all of them were under suspicion.

Gordon Tandy had asked for her assistance and she wanted to help her friends. Two good reasons, she virtuously assured herself, to go out and ask a few questions of her own . . .

Books by Kaitlynn Dunnett

KILT DEAD

SCONE COLD DEAD

A WEE CHRISTMAS HOMICIDE

Published by Kensington Publishing Corporation

SCONE COLD DEAD

KAITLYN DUNNETT

KENSINGTON BOOKS
www.kensingbooks.com

KENSINGTON BOOKS are published by

Kensington Publishing Corp.
119 West 40th Street
New York, NY 10018

All Kensington titles, imprints and distributed lines
are available at special quantity discounts for bulk pur-
chases for sales promotion, premiums, fund-raising,
educational or institutional use.

Special book excerpts or customized printings can
also be created to fit specific needs. For details, write
or phone the office of the Kensington Special Sales
Manager: Kensington Publishing Corp., 119 West
40th Street, New York, NY 10018. Attn. Special Sales
Department. Phone: 1-800-221-2647.

Kensington and the K logo Reg. U.S. Pat. & TM Off.

ISBN-13: 978-0-7582-1646-5
ISBN-10: 0-7582-1646-7

First Hardcover Printing: August 2008
First Mass Market Printing: August 2009
10 9 8 7 6 5 4 3 2 1

Printed in the United States of America

Chapter One

"So," Dan Ruskin said. "Explain this to me."

Liss MacCrimmon shot him an incredulous look. Explain what? The sequence of dance steps that made up a Highland Fling? The years of training that went into creating a professional dancer? Her *life*?

Former life, she reminded herself, and felt a sharp pang in the region of her heart for all she had lost. In a few minutes the lights in the auditorium would dim and the show would begin. Members of *Strathspey*, the company of Scottish dancers Liss had belonged to from the time she was nineteen until a career-ending knee injury forced her into "retirement" seven months earlier, had come to Fallstown, Maine, to perform.

At her urging, Liss reminded herself. This had been her own idea. She'd made all the arrangements to bring the show to the University of Maine's Fallstown campus. Time to suck up any regrets and try to enjoy the evening. Besides, seeing the show from this side of the curtain would bring closure. She hoped.

"Liss?" Dan prompted.

She'd overreacted to his question. He was showing an interest, that was all. Turning her face up to his, Liss forced a smile.

It wasn't really a hardship to smile at Dan Ruskin

under any circumstances. He'd been a childhood friend. Since Liss's return to her old hometown he'd become something more, although she wasn't entirely sure where their relationship was heading. At the moment, they lived in separate houses, each facing the town square in Moosetookalook, a picturesque village just north of Fallstown in the western Maine mountains.

Dan smiled back, showing an engagingly boyish grin. He'd always had that, even when he was a gangly kid who seemed to be all arms and legs. During the ten years Liss had been away, first in a two-year college and then pursuing her career, he'd turned into what one of Liss's friends liked to call "a tall drink of water." He was a pure pleasure to look at— sandy brown hair worn a little too long, eyes the color of molasses, and a lean, well-muscled build. The work he did—construction with his father's company and making custom furniture in his spare time—kept him in shape and gave him the sort of fluid grace Liss associated with lions. Dan Ruskin: king of the jungle.

"What?" The look on his face now was slightly worried.

"Nothing. Just a stray image. You as a big cat."

"You're picturing me as Lumpkin?" Startled, he shifted away, as if he wanted a little distance to take a good look at her. In the process he bumped against the woman sitting on the other side of him. "Sorry, ma'am."

From the row behind Liss and Dan, Sherri Willett stuck her head between them, bringing with her a faint whiff of the flowery perfume she saved for special occasions. Ordinarily, she smelled only of Dove soap and mint toothpaste. "Dan as Lumpkin? Really? When he's biting ankles or when he's catching mice by sitting on them?"

Fighting laughter, Liss tried to rein in the images flooding her mind. Lumpkin was the large yellow neutered tomcat she'd inherited along with her house. Like most felines, he acted as if he owned her rather than the other way around. Sometimes she wasn't too sure but what he had the right of it.

"I said *big* cat, not *fat* cat," she protested.

"No, wait. I can see Dan as a pussycat," Pete Campbell chimed in. He was Sherri's brand-new fiancé, having popped the question just three weeks earlier, on Valentine's Day. Like Liss, Pete had Scottish roots and had long taken an interest in Scottish festivals, Scottish music, and Scottish athletics.

"Meow," Dan said. Then he leaned in to whisper in Liss's ear. "Does this mean I get to sleep with you?"

"On my feet, or curled around my head?" she whispered back, listing two of Lumpkin's favorite spots.

The lighthearted bantering reminded Liss that she was attracted to Dan for more than his looks. He was fun to be with.

He was also steady. Reliable. Safe. She frowned at the last word choice, wondering why she should have thought it, and why such a sterling quality sounded just the slightest bit, well, stodgy.

The life she'd led before returning to Moosetook-alook had been unpredictable. Exciting. Occasionally unsettling and even a little scary. She'd traveled all over the country with a ragtag band of free spirits. She still missed those days and now, right here at home, her old company had come to her. As the lights in the auditorium dimmed to call stragglers to their seats, she finally answered Dan's original question.

"You want to know about *Strathspey*? Think *Riverdance*, only Scottish."

"Yeah, I got that part, but—"

"Shhh! It's about to start." Liss's very mixed feelings about being in the audience instead of on the stage returned in a rush. Dan knew some of what she'd gone through when she'd learned she could never dance professionally again, but he didn't really understand. No one but another performer could grasp what it meant to be denied a means of artistic expression.

As soon as the lights were down, taped music swelled. Just that quickly, Liss was back in the past, waiting in the wings, ready to go on. She could almost smell the rosin that kept their dancing shoes from slipping, and the dust that clung to the theater curtains, and what they still called "greasepaint," even though modern cosmetics had long since replaced old-fashioned stage makeup.

Liss's breath hitched. Someone else was back there now, palms just a bit sweaty, heart racing in anticipation. She forced herself to watch as the curtain rose and a slim blonde of medium height stepped out onto the stage. Her name, according to the program, was Emily Townsend. As Liss once had, she led the rest of the company in the country dance that opened the eighty-minute show.

She was good. Very good. For just a moment, Liss hated her guts.

Then the magic of *Strathspey* caught her in its spell. As well as she knew the production, it still had the power to tug at her heartstrings. Loosely based on stories told by Scots who'd migrated to America, the plot wove together all the traditional Scottish dances— from reels to a sword dance—but they were performed within the tale of a young woman separated from her lover during the infamous "Highland Clearances" of the mid–eighteenth century. At that time, many Scots were deprived of both home and country. Families were rent asunder, friends scattered. In this retelling of history, however, the two sweethearts were reunited. The piece ended happily, with a wedding.

Strathspey was a celebration of Scottish-American heritage, moving and exhilarating. As the first number seguéd into a tune performed by the company's featured vocalist, a soprano, Liss relaxed and began to enjoy her unaccustomed role as a spectator. She'd never fully appreciated how well the dancers looked when seen as a group, or how nicely the occasional song—sometimes in Gaelic, sometimes in English—augmented the visual display. When the lone piper performed "Flowers of the Forest," she had to wipe tears from her eyes.

Without comment, Dan passed her his handkerchief.

Liss had only one bad moment—the point in the program where she had taken the misstep that had ended her career. She caught herself wincing even as Emily Townsend sailed through the routine unharmed.

Of itself, the injury might not have been so disastrous, but it had come on top of years of high-impact activity, all of which resulted in accumulated damage to both knees. In common with other athletes, dancers didn't expect to keep at their profession until a normal retirement age, but Liss had assumed she'd be able to perform until she was in her forties. Her career had ended at twenty-seven.

Oh, stop the pity party! she admonished herself as she rose with the others to applaud at the end of the show. *You've got a new life now.*

As if to prove it, Sherri Willett reached forward again to touch her arm. "I'm so glad you invited us to the show. I've never seen anything quite like that."

"I'm glad you liked it."

"It was wonderful!" Sherri clapped louder as the performers, faces slightly flushed from their exertions but wreathed in smiles, came back out onstage for a final bow.

Apparently the rest of the audience agreed with Sherri's assessment. Someone whistled approval, and from another part of the auditorium, Liss heard the rhythmic stomp of boots, a clear sign of approbation in this part of the world.

When the applause finally died down, Liss turned to collect her winter coat from the back of her seat. Everyone else was doing the same. The March night had been clear and cold when they'd arrived at the campus theater, but there had been the smell of snow in the air. Even those staying for the reception had dressed for the weather and now donned coats, scarves, gloves, and hats over warm and practical indoor clothing.

Standing, Liss towered over her petite blond friend. She was accustomed to that. At five-nine she'd almost always been one of the tallest females around. Half the time she was also taller than most of the males in the vicinity. Dark-haired, dark-eyed Pete Campbell was five-ten but he had a tendency to stoop.

As Dan, who stood a refreshing five inches higher than Liss did, shrugged into his heavy woolen topcoat, she gave herself another little lecture: *Chin up. Smile. Think positive.*

Her nervousness roared back with a vengeance, far worse than the case of jitters she'd suffered through that afternoon. She thought again that she should have found someone to work for her at Moosetookalook Scottish Emporium, the store she co-owned with her aunt, Margaret Boyd. She should have been here in Fallstown to greet the members of *Strathspey* when they arrived on their tour bus. She'd arranged rooms for all of them, but she should have settled them in herself, made sure there were no problems. Instead she'd left them to their own devices.

Sherri would have filled in for her. She worked at the Emporium part-time, when it could be managed around the schedule of her full-time job as a corrections officer and dispatcher at the county jail. Or Liss could have closed up shop for the day. It wasn't as if March was their busy season for walk-in sales. She'd had only one customer all afternoon.

As they made their way out of the auditorium, jostled now and again by the crowd, a blast of cold air reached them through the open outer doors. Had she warned everyone that they'd need warm clothes? Of course she had. And they knew that already. This wasn't the only northern New England gig on their tour.

Stop fussing! she ordered herself. *They didn't need you around earlier.*

In fact, she'd probably have been in the way. Everyone in the company had their own preperformance routine. It did not include taking time to visit with former coworkers. There would be ample opportunity for that now that the show was over.

"You okay?" Dan asked in a voice so filled with concern that she wondered what he'd read in her face.

Liss nodded and continued her silent pep talk as they slowly closed the distance to the exit. She'd survived the first challenge. Only two more to go. Next up was the reception for the entire *Strathspey* company. That shouldn't be too bad. Lots of chatter. Good food. Everyone in a sociable mood. But at the end would come challenge number three. She was taking two members of the company home with her. Two of her dearest friends would be in residence until

Monday morning, when they left on the next lap of their current tour. Liss wondered if she would be able to convince them that she was content with a life in which she stayed in one place, managed a gift shop, and would never again set foot on a stage.

Dan Ruskin was rural Maine born and bred. He'd gone as far as the University of Maine's Orono campus to pick up a bachelor's degree but had returned to Moosetookalook to work for his father right after graduation. He didn't consider himself a hick. He'd attended plays and concerts before . . . but never anything like *Strathspey*. He still wasn't sure what he'd just seen. If pressed, he supposed he'd call it a variety show.

As they walked from the building that housed the theater to the Student Center where the reception was to be held, he watched Liss carefully. At first casual glance she looked just as she always did, a tall, slender, graceful, self-possessed brunette with a flair for wearing scarves and bright colors. Her winter coat was vivid green.

But this evening she was unaccountably nervous. She betrayed herself in little ways—periodically curling a strand of her dark brown shoulder-length hair around her index finger; tugging repeatedly at the bottom of the black velvet vest she wore over a lace-trimmed white blouse. In honor of the occasion she had selected a new outfit from the stock carried by Moosetookalook Scottish Emporium. She wore the blouse and vest with a full-length plaid skirt.

Tartan, he corrected himself. The pattern was called tartan. Personally, he didn't see what the big deal was, but apparently some Scottish Americans got all bent out of shape if you used the P-word.

"You okay?" he asked again, keeping his voice too low for Sherri or Pete, walking just behind them, to hear.

"Just dandy."

It was hard to tell by the security lights that illuminated the pathway, but Dan thought her changeable blue-green eyes looked worried. The too-bright smile and the hint of panic in her voice also betrayed her state of mind.

What was the big deal? She'd worked with most of these people for eight years. Why should she be nervous about seeing them again? She ought to be excited. Happy. Dan was tempted to lump her behavior together with all the other things a man would never understand about the way a woman's mind worked, but something told him the answer wasn't that simple.

The Student Center at the Fallstown branch of the University of Maine had a large function room available for social gatherings. A few months earlier, Dan and Liss had attended their tenth high school reunion there. He hoped this evening turned out better than that one had.

A glance at his companions told him Sherri and Pete were probably thinking the same thing, but Liss clearly had other matters on her mind. The bright lights inside the building showed him that she was worrying her lower lip with her teeth. What next—wringing hands?

"Liss, if you don't want—"

"Hang this up for me, will you?" She slid out of the ankle-length wool coat and just as neatly slipped away from him before he could manage a reassuring touch. By the time he'd located the nearest coatrack and found hangers for Liss's coat and his own less

stylish garment, one of L. L. Bean's Maine Guide
jackets, she'd vanished.

At his questioning look, Pete shrugged. "Said she
wanted to talk to the Scone Lady. Make sure everything is all set with the refreshments."

Janice Eccles, aka "the Scone Lady," was a baker
from the nearby village of Waycross Springs. She spe-
cialized in scones, a particular weakness of Liss's.
Together, Janice and Liss had come up with a new
recipe especially for this reception: cocktail scones.
Dan had sampled the prototype. They weren't bad,
but in his opinion were nothing to write home about,
either. Liss had disagreed. She might not have seen
any of the members of *Strathspey* since she'd left the
company, but she had stayed in touch by phone and
e-mail. She'd sent word to several of her closest pals
that they were in for a new taste treat at the Fallstown reception.

Liss rejoined Dan, Sherri, and Pete some ten minutes later, by which time the function room was filling up nicely. She was just polishing off one of the
flaky pastries, another sign she was nervous. Liss
considered scones the ultimate comfort food.

"Everything in order?"

"Couldn't be better."

"Uh-huh. Listen, Liss—"

"Sandy!" Eyes alight—they flashed more green
than blue—she waved at three members of the *Strathspey* company, two women and a man, who had just
entered at the opposite side of the room. "Zara! Over
here."

The man heard and waved back. He hadn't bothered with a coat and was still in costume—unless he
went around in a kilt all the time. Dan recognized
him, both by his jet-black hair and his outfit, as the

"romantic" lead in the show. From the looks he was getting from the women in the crowd, females apparently found him attractive. He did bear a faint resemblance to Sean Connery in his James Bond days, and Dan had it on good authority—his sister, Mary—that Connery was "to die for."

The two women who accompanied him—Zara and Sandy, Dan assumed—had changed into regular clothing. One, a redhead of the carrot-top variety, wore a short knit dress and high boots that emphasized her long legs. The other had on a more conservative outfit but had topped her plain pant suit with a colorful tartan shawl. Both had an air of sophistication about them.

Liss hurried toward her friends, leaving Dan to follow in her wake. For a moment, as they exchanged air kisses, he had the opportunity to make comparisons. The two dancers were too skinny for his taste, as Liss had been when she'd first come home. She'd filled out in all the right places since she'd been back in Moosetookalook. As far as Dan was concerned, she was just perfect now.

Then she hugged the guy in the kilt.

Dan walked faster. Bracing himself for a couple of hours of chatter on topics he knew almost nothing about, he joined the little group just as Liss broke free of the embrace and turned around to look for him.

"Dan!" She looked flushed, but not with embarrassment. "This is Dan Ruskin, everyone. Dan, this is Fiona Carlson." She indicated the older of the two women. He wasn't good at guessing ages, but Fiona had a strand or two of gray in her light brown hair.

"Hello, Dan," she said in a soft, husky voice.

"We'd be lost without Fiona," Liss went on. "And this is Zara Lowery, one of my house guests."

The redhead startled him by going up on her toes to give him a peck on the cheek. "We've heard a lot about you," she whispered.

"And this is Sandy," Liss said, indicating the man in the kilt.

Dan blinked.

"Alexander Kalishnakof," Sandy said, holding out a hand. His grip was firm, friendly, and brief. "And in case you're wondering about the name, my father was born in Russia but my mother can trace her roots back to Angus the Hammer."

If he noticed that Dan was taken aback by the introduction—to put it mildly—he did not let on.

This was Sandy? The "best pal" Liss had talked so much about? One of the two people staying at her house for the next two nights? Until this moment, Dan had assumed "Sandy" was a woman.

Suddenly all the stories Liss had told him about the two of them took on an entirely new meaning and he felt as if the world had spun off its axis. The conversation around him turned to white noise as Dan tried to tell himself it was ridiculous to feel jealous. If there *had* been anything more than friendship between Liss and Sandy, it was in the past. Besides, Sandy would be leaving Monday morning and Liss would not. She'd stay in Moosetookalook, with him.

He willed himself to relax. Maybe Sandy was gay. That would be good. But even if he was, Dan heartily wished Sandy wasn't going home with Liss tonight. Zara and Fiona as her houseguests would have pleased him much better.

"Dan?" Liss's tone suggested this was not the first time she'd spoken his name.

Belatedly, he realized that Sherri and Pete had joined the group and been introduced, as had a second man wearing a kilt. The stranger toasted him with a nearly empty beer glass. "A pleasure to meet you, my dear chap." He spoke in a British accent so plummy Dan had to wonder if it was real.

"This is Stewart Graham," Liss said. "He's a dancer with the company but he also played that lovely bagpipe solo."

"Lovely" and "bagpipe" were not words that went together naturally in Dan's mind, but he shook hands and mumbled a vague compliment. Stewart was a bit older and a little shorter than Sandy, with a florid complexion and watery blue eyes. Otherwise they were built along similar lines. Dan wondered if there were height and weight requirements to join dance companies. The members of *Strathspey* all seemed to fit the same two sets of specifications, one for males and one for females.

"Go tell Victor how talented I am, there's a good lass," Stewart said when Liss added a few more favorable comments about his musical performance. "According to him I wasn't 'up to par' tonight. If I wasn't such a refined gent, I'd show *him* a birdie!" He sent a glare toward three men, plates heaped high with food, who were standing by the refreshment table on the other side of the room.

Liss groaned at the awful pun and, in an aside to Dan, Sherri, and Pete, identified Victor as Victor Owens, the company manager. "He's the one in the middle, the one gesturing with a half-eaten scone." This portly gentleman, clearly not a dancer, seemed to be lecturing the other two, who just as clearly *were* performers. "He's talking to Charlie Danielstone and Jock O'Brien," Liss continued. "Probably offering a critique of their performance tonight."

"Killing two birds with one scone," Stewart quipped.

"The three of them are pretty much guaranteed to be first in line to get at any refreshments," Liss continued. "Free food is a big draw for anyone in show business, since it's not exactly a profession that lends itself to steady employment or regular meals. Charlie and Jock are living proof of that cliché and they give new meaning to the stereotype of the penny-pinching Scot, too."

"Think Scrooge McDuck," Stewart said, sotto voce.

Liss patted the sleeve of Stewart's green velvet jacket. "Anyway, getting back to your solo—you sounded great to me. I can't imagine why Victor would make such a rude remark."

"Why does Victor do anything?" Stewart gulped down the rest of his beer and excused himself to revisit the cash bar.

Not a bad idea, Dan thought, but he was driving. He settled for offering to get Liss a glass of the white wine she favored.

As the reception wore on and Dan, Sherri, and Pete drifted off to speak with local people they knew, Liss finally relaxed and began to enjoy herself. She hadn't realized how much she'd missed the easy comradery of the *Strathspey* company. Working together, traveling together, they'd had their share of rough spots, but there had also been plenty of good times. Most of all, these people understood what it meant to be a performer.

The troupe numbered thirty in all, including the backstage crew and Victor Owens. Liss wanted to say a word or two to every one of them and chat longer with those she'd been closest to over the years. She hesitated only when it came to approaching Victor. That he'd gone out of his way to insult the company's only piper disturbed her in a way she could not quite define.

In all the years Liss had known him, Victor had usually had a good reason for his actions, even the ones that at first seemed inexplicable. That was why they kept him on as manager. He could find them bookings no one else would have thought of and had kept them solvent—and housed, fed, and paid— through some pretty dicey dry spells.

When she finally took the plunge, Victor was deep in conversation with Emily Townsend. That is, Emily was talking. Victor was making new inroads into the offerings on the refreshment table. Liss planted herself between him and the platters of food to make sure she got his attention.

"Hello, Victor."

"Well, if it isn't our little angel." Victor dabbed at his lips with a napkin before he took a sip from the glass of whiskey Emily had been holding for him. Liss assumed he meant "angel" in the theatrical sense, and his next words confirmed it. "Felt sorry for us, did you? Thought we needed you to convince the local yokels to invite us to this dinky little burg?"

"Victor! Mind your manners!" Emily gave him a playful little slap on the forearm and . . . tittered.

There was no other word for the sound she made. Giggle would have been too dignified. In all other respects, however, Emily Townsend seemed a mature young woman—several years younger than Liss, but exuding the self-confidence of a seasoned performer.

"This is Emily Townsend," Victor said, taking another sip of the whiskey. "Best thing that's happened to this company in a long time. Well, you saw her dance." He reached around Liss to grab another spinach puff.

The implication that Emily was better in her role than Liss had been took Liss aback. Victor had always been a bit irascible, and prone to sarcastic comments when someone screwed up onstage, but he didn't usually go out of his way to be insulting.

Since she'd always found that the best technique for dealing with unwarranted criticism was to ignore it, Liss pretended not to understand the cutting remark. Keeping a smile on her face, she complimented Emily on her performance.

"I'm thinking of giving her Zara's role." Victor smirked at Liss and spoke loudly enough that Zara would be sure to overhear, even with all the crowd noise. Over his shoulder, Liss saw Zara open her mouth, then close it again. She knew as well as Liss did that she was being baited and that if she refused to react, Victor would eventually grow tired of the game.

"Goodness, Victor," Liss said in a mildly reproving tone, "you *are* on a tear tonight. Did someone eat all the mini quiches before you got to them? I ordered them special, you know. I remember how much you liked them." Liss turned to inspect the refreshment table. In fact, there weren't any quiches left, but she suspected that was because Victor had already devoured them all. "Try a cocktail scone." She plucked one up and offered it to him. "It will sweeten your temper."

For a moment he looked almost apologetic. "I have a lot on my mind," he muttered, and took the scone.

"Then it must have been a relief that the show went so well. I thought Stewart's solo was particularly moving."

"Swan song." Victor munched on the scone, devouring it in record time. "He's on his way out. Unreliable. Drinks too much."

Liss couldn't deny the last charge. She'd seen for herself how much beer Stewart had put away in the course of the reception.

"Can't afford to keep anyone around who doesn't pull his weight." Victor took a second scone and bit into it. He gestured at Liss with the remaining portion. "That's *your* fault."

"Mine? How do you figure that?"

"After your knee surgery our insurance premiums went up."

The experience hadn't exactly been cheap for her, either, not with all the copays, but there was no point in telling Victor that. "I lost my career," she reminded him instead.

"You seem to have landed on your feet. I heard about your inheritance."

Liss repressed a sudden temptation to pick up an entire plate of hors d'oeuvres and dump them over his head. Apparently there was no winning with Victor. Not tonight. He might not have had as much to drink as Stewart, but he'd imbibed enough to make him both belligerent and unreasonable. Perhaps having an open bar at the reception had not been one of her better ideas!

"Nice meeting you, Emily," Liss said.

Without another word to Victor, she left the two of them and resumed circulating. It did not take long to find more agreeable companions among the cast and crew. She accepted a bear hug from Ray Adams with good grace. He was a big man in his forties. His nose was big, too—his most prominent feature. His hair was gray at the temples and he had deeply incised laugh lines around his mouth. He'd always been one of Liss's favorite people.

"So, how you doin', Liss?" Ray's voice was a bit on the nasal side, a raspy baritone straight out of New York City. He couldn't speak more than a dozen words without throwing in a rhetorical "y'know?" and his hands automatically went into motion the moment he started talking. "Never figured you for a country girl." His gesture seemed to indicate all of Fallstown.

"If you think a big town like this is the boon-docks, you should see Moosetookalook!"

Too late, Liss realized Dan had come up beside her in time to overhear her flippant remark. He was not smiling. He probably didn't appreciate the criticism of their hometown, but it was too late now to take back what she'd said.

"Dan, this is Ray. He's our stage manager and one-third of our backstage crew. He specializes in running lights on all kinds of systems, some extremely antiquated. He was also the one to provide emergency first aid—ice packs—the night I injured my knee."

Waving off the praise, nodding a greeting to Dan, Ray returned to the one subject Liss wanted to avoid. "You call this a big town? I dunno, Liss. You should pardon the expression, but two days in the back of beyond and I could die of boredom already."

"City boy," she teased him. "Think of it as a chance to catch up on sleep."

Dan, community pride piqued, jumped in with sug-gestions. The Fallstown movie theater offered six screens. There was a potluck supper tomorrow at one of the local churches. And the motel where Ray was staying had cable with NESN.

"NESN?" Ray asked, straight-faced. "Never heard of it."

"New England Sports Network."

Liss kept mum. She knew Ray was just stringing Dan along. He knew perfectly well what NESN was. But he had a point. Not everyone in the company was happy about spending a quiet weekend in rural Maine. Still, they didn't have another booking until Monday evening and it was far less expensive to stay in Fall-

stown than to arrive early and pay exorbitant sums
for an extra night in the Boston area, near their next
gig. Victor, almost as frugal as Charlie and Jock, had
jumped at the chance for two nights at cheaper rates.

Sandy and Zara joined them just as Dan mentioned that the Boston Bruins hockey game would be
televised the next afternoon. Liss headed off Ray's
response—he was *not* a fan of any New England
sports team—and turned the conversation back to what
had been happening among the members of *Strathspey* since she'd last seen them.

Ray recounted a particularly hilarious encounter
with a group of locals during a road trip—what was it
that made some men think a guy in a skirt must be a
sissy? Then Sandy chimed in to tell her about another incident with a similar outcome, except that
he'd ended up with a black eye.

Halfway through the second story, Dan wandered
off. Liss started to call him back, then let him go. It
wasn't as if he didn't know anyone at the reception.

She surveyed the gathering, quietly pleased at its
success. A great many local people had come, in addition to a good number of college students and faculty
members. Liss caught sight of a neighbor, Angie Hogencamp, and her daughter, Beth, at the other side of the
room. Liss had been giving the girl dance lessons
since August and had found the task surprisingly en-
joyable.

A burst of laughter pinpointed Stewart Graham's
location. Good old Stewart—the more he drank, the
worse his puns became. Liss tuned in just long enough
to hear him proclaim that Scottish country dancers
were reel people and had to stifle a groan at hearing
that old chestnut again. None of Stewart's puns were
particularly original and he tended to repeat the
same ones over and over.

"Nice shindig, Liss," Sandy said a short while later, when they found themselves standing together with no one else nearby.

"Yes," she agreed. "Thanks." But she couldn't hold back a sad little sigh.

"What's wrong, kid?" he asked. He was all of three years older than she was, but he'd always called her that. He claimed it was because, during those first few years with *Strathspey*, she'd tended to look at the world through rose-colored glasses.

No longer. That wide-eyed nineteen-year-old innocent had started to grow up a long time ago, and the abrupt end to her career as a dancer had completed the process.

"Kid?"

"I was just daydreaming—wishing there could still be a place for me with the company. A nondancing role, of course. But there isn't. Not unless Victor suddenly decides to resign."

"He'll never do that." Sandy sounded grim. "It would make too many people happy."

Chapter Two

Sherri Willett glanced at her watch. It was getting late and she had a five-year-old son who got up at the crack of dawn. She looked around for Pete, and found him deep in conversation with one of the organizers of the local Scottish festival. Pete competed in some of the athletic events and had a vested interest in when they were to be scheduled. Both Pete and Sherri were deputies with the Carrabassett County Sheriff's Department, she at the jail and he on patrol, and both planned their lives around what shift they were on. It was a crazy schedule in some ways, but did allow for a very long weekend once every three weeks.

Leaving him to it, she wandered back to the refreshment table. Liss had done herself proud. There wasn't a loser in the bunch. Sherri was reaching for one of the crunchy little bacon thingies, since the supply had just been replenished, when someone spoke to her.

"Well, aren't you a pretty little thing," the man said in a slurred voice.

She spared him a sideways glance but didn't respond verbally. He was with the dance troupe, although he wore a plain suit and was clearly not a performer.

Not with that flabby midsection. Victor Something. She remembered that Liss had said he was the company's manager.

Sherri was a little surprised he wasn't at least decked out in a tartan tie. She'd worked part-time at Margaret Boyd's gift shop long enough to know that most people who were into things Scottish flaunted their heritage. Even the ones who wouldn't wear a kilt and sporran tended to have little Scottish lion flags as lapel pins or bagpipe tie tacks.

The man—Victor—took a sip from his glass. It was whiskey by the smell of it. Then he leered at her. When Sherri moved farther along the table, he followed, plucking up bits of food as he went. The servers were still putting out fresh supplies, even though the crowd was starting to thin. Sherri grabbed one of the cocktail scones Liss was so proud of and the man did, too.

"These aren't bad," he said. "I tried a few of them earlier. They have some kind of honey filling."

Sherri bit into hers. Not honey. Not even sweet. She had to force herself to swallow and she quickly discarded what was left of the pastry by chucking it into a convenient trash container. The man didn't seem to be put off by the taste. Or perhaps his scone had a different filling. It disappeared in two bites and he reached for another.

She remembered now that he'd been right here at the refreshment table when Liss had identified him. And later, when Liss had been talking to him, he'd had a blond dancer at his side. The blonde was nowhere in sight now.

"So, sweet thing—what's your name?"

Sherri moved another yard or so away from him. She didn't look his way again, and when there were no heavy footsteps following her she breathed a sigh of relief. Then a burst of song from the other side of the room distracted her. The attempt to render Bobby Burns's lyrics in a Scots accent ended in peals of laughter, equally loud. An odd coughing sound was almost drowned out by the noise of the revelers.

Sherri frowned. The overweight Lothario, gearing up for another try? She told herself not to turn around. She shouldn't even glance over her shoulder at him. Either action would only encourage unwelcome advances. But there was something odd about that cough, and the wheeze that followed it. The hair on the nape of her neck lifted when she heard a strangled, gagging sound.

Sherri looked back, expecting to find him choking on one of the hors d'oeuvres. She was prepared to administer the Heimlich maneuver.

Victor's face was red, his mouth open and gasping, his eyes bulging. He was scrabbling futilely at his jacket pocket.

Shit, Sherri thought. *Heart attack.*

No one else had noticed yet. They were all too busy enjoying themselves. Even as she reached toward him, he collapsed. Sherri knelt at his side, pulling her cell phone from her purse and hitting the button to speed-dial the dispatch center at the jail. At this time of night, the sheriff's department handled emergency calls for the entire county.

Sherri almost lost her grip on the phone as Victor thrashed about on the floor. His flailing hand struck her elbow with painful force. "Donna, this is Sherri," she barked at the deputy who answered. "Send an ambulance to the Student Center ASAP. Possible heart attack."

Victor was still gasping and choking when the blonde who'd been with him earlier reappeared. "Oh my God!" she shrieked. "What happened?"

"Has he got a heart condition?" Sherri asked. In

the mere seconds it took to ask the question, Victor stopped breathing.

Sherri tossed her phone to the blonde, hoping she'd have sense enough to keep the line open, and started CPR. Out of the corner of her eye she saw Pete making a beeline for her and sent up a silent prayer of thanks.

"He's got food allergies," the blonde wailed.

Damn. Realizing that he'd probably been trying to get at an EpiPen, Sherri let Pete take over CPR and shoved her hand into Victor's nearest pocket. She came up empty. She tried the others in rapid succession, but none yielded an epinephrine injector.

This is not good, Sherri thought. If he was severely allergic, he needed a shot, fast, to counteract food-induced anaphylaxis.

Pete continued CPR until the ambulance arrived, but with shocking suddenness Victor moved beyond their ability to save him. When they both stood aside to let the paramedic and the EMT take over, Sherri already knew that whatever Victor had been allergic to had just killed him.

"If only I'd paid more attention," she murmured. "If I'd turned around at that first odd little coughing sound—"

"Guy didn't have epinephrine on him, Sherri." Pete's arm came around her shoulders and he gave her a comforting squeeze. "Not a heck of a lot you or anyone else could have done. Who was he, anyway?"

"Victor Owens," Liss said, coming up beside them. She looked ghastly, and it occurred to Sherri that she must have known the victim well.

"He had a food allergy?"

"To mushrooms," Liss said.

"Mushrooms?" Pete sounded incredulous. "I knew peanuts could be deadly, but *mushrooms*?"

"It's not as common, but . . ." Liss's voice trailed off and she looked down at the body. Seeing was believing.

Sherri hadn't encountered a situation like this before, but she'd read of similar cases. This was the reason peanuts had been banned in so many schools and on most airplanes. They were completely harmless to most people, but absolutely deadly to a select few. Severe allergic reactions were nothing to sneeze at.

Sherri winced at the unfortunate turn of phrase her subconscious had provided. That one was almost as bad as the atrocious puns that guy, Stewart, had been coming up with all evening.

"Mushrooms," Pete said again. "Who'd have thought it?"

"I don't understand," Liss murmured. "There were no mushrooms in any of the refreshments. I made sure of it."

"Did he usually carry epinephrine?" Sherri asked.

"An EpiPen. He always had one on him. And he wasn't shy about letting people know he had to watch what he ate, either. He knew what could happen."

"He was gobbling up everything in sight," Sherri reminded her.

"He trusted me to make sure it was all okay for him to eat." That seemed to shake Liss's composure all over again.

At a loss over how to convince Liss not to blame herself for what had happened, Sherri was glad to see Dan turn up. With him was the punster she'd just been thinking about. Stewart . . . Stewart . . . ? Graham—that was it. Like the cracker. Stewart Graham.

Dan tugged Liss close against his side. Though normally fiercely independent, she looked for once as if she welcomed having someone to lean on. Her arm went around his waist, but her eyes stayed on the body.

Sherri had already searched Victor's pockets. Now she lifted the cloth covering the refreshment table to peer beneath it. It didn't make sense that someone with such a violent allergy would forget, or lose, the one thing that could keep him alive. He didn't seem to have dropped it, though. At least not here.

"What's that in his hand?" the EMT asked.

Sherri leaned forward. "That's a partially eaten cocktail scone."

And he'd just consumed a whole one.

Stewart Graham, beer in hand and staggering a little, took a wobbly step closer to the body and peered down at the bit of food.

"Are you sure he's dead?" someone asked. The older woman. Fiona Something.

"Indeed he is," Stewart Graham proclaimed in a ringing British accent. "Scone cold dead."

Victor Owens's death brought the reception to a sudden and sobering close. Liss stayed until the medical examiner had made it official, but even after Victor's body had been taken away, she was still struggling to come to grips with what had happened.

"One moment he was fine," she murmured, "and the next—"

"We all knew Victor had that food allergy," Sandy reminded her. "He always knew there was a risk he'd have a bad reaction."

"I can't understand how this happened. I took special care that no mushrooms be included in the menu for the reception. I even went so far as to specify that no pan previously used to cook mushrooms should be used in the food preparation. Remember? Victor told us once that he almost died from eating a cheese omelet made in a pan that hadn't been properly cleaned after making one that contained mushrooms and onions."

"If you're blaming yourself, stop it right now," Sandy said. "This was nobody's fault but Victor's. He was careless. Probably left the EpiPen in his motel room."

That did not make her feel any better.

Dan took her arm and steered her toward the exit. "There's nothing more you can do here, Liss. We may as well head home."

"I'm really anxious to see your place." Zara's tone made it clear she was changing the subject. "You've been gushing about it in your e-mails for months now."

Liss produced a faint smile, but her heart wasn't in it. She reminded herself that she'd been looking forward to showing Sandy and Zara around her part of the western Maine mountains. Victor's death wouldn't change that plan, but it had certainly cast a pall over their reunion.

"Give us a hug," Sandy said when Dan went to collect their coats. "You'll feel better."

As they embraced, tears sprang into Liss's eyes. She wiped them away, embarrassed. "He wasn't such a bad guy. He didn't deserve to—"

"Don't dwell on it, Liss. If you'll forgive the platitude, maybe it was just his time."

"It was so *sudden*."

"Kid, there's no good time to kick the bucket. At least it was quick and relatively painless."

He was right. Especially about not dwelling on

what had happened. She couldn't change anything by wallowing in guilt.

"I've missed you," she whispered as she finally eased herself out of Sandy's comforting arms.

Dan cleared his throat. Liss didn't even look at him as he helped her into her coat. Sandy held her attention by saying, "On a much brighter note, I've got a surprise for you, kid."

"Oh, goodie. I love surprises." She managed to coax some enthusiasm into her voice. "What is it?"

"Later. If you're very, very good."

They collected their luggage, which had been left on the company bus, and piled into the five-year-old station wagon that belonged to Liss's aunt.

By unspoken agreement, Victor's name was not mentioned again as they drove north to Moosetookalook through a light snowfall. Sandy told a story about a mix-up in room reservations at a gig in the Midwest two months earlier. Then Zara chimed in with an amusing tale of her own. It wasn't that they were cold or unfeeling about Victor's death, Liss knew. They were trying to take *her* mind off that dismal subject.

They were halfway home before Liss realized that Dan, who was behind the wheel, hadn't said a single word since leaving the Student Center.

Moosetookalook was a small, quiet community—population 1,007—with a picture-perfect town square surrounded, for the most part, by white clapboard houses. A majority of them were no longer one-family homes but rather had businesses on the first floor and apartments above. Liss's house was one of the exceptions. Situated next door to the building that housed Moosetookalook Scottish Emporium, it had a wide front porch and a bay window that looked out over most of the neighborhood.

"It's a Christmas card!" Zara exclaimed in delight.

It *was* pretty, Liss acknowledged, now that a fresh white dusting covered the rusty piles of snow that had been such a blight on the landscape earlier in the day.

Liss unlocked and opened the door and flicked on the lights in her foyer to reveal a flight of stairs off to their right. Lumpkin occupied the second step. All of it. The enormous yellow cat effectively blocked the way up.

"Wow!" Zara exclaimed. "That's some welcoming committee."

"Meet Lumpkin. He came with the house."

"Cute name," Sandy remarked, "but not very flattering."

"My theory is that he was named after a family that appears in some of Charlotte MacLeod's mysteries. His former owner was a big fan."

Liss expected Dan to chime in with a warning about Lumpkin's tendency to bite unsuspecting victims in the ankle—although there had not been such an incident for months now—but he remained silent. She lifted the cat into her arms to get him out of the way, thankful that he'd slimmed down a bit since she'd had charge of feeding him. He'd originally weighed in at twenty pounds. Now he was closer to fifteen, but still an armful. When he kicked her in the stomach, she let him go, giving him a shove toward the living room.

"Why don't you two go on upstairs and settle in?" she suggested. "Zara, you're in the back bedroom. Sandy, hang a left at the top of the stairs and you end up in my spare room. The love seat folds out into a bed."

"No need for that," Sandy said with a grin. "I don't mind sharing one of the big beds."

Liss distinctly heard Dan's teeth grind together.

"Come back down when you're ready for cocoa," she called after her two houseguests. "I just want to say good night to Dan."

Liss waited until Sandy and Zara reached the second floor before she turned to look at him. She'd never before seen such a surly expression on his face. "What on earth is bugging you?"

"That spare room connects to yours."

"So?"

"So just where is your good friend Sandy *really* going to sleep tonight?"

"With Zara, I presume." Liss felt her eyes widen as she finally caught on. "You thought he was planning to sleep with *me*? Get a grip, Dan. Sandy and I are friends. I've told you tons of stories about scrapes we got into on the road. How could you possibly—"

"I *thought* Sandy was short for Sandra, not Alexander. It's not that easy to shift gears." He looked away, then back at her. "I was kind of hoping the guy would turn out to be gay."

"Well, he's not."

That seemed to set him off all over again. "You know this from personal experience?"

"That is none of your business!" How could she possibly explain what she had with Sandy? She could hardly say they'd "dated." Surely that was a misnomer when two people traveled together with a troupe of dancers for months on end.

"I thought we were in a relationship, Liss."

"That does not give you the right to question me about my friends." Exasperated, she jerked open the closet door to hang up her coat. "I don't even know why we're having this discussion. This is so high school!"

"You called him your 'best pal.' Exactly what does that mean?"

"You're out of line, Dan." Besides, he didn't deserve an answer if he thought so poorly of her that he'd assume she'd sleep with someone else at the same time she was involved with him.

"I just want—"

"Oh, for goodness' sake! Dan, go home. Come back when you decide to have a little faith in me." Put out at his attitude, angry with herself for arguing with him about it, and suddenly completely exhausted from a long, harrowing evening, she opened the front door, shoved him through it, and slammed it shut behind him. She could still see him through a side panel. He didn't move until he heard her lock the dead bolt with a resounding click. She flicked off the outside light, plunging the porch into shadow, just as he started to turn her way.

Liss leaned her forehead on the door, resisting the temptation to bang her head against the wood. *Dan* was the one who needed some sense knocked into him.

"Trouble in paradise?" Zara asked from the stairs.

"Nothing that won't blow over when he's had a chance to come to his senses." She hoped.

As far as Liss was concerned, her relationship with Dan Ruskin was still at the fun, getting-to-know-you-better stage. She was a long way from being ready to plan a future together and she had no idea where this ridiculous jealousy had come from. What really hurt, though, was that he didn't automatically trust her.

She led Zara past the open living room to their left and the closed doors of closets and a bath on the right, down a narrow hall, and into the kitchen. It took up the entire back end of the house and included a dining area. This was the room in which Liss had made the greatest number of changes since moving in. New appliances had been a must—the ones al-

ready there had been at least forty years old—and
she'd splurged on a small wooden drop-leaf table and
four chairs because Dan had assured her the work-
manship was excellent. The walls, those not taken
up by cabinets, were decorated with framed prints of
various cooking herbs set off by the pale green wallpaper she'd hung herself.

"There used to be a formal dining room," Liss remarked as she ran water into a large glass measuring
cup, "but the last owner decided she'd rather have a
combination library and office. She closed off the
doors that opened into the kitchen and the hall, and
now the only entrance is through the living room."

"It's a great house." Zara gravitated toward the
back door, which looked out across a narrow strip of
land at Moosetookalook Scottish Emporium. "Does
your aunt live above the store?"

"She has an apartment there, yes, but at the moment she's visiting my parents in Arizona."

Liss put the water in the microwave to heat and collected packets of hot chocolate and mugs, taking
them to the table. Some of the troupe preferred a night-
cap after a performance, but she and Sandy and Zara
had usually opted for a soothing drink of the nonalco-
holic type. So much for the sophisticated image!

Lumpkin wandered into the kitchen just as the timer
on the microwave dinged. He jumped a good foot
and came down wild eyed, claws extended, and the
fur on his tail puffed up to twice the size it had been.

"Settle down, Lumpkin," Liss told him.

"Nervous for such a big lug."

"He has his little quirks. Try to avoid sneezing if
he's in the room. That startles him, too." She finished pouring the water into the mugs and got out a
cat treat. Panic attacks never seemed to dull Lumpkin's appetite.

Sandy appeared just as Liss joined Zara at the table. He'd changed from the kilt into a comfortable fleece sweat suit that was the twin of Zara's.

Liss lifted a brow as she looked back and forth between them. "Cute."

He grinned and took a moment to absorb his surroundings before he turned one of the remaining chairs backward and straddled it. "You've done all right for yourself, Liss MacCrimmon," he said as he reached for the steaming mug on the place mat. "I knew you'd bounce back."

"Even when I hit the floor of the stage with a splat?"

"Even then."

"So, what's this surprise you promised me?"

Sandy reached across the table to take Zara's hand. She always wore rings, when she wasn't onstage, but the gesture called Liss's attention to a new one.

"We're getting married," Sandy announced, fingering the square-cut emerald. "In two months. And we want you to be in the wedding party."

"We had to flip a coin," Zara said over Liss's delighted congratulations, "to decide which one of us you'd stand up with. I won. You'll be wearing a dress instead of a kilt."

As they sipped hot chocolate, the conversation slowly turned from wedding plans back to *Strathspey*. "So, how did we look from out front?" Zara wanted to know.

"Pretty darned good. I have to tell you, though, that it was strange seeing someone else dance my part."

"Emily's not bad," Sandy conceded. "Sarah was better, though."

"Sarah?"

"The first dancer Victor hired to replace you."

"I thought Emily was—"

"No, she came in when Sarah left, at about the same time you sent word that you wouldn't be back at all."

"So this Sarah was just hired as a temp?"

Sandy and Zara exchanged a glance. Then Zara shrugged. "I never was a believer in 'speak no ill of the dead.' She would have been your permanent replacement if Victor hadn't told her she'd have to sleep with him to get the job. She smacked him upside the head, accused him of sexual harassment, and threatened to bring formal charges against him. I'm not sure what changed her mind."

"I guess I'm not surprised," Liss said. "Victor made a pass at me shortly before my accident. That was just after you broke up with him, Zara."

"I swear I don't know what I ever saw in the man, although he could be charming when he wanted to. He didn't pressure me into a relationship, in case you're wondering." She reached for Sandy's hand and he gave her fingers a reassuring squeeze. "But after it was obvious Sandy and I were developing feelings for each other, Victor went out of his way to make things difficult for us on the road. We've been considering leaving *Strathspey*."

"I don't understand. Victor was always a pain, but he wasn't petty."

"He'd been under a lot of pressure," Zara said. "My guess is that the company is on shaky ground financially."

"Has attendance fallen off?"

"Not so's you'd notice, but expenses are up. Gas for the bus, for instance."

And rates for health insurance, Liss thought, remembering Victor's complaint. "I can sympathize. I've learned more about finances than I ever wanted to know since I started running the gift shop. My aunt was barely making ends meet before we restructured her mail order business and made the entire inventory available online."

Encouraged by questions from Sandy and Zara, Liss talked a bit about what she'd done to turn the business around. She hoped she didn't sound as if she were boasting, but she was extremely pleased with the success she'd had so far.

Sandy took a thoughtful bite out of one of the molasses cookies he'd found by foraging in her cupboards. "Sounds like you might be able to work the same magic on *Strathspey* if you were to step in as manager."

"You did say you'd love a chance to come back," Zara reminded her.

"Well, yes, but—"

"Someone's going to have to take Victor's place."

She temporized. "It seems a little callous to talk about this now."

"The man's dead. The show isn't," Sandy said bluntly. "Not yet."

They were watching her intently, making Liss extremely self-conscious. Then a yellow paw appeared over the edge of the table. It patted the surface, reached farther, found the plate with the cookies, and had almost snagged one when Liss tapped it lightly with one finger.

"Bad boy, Lumpkin."

"Does he do that often?" Zara asked.

"Every chance he gets. And anything he finds goes straight into his mouth. Even lettuce. Even, once, a pearl onion. He spit that back out, though." Liss glanced at the clock, then stood and collected their mugs, dumping them in the sink to deal with after she'd slept. "I don't know about you folks, but I've just hit the wall."

Sandy and Zara exchanged a look but they didn't say any more about Victor's job. Liss knew she'd made her point—she wasn't prepared to make any decisions tonight.

Ten minutes later, they had all retired, but the sleep Liss craved was slow in coming. What Sandy had proposed intrigued her. She wasn't sure why she'd hesitated. They were right. She had been looking for just such an opportunity . . . before she'd settled into life in Moosetookalook.

What she'd said at the reception had been a holdover from those first days here, when she was still mourning her lost career. Things were different now. As much as she might enjoy returning to the road, it would not be the same. She wouldn't be dancing again. She'd be handling the business end of things, just as she was in Moosetookalook. Where she was settled. Productive. Content.

Besides, she had responsibilities to her aunt, to the shop, to Lumpkin. She refused to add Dan into the equation, but even without him, and in spite of a certain wistful longing to return to what had been, Liss told herself she was happy in her new life. Wasn't she?

Three hours after Liss, Dan, and everyone else had left the Student Center, Sherri Willett was still in the building. With Pete's help and that of a campus security officer, she was meticulously searching every nook and cranny.

She was playing a hunch. There had been something distinctly odd about Victor Owens's death. That's why she'd grabbed the plate with the remaining cocktail scones and suggested to the Fallstown police officer who'd shown up to take charge of the scene that its contents, and the scone Owens had been eating when he died, be analyzed. She'd tasted one herself and could well believe that the filling had contained mushrooms.

But who made scones with mushrooms? Nobody, that's who.

Sherri was no great shakes in the kitchen, but Liss's experiments with making her own scones over the last seven months had taught her friend a thing or two about the ingredients that went into that particular flaky pastry. She wished Mrs. Eccles, "the Scone Lady," hadn't left the reception before Owens died, but Sherri was certain she wouldn't have put mushrooms into her scones, either, especially after Liss had specifically told her, and all the others who'd provided food for the reception, that one of the guests was allergic to them.

"We've looked everywhere," Pete said, breaking into her thoughts. He sounded tired and a trifle exasperated.

The campus security officer looked bored, but he pointed to an alcove Sherri would otherwise have missed. "There's one more office off there."

"Think maybe you might be taking that online course of yours a bit too seriously?" Pete had to stifle a yawn halfway through asking the question.

"No."

And thank God she'd signed up for it. She'd learned more about investigative techniques in the last couple of months than she'd ever dreamed possible. Most of it was plain hard work and boring to boot, but it had to be done. In the end it usually yielded results.

"If there's nothing here," she said, "then I want to go to the motel where he was staying."

"I doubt they'll let you into his room, and they certainly won't let you search any of the others."

"Then I'll go through the Dumpsters." She tried the office door and to her surprise found it was unlocked. She went in, flicking on the light. Pete and the security guard stayed in the hall, since there was barely room for one person to turn around inside the cubicle.

Sherri heard the guard mumble something about watching too many crime dramas on television.

"Yeah," Pete agreed.

Traitor! Ignoring both of them, she peered into the wastepaper basket beside the desk.

"Not every death is a murder," Pete added in a louder voice—a blatant attempt to convince her to give up the search.

"But some are," Sherri murmured. "Uh, Pete?" She raised her voice as she lifted the receptacle. "You want to come in here and take a look at this?"

Chapter Three

L iss was barely awake the next morning when her doorbell rang. Deciding what to wear had been beyond her when she'd rolled out of bed twenty minutes earlier, so she'd thrown on the brightly colored silk caftan Dan had once said made her resemble a circus tent.

That hadn't been the look she'd been going for, but the comment made her smile every time she remembered it. She could count on Dan to be up-front with her. That was a good thing. Wasn't it?

Liss had not passed a peaceful night. Every time she closed her eyes, an instant replay began. First it had been of that ridiculous quarrel with Dan. Then she'd been back at the reception, watching helplessly as Sherri and Pete tried to revive Victor Owens. She felt a nagging sense of wrongness about the way Victor had died. It should not have happened, especially not on her watch.

Liss knew it was absurd to feel guilty about his death. She'd done everything she could to keep mushrooms off the menu. Nor was it her fault that Victor had evidently forgotten to carry an EpiPen. But he'd died at a function she'd arranged. She couldn't help thinking that there might have been something she could have done to prevent the senseless accident that had taken his life.

Was it any wonder that the idea of taking his place with the company no longer appealed to her?

The ringing changed to banging.

"Coming!" Liss fumbled with the chain, the dead bolt, and the brass key in the old-fashioned lock beneath. Nothing worked right with only an ounce or two of caffeine circulating through her bloodstream. She hadn't managed to consume more than a few sips from her first mug of coffee of the day.

A blast of icy air swirled inside when she jerked the door open. A man wearing a ski jacket open over a sports coat and dark slacks stood on her porch. He was holding up a badge, as if he expected her to ask to inspect it before she let him in. "Amaryllis Mac-Crimmon?"

"Yes?" She wrapped her arms around herself, but that didn't stop a chill from running up her spine. She suddenly wished she'd taken the time to look through the side windows first. Then she might have been able to pretend she wasn't home.

"I'm State Police Detective Gordon Tandy. I wonder if I might talk to you for a few minutes. It's about the incident at the Student Center last night."

Liss hesitated. It seemed odd to her that the state police would interest themselves in an accidental death, but she told herself there must be formalities to go through when the deceased had been a visitor to the area and had no family near at hand. She wasn't sure how much help she'd be. She had no idea where to find Victor's next of kin.

"Come in out of the cold, Detective Tandy." As she said his name, it belatedly rang a bell. "Tandy's Music and Gifts?"

"My brother's place." His glance strayed next door

to Moosetookalook Scottish Emporium. "Ah. I should have guessed. You're the little girl who used to win all the dance competitions."

Liss frowned at the "little girl" part as he moved past her into the foyer. "And you're one of the bagpipe-playing Tandy brothers. Small world."

She studied him as he shrugged out of the ski jacket. She knew he must be at least a dozen years older than she was, but he didn't look it. He had the kind of face that made people think "boy next door" at any age. The body wasn't bad, either.

Liss decided she must be more sleep deprived than she'd thought if she was ogling a strange man at this hour of the morning. That didn't stop her from admiring the thick, reddish brown hair Tandy revealed when he took off his hat. He wore it trimmed very short, a good match for his almost military bearing.

Definitely *not* her type!

"This way," Liss said when she'd hung his coat and hat in the closet, and led the way to the kitchen. Lumpkin, she noticed, was still sound asleep on top of the refrigerator. "Coffee?"

"That would be great. Thanks."

His smile was warm, and there was something in his eyes—so dark a brown that they almost looked black—that made Liss think he might disagree with Dan's opinion of the way she looked in the caftan.

She found the notion that he thought her attractive an agreeable one, but suspected it was a delusion induced by lack of caffeine. "You'll have to forgive me if I'm not too coherent yet," she apologized as she reached for the coffeepot. "It was a late night and I'm not fully awake. I have two houseguests. Members of the dance troupe. Do you want to talk to them, too?"

"I'd like to ask you a few questions first. Alone."

Something in his tone sounded ominous. Frowning, Liss filled another mug and topped off her own. She gestured toward the table, brought the coffees over, and took a chair for herself.

"Victor Owens's death was not an accident," Tandy said as soon as he was seated.

Liss heard what he said but her mind refused to take it in. "He had food allergies—"

"Yes. And that's how he was killed. There was mushroom filling in the scone he was eating just before he died."

Very slowly, Liss lowered her coffee mug. The small sip she'd taken had turned to acid in her mouth. With an effort, she swallowed. "That's impossible. The cocktail scones Janice Eccles supplied were made with sweet fillings. And she knew about Victor's mushroom allergy. Everyone who supplied food for the reception knew. I told them myself. None of them are idiots. They know how careful they have to be about things like that."

"As I said, this wasn't an accident. Our best guess right now is that someone slipped a batch of their own scones in with Mrs. Eccles's creations."

"You're saying someone *murdered* him?"

"I'm saying someone murdered him."

For a moment Liss didn't say a word, although several unprintable ones were whirling around in her head. Victor's death had been bad enough, but this . . .

Tandy cleared his throat. "There's more. It doesn't appear to have been just a tragic oversight on Mr. Owens's part that he didn't have epinephrine on him when he needed it. An EpiPen was found in a wastepaper basket in the Student Center, wiped clean of fingerprints."

"Good Lord!" In her pleasant kitchen, redolent with freshly brewed coffee, Liss found this new revelation even harder to accept than the idea that someone had deliberately planned Victor's death. She toyed with the nubbly edge of her place mat, trying to wrap her mind around what Gordon Tandy was telling her. She didn't want to believe him, but what choice did she have? He wouldn't be here if it weren't true. Victor had been murdered.

"I understand you knew the victim fairly well," Tandy said.

"I worked for him for about eight years, if that's what you mean. He was the manager of *Strathspey*."

"Did you get along with him?" Tandy did not have a notebook out or a tape recorder turned on—unless it was small enough to be hidden in his jacket pocket—but Liss had the feeling he was keeping close track of everything she said. He drank his coffee, watching her over the rim of the bright green ceramic mug.

"Most of the time. He was . . . temperamental." She leaned closer to the table. "This doesn't make any sense. Victor could be a pain in the ass, okay? And he came on too strong with women sometimes. Not exactly politically correct. But I can't think of a single reason why anyone would want to *kill* him."

"You may know more than you think, Ms. Mac-Crimmon. After all, you are familiar with all the members of the dance company."

She'd been afraid that was where he was going with this. "You think one of them murdered Victor?"

"I think that's a more likely explanation than it having been a random act by someone local who'd never met him before last night."

He had a point.

Tandy set his empty coffee mug aside. "I'll level with you, Ms. MacCrimmon. My predecessor here in Carrabassett County did not cover himself with glory investigating the last murder in these parts. You, on the other hand, came up with several viable leads and eventually discovered the killer's identity."

She grimaced. "I didn't have much choice. Your idiot of a predecessor was convinced I was the one he was after. He didn't look for anyone else." In retrospect, Liss wished she hadn't, either. She hadn't liked what she'd found.

Then those compelling dark eyes locked on hers. "I don't intend to make the same mistakes he did, and it has been suggested to me, by the person who had the foresight to look for the missing EpiPen, that you may be able to help me avoid some of them."

A harsh jangle from the wall phone interrupted Tandy in midpitch.

"Excuse me," Liss said, and grabbed it on the second ring.

Fiona's voice, agitated, exploded in her ear. "Do you have any idea what's going on?" she demanded. "I'm getting the runaround from these people. They won't let me have Victor's body."

"They're probably still trying to locate next of kin."

Tandy's eyes narrowed when he overheard Liss's words.

"He had no kin left," Fiona said. "Look, all I want is to arrange for a memorial service on Monday morning so we can all attend before we leave."

"Fiona, I'm going to give you to a state police detective. His name is Gordon Tandy." She put her hand over the receiver. "This is Fiona Carlson." As Fiona was the senior member of the company, it made sense she'd be filling in for Victor to handle practical details. She'd helped out before with bookkeeping, scheduling, and other management tasks.

Liss refilled both her coffee mug and Tandy's

while he explained the situation to Fiona. She heard him tell Fiona it would be helpful if she could make arrangements for the troupe to stay in the area longer. Liss expected he'd get an argument about that, but to judge by the one side of the conversation she could hear, Fiona readily agreed to cancel Monday night's show in Lowell, Massachusetts.

After asking Fiona not to tell anyone yet that Victor had been murdered—he wanted to break that news to each individual himself—Tandy handed the phone back to Liss. She assured Fiona she could make arrangements to hang on to the rooms the members of *Strathspey* currently occupied. It made sense for her to handle that, since she'd been the one to make the reservations in the first place.

"Was Ms. Carlson close to Victor Owens?" Tandy asked when she hung up.

"Not the way *you* mean. They worked together."

"Okay. No romantic overtones. So noted. That's the sort of information it's helpful for me to have. I can get personnel records but you're acquainted with these people. You can help me understand them. You may even be able to persuade them to be honest with me if they're inclined to leave out a detail or two."

For a moment Liss just stared at him. All the air seemed to have been sucked out of the room. Her chest felt tight. "You want me to . . . ? *What* do you want me to do?"

"You'd be a liaison."

"And that entails what?"

Tandy produced a spiral-bound memo pad from the inside breast pocket of his sports coat and flipped it open to a list of names—the members of *Strathspey*. "For starters you can identify each of these people and tell me how they got along with the victim."

"So what you really want is a snitch. And maybe later a spy?" Clearly he saw her as a source of inside information. He expected her to dish the dirt on her former colleagues. The suffocated feeling was replaced by a hot spark of resentment. He was trying to manipulate her into betraying her friends.

"It's in everyone's best interests to clear this up quickly," Tandy said, his tone reasonable. "You'll be doing these folks a favor if you help me rule them out one by one."

Liss stalled by taking another sip of her rapidly cooling coffee. Maybe she shouldn't jump to conclusions. In theory, Tandy was one of the good guys—she'd give him the benefit of the doubt about that.

A rhythmic thump intruded on her internal debate. She recognized it at once—Lumpkin, playing with the cabinet doors above the refrigerator. He liked to use his paw to pry them open an inch or two, then let them thud closed on their own.

Gordon Tandy's attention had also been caught by the sound. He grinned when he spotted Lumpkin. "Does your cat do that a lot? Clever kitty."

Liss glanced up. "Wait a minute and he'll prove you wrong."

True to form, Lumpkin tired of the first set of cabinet doors and reached over to try his luck with the one to the side of the refrigerator. This time nothing happened. He was trying to open the hinged edge.

"He hasn't been able to figure out what he's doing wrong," Liss said. "That's the only thing that gives me hope that he's not really smarter than I am."

Abruptly tiring of the game, Lumpkin hopped down from his perch and, ignoring both humans, left the room. Liss sighed. She'd welcomed the distraction. Now she had no choice but to once more focus on the reason Gordon Tandy was sitting in her kitchen and drinking her coffee.

Had someone she knew deliberately poisoned Victor? Had one of her friends taken advantage of the reception she'd arranged to carry out premeditated murder?

Liss tamped down a spurt of anger at the thought. If it was true, she wanted that person caught and punished. She didn't have any alternative but to help the police because she was partly responsible for what had happened to Victor. She'd provided the killer with the opportunity to take a life.

There was a second reason to cooperate with Gordon Tandy, too. The longer his investigation dragged on, the worse things would be for everyone in the troupe. Even now, Fiona was canceling their Monday night performance. Sandy had told her that *Strathspey* was booked solid for several weeks after that. What happened if the police weren't satisfied with their answers? Would they be allowed to resume the tour or would they have to miss even more shows?

If the company's financial situation was as bad as Sandy and Zara seemed to think, *Strathspey* couldn't afford to take that route. Lost revenues combined with refunding what they'd been paid in advance would ruin the company in record time.

Liss held out a hand. "Let me see that list."

Tandy slid it across the tabletop. "She said you'd want to help."

"She?"

"Officer Willett. She's the one who realized the death was suspicious. And the one who thought to look for the EpiPen in the Student Center." Gordon Tandy's smile was a real heart-stopper. "Seemed to me, when she suggested recruiting you to assist in our inquiries, that I'd do well to listen."

* * *

On Sundays, Dan Ruskin worked at The Spruces, the hotel his father was renovating. It had been a landmark in Moosetookalook when it first opened in 1890, sitting on a little hill above the town and providing jobs for fully half the residents. By the time it had celebrated its hundredth anniversary, however, like so many other "grand hotels," it had retained only a faint echo of past splendor. Later, standing empty in all its faded glory, it had seemed likely to fall victim to a fire caused by mice chewing on matches, or to be bought by a developer, leveled, and replaced with condominiums.

That's when Joe Ruskin, owner of Ruskin Construction, had stepped in. He'd worked at the hotel one summer forty years earlier and fallen under the spell of the place. He was determined to restore as much as possible of the building to its former grandeur and once again open it as a destination resort.

The project was a labor of love, worked at in every spare moment by Joe and his two sons, Sam and Dan. The money for the project came out of Joe's pocket, from local investors who believed the hotel could rejuvenate the economy of the entire community, and from a few small historical preservation grants. Somehow, they were scraping by. If their luck and the money didn't run out, the hotel would reopen on Fourth of July weekend, less than four months away.

Dan was thinking about that as he gently removed layers of varnish from the decorative ceiling molding in the second-floor ballroom. Taking it down to work on would have been easier, but the wood might have split if they'd tried.

He was distracted from the task, and his thoughts, by the faint hum of an approaching vehicle's engine.

Curious, since they weren't expecting anyone else to show up this morning, Dan gave the section he'd been working on one final swipe, descended the ladder, and headed for the nearest window. When he recognized Pete Campbell's pickup truck, he raised the sash and leaned out.

"Hey, Pete! Up here. Take the main stairs and hang a left."

Pete signaled that he understood and a few minutes later stepped into the room. He gave a low whistle. "You've done a lot since the last time I swung by. Lookin' good."

"Thanks. What brings you out this way? You know if Dad sees you you're likely to be roped into wielding a paintbrush."

Pete looked uncomfortable. "You talk to Liss today?"

"No." The one-word answer sounded a bit abrupt, even to Dan's own ears, but he let it go. It was none of Pete's business that he'd made a fool of himself last night.

"Then I guess I'd better fill you in."

By the time Pete was done, Dan had forgotten all about the stripping he'd planned to complete that day. "Please tell me they don't suspect Liss."

"Not this time, but you're not going to like what *is* going down much better. I'm not too thrilled about it myself, but I swear I didn't know what Sherri was up to until it was too late to stop her."

"You said she talked to the state police, to the detective who covers this area." He knew they'd transferred the officer who'd been in charge the previous summer. Good thing, too. He'd been an incompetent jerk.

"Right. And she says he seems to know what he's doing. He actually thanked Sherri for sticking her nose in, and he took the suggestion she made about Liss."

"This is the part I'm not going to like, right? What did Sherri suggest?"

"That Liss could help with the investigation. Because she knows all the likely suspects pretty well. And the victim, too. And Tandy went for it. That's the detective—Gordon Tandy. He's from over to Waycross Springs originally. Used to be on the police force there before he went to work for the state."

The name meant nothing to Dan, but he was ready to take a piece out of the guy for even thinking of putting Liss on the spot. She'd almost been killed meddling in murder last year. He didn't want her getting involved in something so dangerous again.

Dan shook his head. Like he'd have anything to say about it! Especially after that fiasco last night. He could hardly go charging in this morning to lecture Liss about being careful.

"Maybe she'll turn him down. She won't want to rat out her friends."

"Maybe." Pete sounded doubtful. "But what if Sherri won't let this one go? She and Liss are pretty tight."

"What are you talking about? Just because Sherri's the one who found that evidence—"

"She looked in the first place because she was upset at not being quick enough to figure out what was wrong with the guy. She couldn't save him. Guess she figures she owes him to find out why he died. And she's been taking that course in criminal investigation . . ." His voice trailed off and he shrugged. "Being a corrections officer at the jail is a dead-end job. And boring. Sherri wants to go on the road. Be a patrol deputy like me. Anyway, she's been learning about crime scenes and something didn't feel right to her. Guy like that, she figured, doesn't just forget the antidote he needs to save his own life. So we hunted and she found it."

Dan heard the note of pride beneath the frustration.

"Trouble is, now that she's got the bit between her teeth, I'm afraid she's gonna run with it."

An hour after Detective Tandy's arrival, when Sandy and Zara wandered into the kitchen in search of coffee and breakfast, Tandy's notebook was closed, he was on a first-name basis with Liss, and the two of them were laughing over a mutually remembered incident involving the escape of some sheepherding dogs at a Scottish festival they'd both attended. The dogs had encountered the Clan Chattan mascot, a rather formidable-looking, though tame, Scottish wildcat, and discovered that cats, domestic or otherwise, tend to resist being herded.

"What's up?" Sandy asked.

Liss's stomach lurched. For a little while there she'd forgotten what it was Gordon wanted her to do. When they'd been talking about Scottish festivals and bagpipe competitions, she'd almost been able to ignore the fact that he was also a detective. They'd simply been two people with common interests. They'd discovered they had a good many mutual acquaintances, both in Carrabassett County and around the country.

It was a jolt to come back to the present and remember what had brought *Detective* Tandy to her door. "Victor was murdered," she blurted.

Zara almost dropped the mug she'd just filled. Hot coffee sloshed over the sides and onto her hand, making her gasp.

"You okay?" Sandy asked, reaching for her.

"I'm fine." Hastily cleaning up the spill on the countertop, she doctored her coffee with artificial sweetener and nondairy creamer and took a seat at the table. She smiled at Gordon Tandy. "Hi. I'm Zara Lowery. I'm guessing we're all suspects, right?"

"Yes, ma'am. For the moment."

Sandy remained standing, one hip propped against the kitchen counter, as he sipped coffee from a mug that was the twin of Zara's. "Maybe you should fill us in. Last we knew, Victor's death was an accident."

While Gordon obliged, Liss watched Zara. The other woman listened in tight-lipped silence, her fingers clutching the handle of the coffee mug as if it were a lifeline.

"I need to talk to each member of *Strathspey* separately," Gordon said when he'd given them the bare essentials. "I know what happened, but I don't know who was behind it or why. I'm hoping you can help me figure that out."

Liss offered them the use of the library and led them along the hall and through the living room to the book-lined room. Lumpkin was sleeping on a cushion on a high shelf. He opened one suspicious eye when they walked in, then ignored them.

"Ladies first?" Gordon waved Zara toward the room's most comfortable chair. Then he ushered Liss and Sandy back into the living room before he closed the library door.

"I don't like this," Sandy muttered.

"He's just doing his job. He's got to ask questions in order to find out what happened. And I've got to make some phone calls. Fiona asked me to arrange for rooms for another night. It's going to take a while for the police to question everyone."

Three brief conversations later, Liss had completed her assignment. The members of *Strathspey* could remain where they were until Tuesday morning. She sincerely hoped this would all be settled by then.

"Someone murdered Victor," Sandy said as Liss plunked herself down beside him on the living room sofa. He shook his head. "Unbelievable."

"He pissed off a lot of people." She shifted on the cushion, curling her legs beneath her and turned so she could see Sandy's face.

"Well, yeah, but to kill him like that . . . I mean, I can see one of us—me, even—hauling off and slugging him if he went too far. But this? This was . . ."

"Premeditated?" Liss suggested.

She understood what he was saying. He wasn't exactly grieving for Victor Owens, but even the nastiest people didn't deserve to die before their time, and to kill in such an underhanded manner seemed particularly vicious. The person responsible must not be allowed to get away with the crime, no matter who he or she was.

"What's he doing in there?" Sandy glared at the library door. "How many questions can he possibly have for her?"

When Liss didn't answer, he turned an accusing gaze on her.

"Don't look at me like that!" Her hand clutched in the soft wool of the afghan thrown over the back of the sofa. "I know it's frustrating waiting in the wings, but I'm sure Gordon isn't giving her the third degree."

"What did you tell him about her?"

"The truth, with no elaboration. She *did* have a relationship with Victor, Sandy."

"And now she's engaged to me."

"I told him that, too, and that you'd been making tentative plans to leave *Strathspey* because Victor was being such an ass."

"Crap."

He might have said more, but at that moment the door opened and Zara emerged. "He wants to talk to you next, Sandy."

"You okay?"

"Of course. It's just routine. And he's a charming man." She winked at Liss.

"Can I get you a fresh cup of coffee?" Liss asked Zara when the other woman sank down onto the overstuffed easy chair opposite Liss's equally comfortable sofa.

She got no answer. Shrugging, Liss got up and went into the kitchen to refill her own mug. When she returned, Zara was gone. Upstairs, Liss presumed. Had she been more upset than she'd looked? It was hard to tell with Zara. Like so many professional performers, she could look poised and self-confident and be shaking like a leaf inside.

Liss took her coffee to the Canadian rocker in the bay window and put her feet up on a small hassock. The mystery novel she'd been reading, the latest installment in Kathy Lynn Emerson's Face Down series of cozy historicals, lay on the round table at her elbow, but Liss wasn't in the mood to read. Instead she stared out at the neighborhood. She had a clear view across Pine Street to the town square and the brick municipal building on the other side. She could also see more than half the buildings that surrounded the square, including Dan's house, off to her right in the middle of the Birch Street block.

His truck was gone from the driveway. Since this was Sunday, he was probably working at The Spruces. Liss still had doubts about Joe Ruskin's chances of making a success of the place, but there was no questioning his devotion to his pet project. During the week his construction company might build homes, garages, and extra rooms on existing structures, but Joe and his two sons spent most of every weekend at the hotel site, repairing, rebuilding, and retrofitting.

"That does it for now," Gordon Tandy said from behind Liss, interrupting her musings. "I'm headed back to Fallstown to talk to each of the others in the company."

"Do you want me to come along to introduce you?"

Gordon actually seemed to consider it before he shook his head. "No. Better do this on my own. But I may want to talk to you again after I've had a chance to question everyone and I may want you with me when I talk to one or two of them a second time."

"I'll do anything I can to help," Liss assured him. Collecting his coat and hat, she showed him out. She could feel Sandy's stare boring into her back the whole time and wheeled around to face him the moment she'd closed the front door. "What?"

"Kind of chummy, aren't you?"

"He's not the enemy, Sandy. He's trying to find a murderer."

"He's after one of us."

She returned to the bay window to watch the state trooper get into his car and drive away. If she'd understood Gordon correctly, he'd call on her only if he needed help persuading one of the troupe to cooperate, or if he needed more information about someone in order to judge if that person was telling him the truth. "Conflicted" pretty much summed up her feelings about the role she'd agreed to play.

"So what happens now?" Sandy asked.

"He talks to everyone. He tries to figure out who killed Victor. If no one confesses and he can't find any hard evidence, things will be in limbo. That could be worse than discovering one of us is a murderer."

"How so?"

"The police will probably want everyone to stay in the area until they figure out who did this."

"I don't think they can enforce that, but even if they can, what's the big deal? I like your part of the world, Liss."

"I'd love to have you and Zara stay longer, too, but that won't help the company's bottom line. You're the one who told me that *Strathspey* is in financial trouble."

"I also told you Zara and I were thinking of leaving. Thanks so much for sharing that with the cop, by the way. He seemed to think our plans were highly suspicious and that we had an ax to grind with Victor."

"There's no point in trying to hide things, Sandy. Keeping secrets, even silly little ones, just makes people look guilty."

"Maybe. Anyway, I think I put him straight. I told him that if I'd wanted to bump Victor off, I'd have done it up-front and personal, so I'd have the satisfaction of seeing his face when he realized the worm had turned." He grinned. "I told your cop friend that I'd have used one of the swords from the sword dance. I thought that was a nice touch."

"Don't joke about it," she warned. "I've been a suspect in a murder case. It's no fun."

"You're serious, aren't you?"

"Dead serious."

"Has he left?" Zara's disembodied voice floated down from the head of the stairs.

Liss exchanged an anxious look with Sandy. Zara

sounded as if she was on the verge of tears. As one, they moved to the stairwell.

"It's okay, hon," Sandy called up to her. "He's gone."

Before their eyes, Zara seemed to wilt. She sank down onto the top step in a graceful collapse, grasping the railing with one hand and letting her head fall limply forward until it rested on her forearm. "He'll be back," she whispered in a broken voice. "He's going to come back and arrest me. I just know it."

This time the look Liss and Sandy exchanged was incredulous. Sandy took the steps two at a time and dropped down onto the step below Zara, taking hold of his fiancée's free hand. "Honey? What are you talking about?"

"That cop. He's going to blame me for Victor's death."

"*Did* you kill him?" Liss, following more slowly, stopped climbing when her head and shoulders were level with Zara's.

"Liss! Zara wouldn't—"

"Zara? Did you kill him?"

Tears welled up in the dancer's eyes. "No, but I can't prove that I didn't do it. And when they find out . . ."

"Find out what?"

But she just shook her head. The waterworks came on in earnest and she bent forward over her knees, burying her face in the long skirt she wore. Sandy slid up to sit beside her, slipping an arm around her thin, shaking shoulders, and she turned into his embrace, clinging to him and sobbing as if her heart would break.

At a loss, Liss simply watched them, waiting for the deluge to end. Zara had denied killing Victor. That was good enough for her, but there was more in play here. Liss had a hunch that it was not something she was going to be able to share with Gordon Tandy.

Sandy glanced up from stroking Zara's hair. "We can't let this go, Liss."

"What do you suggest we do?"

"Find out who really killed Victor."

"We aren't detectives, Sandy. Let the pros do their job."

"What if Zara's right? What if they decide she did it?"

"Zara?" She spoke sharply to the other woman, hoping to startle her into answering. "Why would they?"

But Zara still wasn't talking. Although the sobs had diminished, tears continued to stream down her pale cheeks.

When Sandy had taken Zara into the guest room to try and get her to rest, Liss went back downstairs. She didn't want anyone in *Strathspey* to be guilty, but even less palatable was her knowledge that, until the killer was caught, all of them were under suspicion.

Gordon Tandy had asked for her assistance and she wanted to help her friends. Two good reasons, she virtuously assured herself, to go out and ask a few questions of her own.

Chapter Four

The remaining twenty-seven members of the *Strath-spey* company were lodged in three places, the Fallstown Motor Lodge, Lakeside Cabins, and the Lonesome Stranger B&B. Liss knew all the room numbers because she had been the one to make the arrangements. There was only one thing she needed before she talked to each of them—another pair of eyes and ears.

Sherri Willett lived with her mother and young son in a trailer park halfway between Moosetookalook and Fallstown. Fortunately for Liss, this was one of Sherri's rare Sundays off.

Unfortunately, Ida Willett answered the door. "What do you want?" she demanded ungraciously, blocking the door with her body. "Shame on you, Liss Mac-Crimmon. Keeping my daughter out till all hours and now here you are again, disrupting the only time all week she has to spend with her son."

Trust Mrs. Willett not to mince words! Liss felt bad about asking Sherri to abandon Adam, but it wasn't as if she hadn't just spent several hours playing with him. It was already well past noon and she knew her friend's habits. No matter how late she'd gotten home, Sherri would have risen when the boy did—the crack of dawn. In fact, Liss might be doing her a service. Sherri was probably ready for a break from nonstop motherhood.

"Shouldn't you invite me in?" Liss asked. "I'm letting all the heat out."

For a moment it was touch-and-go whether Mrs. Willett would step aside and let her pass or simply slam the door in her face. Evidently she decided that Sherri would be upset if she followed her own inclinations. Grudgingly, she allowed Liss to enter.

The living room was littered with toys, but there was no sign of either Adam or his mother. Liss followed the soft murmur of voices toward the back of the trailer where the bedrooms were. Sherri and her son were in the smaller of the two rooms, a bedsheet stretched out between them. Adam kept dropping his end but gamely tried again and again until they'd managed to fold it into a neat square.

"Now go put it in the linen closet," Sherri told him, and he raced off toward the other end of the trailer.

"Linen closet?" Liss asked, amused, as she shrugged out of her jacket. It was warm in the trailer, especially after coming in from the chill outside, and the room smelled of bleach and flower-scented fabric softener.

"All-purpose storage closet." Sherri shrugged and pulled a pillowcase out of her laundry basket. "Today it's the linen closet. So, what's up?"

The glance Sherri sent Liss's way was a trifle wary, as if she wasn't sure how much Liss knew about her activities the night before. She also looked tired. No—exhausted.

"Did you get any sleep at all?"

"Maybe four hours. I've managed on less."

Liss reached for the matching pillowcase and they folded laundry together in companionable silence until the task was complete.

"I thought you had houseguests," Sherri said.

"I do. They'll be okay on their own for a few hours. I thought it was more important to check on the rest of the company. I wondered if you'd like to go with me, but if you're too tired, I can—"

"I'm not too tired. And you probably shouldn't go on your own."

Liss felt a twinge of guilt. She knew how hard it was for her friend to carve out blocks of quality time with her son. There was no husband in the picture—never had been—and between Sherri's full-time job at the jail, changing shifts every seven days, and her part-time job at Moosetookalook Scottish Emporium, she had little free time. It wasn't as if Sherri had a choice about working that much, either. Even with two jobs she only just managed to make ends meet.

"There's no danger," Liss assured her. "I'm just going to . . . talk to people."

"You're going to meddle in an official investigation." Sherri put the last of Adam's T-shirts away in a drawer and turned her sharp-eyed gaze full on Liss.

"You're a fine one to talk! There wouldn't be an investigation if you hadn't stuck your nose in." Liss clapped her hands over her mouth, horrified. Her words had come out in an accusing tone, as if she blamed Sherri for finding out the truth about Victor's death. "I didn't mean that the way it sounded. Honest. It's just that . . . well, now I've got a lot of friends who are suddenly under close scrutiny by the law. Been there. Done that. I wouldn't wish the role of prime suspect on my worst enemy."

"I have a feeling you would have started to think

something was fishy before long yourself," Sherri said. "You knew there were no mushrooms in the food, yet that's what must have killed him."

"I was trying not to think about Victor's death one way or the other, but that's a lost cause now. Gordon Tandy came and talked with me this morning."

Sherri's grin was impish. "Cute, isn't he? He's one of those guys who just gets better looking as he gets older. If I wasn't already engaged to Pete, I might be sorely tempted."

"He's not married, then?"

"Not that I know of." Sherri's eyes narrowed. "Oh-ho! So you think he's cute, too."

"I don't think 'cute' is precisely the word I'd use. And that's not the issue here. Because you went snooping, he's got a murder case to solve and he asked for my assistance and I'm asking for yours."

"I'm not sure how much help I can be. I'm only a dispatcher for the county sheriff's department. I've got zero training in anything else except for what I've learned in my online courses in criminal justice."

"Oh, please! You're dying to put what you've learned to use."

Sherri avoided meeting her eyes. "Maybe."

"At least you *have* some training. And that's exactly why I want you to watch my back. This whole mess needs to be resolved as quickly as possible. Every canceled booking means the company comes closer to financial ruin. I can't let that happen to *Strathspey*. To be trite, the show must go on."

"So you're going to question people. I don't know, Liss. Remember what almost happened the last—"

"Don't say it! This time it will be different. That's why I stopped here to get you."

"And if we stumble over the most likely person to have killed Victor Owens?"

"We call in the troops. No heroics. No trying to talk that person into surrendering." She really had learned her lesson. Anyone could be a killer, and killers tended to go to great lengths to keep from getting caught.

"Okay, then." Sherri hadn't really needed much convincing. She snagged her parka off a peg on the back of the door, stopping only to address Mrs. Willett, who was in the living room, building a castle out of blocks with Adam. "Mom, I need to go out for a while. Can you watch Adam for the rest of the afternoon?"

No answer. Mrs. Willett didn't even look up.

"Mom?"

"Are you going to miss supper?" The words were muffled but loaded with acid.

"I don't know. Don't wait for me, okay? Go ahead and eat when you and Adam get hungry."

Mrs. Willett glared at Liss.

Despicable old witch, Liss thought. But since Ida Willett *was* Sherri's mother, she kept her opinion to herself.

"So, what's the plan?" Sherri asked once they were on the road.

"I made a list." Liss handed it over. "The ones with checkmarks are those who had particular reason to dislike Victor."

Sherri gave a low whistle. Just over half of the twenty-nine names were marked.

"Of course I told Detective Tandy all this, and by now he's talked to everyone, but I can't help but think there may have been something he missed."

"Or they just might be more willing to open up to you."

"Right." And didn't that make her feel like a turncoat! "I thought we'd start at the Fallstown Motor Lodge. Most of the company have rooms there." She'd booked twenty people into the fifteen-room motel, including Victor.

"What's your excuse for stopping by?" Sherri asked.

At least that was open and aboveboard. "I'm letting everyone know they can stay another day where they are."

"And that gives you a good lead-in to bring up the reason they're staying longer. Good thinking."

"Sherri? Can Gordon compel them to stick around indefinitely?"

"Not really, no. He can make it sound like they have to stay put, but there's nothing he can do if they all decide to get on the company bus and head out. Of course, if he arrests someone and there's a trial, they'll subpoena people to come back and testify."

"What about material witnesses?"

"You've been reading mysteries again, haven't you? I don't know what Gordon Tandy's turned up since I last saw him, but all he had then was a suspicious death to investigate. I expect the autopsy will prove Victor Owens died from a reaction to mushrooms. Analysis will show there were mushrooms in that one batch of cocktail scones—and by the way, yuck!—and interviews will establish that Mrs. Eccles didn't bake them. I found an EpiPen in a wastepaper basket that turned out to have no fingerprints on it, indicating that someone wiped it clean. Can't prove it belonged to the victim, but it's a good bet someone took it off him to prevent him using it, then dumped it in case anyone got suspicious and ordered the people at the reception searched."

"So no one person is suspected more than any other at this point?"

"As of around three this morning, no. A confession would be nice, but it's unlikely. And maybe someone saw something suspicious, but ditto. There was quite a crowd there last night. It wouldn't have been hard for the killer to slip away to add a few extra scones to the ones Mrs. Eccles baked or to get rid of the EpiPen—a trip to the bathroom, or out for a breath of fresh air, would do it."

"But where did the scones come from?"

"Prepared in advance, I imagine. The food services people were the ones putting out the goodies. They'd have taken whatever was delivered, heated it up if it was supposed to be served hot, and taken it into the function room. Time it right, and they would have been too busy to notice a few extra scones. There's no way to tell what the filling is until you bite into one."

It *would* have been easy, Liss thought. Too easy. It had taken careful planning, and a certain amount of luck, but Victor's murderer would have needed only a minute or two when the kitchen was empty to slip in and make a deadly addition to the menu. As for getting hold of the EpiPen, that would have been even simpler. Victor customarily kept it in his outside jacket pocket. In a crowd, a jostle could easily go unnoticed. As far as Liss knew, no one in the company had experience as a pickpocket, but how hard could it be, especially when the victim had been drinking?

"Dumb luck factor," she murmured.

"You betcha. Could just as easily have ended up without him so much as tasting one of the poisoned scones. Or someone could have sampled one and realized how awful the flavor was and tossed the whole batch. Owens must have been pretty drunk to reach for a second one. Then again, he all but inhaled the first. Maybe he didn't even taste it."

"He *was* kind of a glutton."

"One of the seven deadlies."

"He didn't deserve to die for it!"

A little silence fell in the car as Sherri studied the list again. "Are any of these suspects way more likely than the rest?"

Liss debated with herself for a moment, but decided Sherri would be more helpful if she knew everything. "There is one thing. After Gordon left my house this morning, Zara broke down. She's sure she's going to be charged with Victor's murder, but she won't say why the police should think she's guilty. She swears she didn't kill Victor, and I believe her."

"Zara's the woman who's staying with you?"

Liss nodded. "I invited her and Sandy to bunk at my place. They're engaged to be married," she added. "They were thinking of leaving the company because Victor was giving Zara a hard time. Victor and Zara were a couple for a while, maybe a year or so ago. Nothing all that serious, though. Victor had a tendency to take up with any new addition to the troupe."

Sherri didn't comment. She didn't have to. Any time a romantic triangle existed, there was potential for tragedy. Some pretty deep and desperate emotions could lurk just beneath a polished surface.

"So, who's first?" Sherri asked as Liss pulled into the parking lot of the Fallstown Motor Lodge. She unfastened her seat belt but made no effort to get out of the station wagon.

Liss glanced at her watch. It was a few minutes before three in the afternoon. "Let's try Stewart Graham's room, although I'm guessing he won't be there."

"The punster?"

"Yes. Stewart likes what he calls his 'afternoon libation.' By now he's probably discovered that the Meandering Moose is walking distance from here." The Moose was the local brew pub.

"Almost everything of interest in Fallstown is

walking distance from here. Isn't that why you picked the Motor Lodge?"

"Yes. The company travels by bus, so no one has transportation of their own. Unfortunately, there wasn't room here for everyone in the company. The rates were so low that a lot of people who'd usually double up with a roommate to save money opted for singles. I booked the overflow into the Lonesome Stranger Bed-and-Breakfast and out at Lakeside Cabins. The B-and-B is just around the corner, but I had to find volunteer drivers to play taxicab for the other six."

"Did the bus take them back and forth last night?"

"Yes, but I didn't want them to feel stranded out there. I gave each of them a number to call if they wanted a ride anywhere. That was the best I could do short of renting cars for everyone. The budget wouldn't quite stretch to that."

They tried Stewart's room first, and as Liss had expected, no one answered her knock. Lee Annie Neville, the featured vocal soloist, poked her head out of the room next door and reported that Stewart had gone out half an hour earlier.

Lee Annie Neville would never be mistaken for a dancer. She was a big-boned woman in her midthirties and although she was far from obese, she looked heavy in comparison to the bevy of lithe, lean, athletic young women she traveled with. Her hair was red, a shade between mahogany and auburn, and she favored bright colors in her clothing and flashy stones in the many rings she wore. She was fluent in Gaelic and sang with the voice and the soul of a true daughter of Scotland. In the ordinary way of things, she had a cheerful disposition and a positive outlook on life. Just now she looked a bit haggard and out of sorts.

"Talk to you a minute, Lee Annie?" Liss asked.

* * *

Sherri let Liss ask the questions. With each troupe member at the motel, the patter was the same: *How are you holding up? Don't worry about a place to stay. Everyone has housing for another night. Looks like Fiona's taken charge, and that's a good thing. Did the state police talk to you? Had anyone had any run-ins with Victor lately?*

The comments people made gave Sherri the impression that most of the differences between Victor and various members of the troupe were pretty petty. No one, of course, confessed to killing him.

It was getting dark by the time they worked their way around to the last of the lot staying at the motel. "Ray Adams is our stage manager," Liss said as she knocked on his door. "Head of a two-man crew responsible for lights, sound, scenery, and just about everything else backstage except costumes and props."

When Adams absently waved them into his room, Sherri remembered seeing him at the reception. How could she forget that nose? It rivaled Jay Leno's in size. Fortunately, Ray's chin was of normal proportions.

He'd been watching a hockey game on television. He muted the sound, but made no other concession to their presence. His gaze returned to the screen as soon as they entered. He left it to Liss to close the door against the chilly March twilight.

"Ray's a rabid Islanders fan," Liss said, sotto voce.

"What are you, nuts?" Ray yelled at the screen. His voice was deep and raspy. Sherri would have said it was a smoker's voice, except that there was no smell of cigarettes in the room.

"He roots for the Yankees during baseball season and the Giants when football games are on. Hates both

the Red Sox and the New England Patriots with
equal passion."

"And you two still speak to each other?"

Neither Sherri nor Liss was a big sports fan, but
anyone hailing from Maine knew where their loyal-
ties must lie, especially when, miracle of miracles, a
New England sports team actually managed to win a
championship.

"Ray is backstage during every performance,"
Liss said, "and I have a feeling that he sees a lot that
the rest of us miss."

"Shoot, already!"

"Uh, Ray?" Liss touched his arm.

"What?"

"Cops talk to you earlier?"

"Yeah. All right! Hat trick!"

"Ray!"

A commercial came on. He swung around to face
them, blinked once, and grinned. "What?"

"Victor was murdered. You're all stuck here for
an extra day."

"Yeah, yeah. Heard that already."

Sherri watched his face intently as Liss questioned
him, just as she'd watched the others they'd talked to.
So far everyone had agreed Victor had been more ir-
ritating than usual lately, but no one had admitted to
being ticked off enough to want him dead.

"Tell me about the last week or so," Liss urged
Ray. "Did Victor clash with anyone in particular?
Was someone grumbling about him?"

Distracted by the game, Ray just shook his head.

"Come on, Ray. Help me out here."

Sherri couldn't tell if he was frowning because of
the goal the Islanders had just missed or because it
had finally dawned on him that Liss was pumping him

for information. Maybe both. He shot her a sharp look. "Victor was always pissing somebody off, y'know? You want I should list every time? I should live so long!"

"Ray . . ."

"All right, already!"

With ever-increasing frequency, "y'know?" ended Ray's sentences as he reeled off accounts of half a dozen clashes between Victor and various members of the company. All were minor incidents except the last, which had taken place earlier that week in the parking lot of a high school they'd been playing in Vermont.

"Let me get this straight." To Sherri, Liss's voice sounded shaky. "Victor and Sandy got into it a couple of days ago but you didn't hear what they said to each other, you just saw that they were shouting?"

Ray nodded. "A lot of arm waving, y'know? Sandy shook his fist right under Victor's nose. Victor knocked his arm aside, y'know? And they both stalked off in different directions." His attention drifted back to the television.

Liss looked stricken. It was clear that although she didn't want Zara arrested, she wouldn't be happy if suspicion shifted to Sandy, either. After a moment, she gathered her wits and smacked Ray on the arm to regain his attention. "Did you tell the cops what you just told me?"

"You want I shoulda lied?"

"No. No, of course not." She sighed. "Thanks, Ray. Talk to you later."

They were at the door before Ray said anything else. "Victor got what he deserved, y'know." The words sounded heartfelt. "You should let it go, already."

* * *

When he got home from The Spruces, Dan took a quick shower, then headed for Liss's house. That he owed her an apology was only half his reason for going there. He also needed to make sure she was okay. He knew her well enough to be certain she'd involve herself in any trouble the members of *Strathspey* were in. She'd think them her responsibility, since she'd been the one to invite them to perform in Fallstown.

He didn't see Margaret Boyd's station wagon on the street in front of the Emporium, but didn't let that alarm him unduly. It might be parked in Liss's garage. Given the likelihood of more snow, it probably was.

When Sandy Kalishnakof answered the door, Dan gritted his teeth and greeted him cordially. He could hear recorded bagpipe music coming from the living room and recognized Beth Hogencamp's excited, high-pitched voice. She'd come for a dance lesson. Liss must be home.

But when he advanced into the house, he saw that it was Zara Lowery, not Liss, who was demonstrating a step for the girl. Liss was nowhere in sight.

Zara turned the music off and watched while Beth imitated what she'd just been shown. "That's it," Zara said encouragingly. "The third step is the toe-and-heel." She watched for a moment. "No. Spring, then hop on the right foot, and execute the toe-and-heel movement with the left foot in fifth position. Good. Spring. Then hop on the left foot. Toe-and-heel with the right foot in fifth position. That's it! Now repeat."

Beth's smile was triumphant as she went through her paces. When her movements brought her around to where she could see Dan, however, she faltered. A shy child, she wasn't quite ready to perform for an audience.

Zara glanced at him, then at her watch. "That's it for today, Beth. I hope you didn't mind having me as a substitute teacher."

"Oh no. You were great, Miss Lowery. Thank you." All the while avoiding looking directly at either Dan or Sandy, she traded her dancing shoes for sturdy boots and bundled up in her winter coat. Moments later she was racing toward home, the apartment above Angie's Books on the other side of the town square.

"Nice kid," Zara said. "She's going to have to get over that shyness, though."

An awkward silence fell. They were probably wondering how much he knew, Dan thought. And he'd certainly like to know what Liss was up to. He cleared his throat. "Liss around?"

"She went to Fallstown to talk to the rest of the company. We're staying an extra day."

"Ah. I see. And she asked you to take over Beth's lesson?"

"Actually, she forgot all about Beth, but since that was our fault . . ."

Sandy must have seen the flash of anger in Dan's eyes. He moved protectively in front of Zara. Dan held up a hand. "Whoa. Sorry about that. I'm not upset with you two. Guess you know the police are taking an interest in Victor Owens's death. They've been here, right? Talked to Liss?"

Zara sank into the nearest chair and let her head fall back against the cushions, closing her eyes. Sandy settled in on the arm of the same chair, taking one of her hands in his. "We've all been interviewed," he admitted.

"And that's why Liss went to Fallstown to talk to

the others in the company." Dan frowned. No sense beating around the bush. "Did she go to talk to them or to interrogate them? If one of you people is a cold-blooded killer, it isn't exactly safe for her to go snooping around."

"You'll have to take that up with Liss. We certainly have no control over her actions."

"Nobody does. That's the problem. She's too damned impatient to let matters work themselves out. She'll take a hand, hoping to hurry things along. I don't like to think what could happen if she corners the wrong—or in this case, the right—person."

"She's got a good head on her shoulders," Sandy said. "She knows how to take care of herself."

"She knows one self-defense move." Granted, it was a good one. He'd ended up flat on his back himself when she'd demonstrated it to him. But it wouldn't help her against a man with a gun or a woman with a knife or poison—real poison, not just something only one person in the group was allergic to. "Any idea when she'll be back?"

"None. Truthfully, we expected to see her by now. I mean, it's not like her to forget that she had promised to give Beth a dance lesson this evening."

Dan didn't like the sound of that at all. Reaching for the phone on the end table, he punched in Sherri Willett's number. He got her mother, and an earful, but no information on where either woman might have gotten to.

"Whatever she's doing, it's to help us," Sandy said when Dan hung up.

"You sure you don't know anything? The sooner someone's arrested, the better, and I personally don't care who it is. None of you mean squat to me."

To his surprise, Sandy found that amusing. Chuckling, he eased himself off the arm of Zara's chair and urged her to her feet. "You feel like fixing us something to eat?" he asked her.

She narrowed her eyes at him. "No."

"Do it anyhow." It was a gentle-voiced suggestion, not a command, but she sighed and drifted off toward the kitchen. Sandy waited until she'd disappeared down the hallway before he turned back to Dan.

"More than one person had reason to wish Victor gone from the company, but killing him is a little drastic. He'd probably have been fired at the end of this tour. He was causing a lot of morale problems and getting careless about finances."

"You one of the ones who wanted him gone?"

"Yes. And if there hadn't been a risk that the company's backers would simply disband *Strathspey* rather than find a new manager midtour, several of us would have filed formal complaints before now. We were biding our time. And Zara and I were looking for another dance company to join, just in case they decided to keep him and not us."

The smell of frying onions drifted into the room and Dan heard the clank of spatula against pan. Maybe he would stick around for supper. See what he could find out about these people.

"How's *Strathspey* set up?" he asked Sandy. "You said something about backers?"

"Yeah. A group of self-styled patrons of the arts put up the seed money and act as a board of directors. First couple of years, they paid most of the expenses. Since then we've been self-supporting. No big profits, but holding our own."

"You said you and Zara were looking for new jobs. Are there a lot of companies like yours?"

"Not really. *Riverdance* runs a couple of tours. Irish dancing and Scottish dancing aren't the same, but we could adapt." His gaze was unfocused, as if he were trying to see into the future. After a moment he shook his head and shot a rueful look in Dan's direction. "Yeah. Okay. Pipe dream. Especially when there are two of us. But we had feelers out. Musical theater's a possibility. Summer stock. Lots of shows employ dancers of one sort or another."

It didn't sound like they had much in the way of job security to Dan, and he knew from Liss's experience that the career of a professional dancer could be a short one. "How'd you get into this line of work, anyway?"

"Dancing? It's in my blood. My father was with a ballet company before he left Russia for this country. My mother, like Liss, competed in Scottish dancing from the time she was a kid. When they married they opened a dance school. Taught everything, in fashion or not. Ballet. Tap. Modern. Folk dances and Celtic dancing."

"And Zara?"

"Victor found her at a Scottish festival two years ago, winning all the dance competitions. He recruited her for the company."

"Victor, huh?"

"Victor Owens was hired as manager when *Strathspey* was organized. He was a dancer, too, at first. Better at running things. He had a good eye for talent and could pinch a penny till it squealed. Until recently, nobody had any real complaints about him, except a lady or two who also got pinched."

"So Victor was with the company from the beginning, just as Liss was. Anyone else go back that far?"

"Four of us," Sandy said. "Fiona, Ray, Stewart, and me."

Chapter Five

Fallstown wasn't the sort of place that went in for disreputable bars. Instead it had a brew pub called the Meandering Moose that was half lounge and half restaurant. There was no smoking in either section, thanks to a strict state law, and the clientele was a mixture of couples, singles, and college seniors who were finally old enough to buy themselves a drink.

Liss and Sherri found Stewart in the lounge section, where he had commandeered a four-person booth. Only one beer bottle and one glass mug sat in front of him, but Liss was fairly certain he was well past his first drink of the day. His color was high and his watery blue eyes looked a trifle unfocused even after he recognized her.

"Ah, Liss!" Stewart grinned widely. "Who would have imagined that such a delightful establishment could exist in the back of beyond? Look—this is a place after my own heart. Will you join me in a lager?" He turned the longneck around so that she could read the label. The brew pub had named this particular beer Fallstown Logger.

Liss refused to dignify such a pitiful pun by acknowledging it. Instead she gestured toward Sherri.

"You remember my friend Sherri Willett. I'm pretty sure I introduced you two at the reception last night."

Stewart rose, bent over Sherri's hand, and kissed it. Sherri's brows lifted and she sent a questioning look in Liss's direction.

Liss shrugged. "Stewart was born in England. His accent becomes more pronounced after a few beers and the lord of the manor manners seem to increase along with it."

"And I believe I'm in need of another. Ladies?"

"I wouldn't mind a beer," Sherri said.

Liss asked for a ginger ale.

"Excellent, my dears. Oh, waiter!"

"So, what do you do with the company, Stewart?" Sherri asked when they had been served. Her first cold gulp of Snowe's Pale Ale, another local special, went down a treat.

"He plays the bagpipes when the show calls for live rather than taped music and he dances." Even as she spoke, Liss realized that last night Stewart had *not* danced. "At least he usually does. Injury?"

"Victor," Stewart growled. "I had a much bigger role in the show until he started making changes."

"Why did he do that? I mean, why mess with what works?"

"Said I was unreliable. Ha! I'm as reliable as good clockworks. Just wind me up and I can do my stuff no matter how I spend my time off. Get it? Time?"

Liss and Sherri exchanged a glance. Liss put one hand over Stewart's on the table. "You've been . . . partying lately, haven't you? Staying out late? Showing up late? Missing the bus?" It was an old pattern with Stewart, but Liss had been under the impression that he'd licked it. They'd staged an intervention about three years ago, after which he'd cut way back on the drinking.

"Man's got a right to enjoy life," Stewart grumbled.

Sensing that there was no point in being subtle with Stewart when he was half-plastered, Liss asked right out if he knew of anyone, besides himself, who had a bone to pick with Victor.

If Stewart knew about Sandy's quarrel with the company manager, he didn't mention it. Nor did he come up with any other useful suggestions.

"Okay, Stewart. I'll talk to you again when you're sober." Liss stood and Sherri followed suit. On the way out, Liss asked the bartender to call a cab for Stewart when he was ready to leave.

"You don't want to give him a lift to the motel now?" Sherri asked.

"I know him too well. He'll just take off again on his own, end up in worse shape, and try walking back. I'd hate for him to get hit by a pulp truck."

Four members of *Strathspey* had been booked into rooms in the Lonesome Stranger B&B, a charming old Victorian house decorated in the style of that period. Sherri was almost afraid to move for fear of breaking something. The rooms were stuffed with furniture and every level surface seemed to be littered with breakable knickknacks. Keeping a wary eye on her surroundings, she followed Liss upstairs.

There was no answer when Liss rapped on the first door they came to. She knocked again, then tried the knob, which turned easily in her hand. "Emily?"

She flipped the light switch, revealing a heavily carved bed, a massive dresser, and huge cabbage roses marching across what wallpaper could be seen around a profusion of framed sketches, portraits, and landscapes. Of Emily, however, there was no trace.

"I thought she might be lying down," Liss explained, turning the light off again and backing out of the room. "Emily Townsend dances my old role in the show. Apparently she was romantically involved with Victor. His death must have been a terrible shock to her."

"The blonde?"

"Yes."

"Lot of help she was. I handed her my phone so I could start CPR. She turned it off and left it on the refreshment table." Sherri hadn't seen her again.

"Unless you told her what to do with it, she probably didn't have a clue. Most civilians don't, you know."

The next room along the upstairs corridor was occupied by a snub-nosed, sloe-eyed older woman Liss introduced as Winona West. She was in charge of costumes and props for the company. She was wearing what appeared to be a costume herself, a long flowing skirt of apricot-colored velvet and a military-style black velvet jacket.

Her room, like Emily's, was all lace and flowers and smelled faintly of potpourri. Only one lamp had been turned on. Since its glass shade, in the shape of an owl, was amber colored, the light it offered was feeble. Winona didn't seem to need more. She'd been playing solitaire on her laptop when they'd interrupted her.

Liss asked the usual questions, then added one. "Do you know where Emily is?"

"I haven't seen her all day."

"Did you talk to her last night after the reception?" Sherri asked.

"Only to tell her how sorry I was." She shifted her attention to Liss. "You heard she and Victor were an item, right?"

Liss nodded, frowning. "If they were so tight, why was she staying here instead of at the motel with him? I went by requests from individuals as to what type of lodging they preferred. If I'm not mistaken, Emily specifically asked for a B-and-B."

"Asserting her independence? About time, if she was." Idly, Winona resumed her virtual card game.

"Did anyone have a particular grudge against Victor, Winona?"

"Particular enough to make them kill him, you mean?" She didn't look away from the glowing screen. "That's what that cop wanted to know, too. I'll tell you the same thing I told him. Everybody cussed Victor out at one time or another, but it was just talk. You know us. We're just one big, happy family."

"Uh-huh."

"That's my story and I'm sticking to it." She met Liss's eyes and grinned, then went back to her game.

Liss winced, but accepted the dismissal. "Well, thanks, Winona. I'm going to talk to Josie and Cal, then go out to the cabins. If Emily shows up, will you have her call me on my cell? I want to make certain she doesn't need anything."

"Sure thing, sweetie."

Liss headed for the door. Sherri scrambled off the high bed where she'd perched—she'd decided it was the place from which she could do the least damage to the overflowing clutch in the room—but she wasn't ready to leave just yet. "Do you know anything about a quarrel between Victor and Sandy?" she asked Winona.

The wardrobe mistress didn't answer right away. She seemed to be weighing the question. Or perhaps she was just involved in the card game. Finally, she shook her head. "Nope. Don't know a thing about it."

"What about Stewart? It's pretty obvious he resented Victor for cutting his part in the show."

Winona played one last card, gave up on winning, and closed the laptop. Setting it aside, she narrowed her dark, exotically slanted eyes at Sherri. "You've met Stewart, right?"

Sherri nodded.

"How likely is it that he'd have been able to plot a murder?"

"Good point," Sherri conceded. Given the beer-soaked state of his brain, she doubted Stewart Graham could devise a complex plan to poison anyone, let alone carry it out.

Josie Malone, just across the hall, was even less help than Winona. She didn't seem to mind having an extra day off, though. She was already comfortably dressed in an old football jersey that came down to her knees and told them she intended to go to bed early and sleep late, an unheard-of luxury when they were on the road. The smell of onions and french fries had Sherri scanning the room—yet another tribute to the Victorian penchant for clutter—until she found the wastepaper basket. The distinctive bag, wadded up and tossed away, confirmed that Josie had bought her supper at a nearby fast food restaurant.

The last room was occupied by yet another dancer, Calvin MacBain. Liss introduced him as her erstwhile partner in the country dances.

"Does that mean you're paired with Emily now?" Cal's room was just as frilly as the others. A Victorian doll with a painted china head sat in a small wooden rocking chair in one corner.

"For my sins, yes, we're partners." Cal had a smooth tenor voice and a friendly smile. There was a slight but distinct gap between his two top front teeth.

"Any idea where she is now?" Liss asked.

"In her room?"

"Guess again."

"No idea. Haven't seen her since last night and she wasn't exactly in friendly mode then."

Same questions. Same lack of answers. Once again, Sherri had to be the one to ask about Sandy and Victor's quarrel. She believed Cal when he said he didn't remember witnessing any such thing, or hearing about it from anyone else afterward.

"What about Victor harassing people, especially women?" she asked.

"Sexually, you mean?" Cal grinned. "In Victor's case, it would *only* be women. Back when he was dancing, he was petrified someone would think he was gay. He made a big point of always having a lady on his arm."

"I'd forgotten you knew him when he was a dancer," Liss said. "Victor managed and danced the first two years we were on the road," she said in an aside to Sherri.

"So you two go way back," Sherri said to Cal. And that meant Liss would have a blind spot where he was concerned, just as she seemed to about Sandy, Zara, and Stewart. Sherri wondered if that was another reason Liss had wanted her along—she needed a "bad cop" to her "good cop," someone who wouldn't care about ruffling feathers or stomping on egos.

"I've been with *Strathspey* about six years," Cal said.

"Were you two partners all that time? Till Liss left, I mean."

It was Liss who answered. "Not until about three years ago when I took over the featured dancer's part in the country dances. There are twelve male and twelve female dancers in the company, so we can form three circles of four couples each. That's what looks best on a small stage."

"What do you do if someone is sick?"

"It depends. In a pinch the singer and piper would fill in, just as a couple of the dancers could fill in for one of them if they had to. That's why Stewart ended up dancing on a regular basis until recently. If we couldn't manage that, we'd sometimes have to cut back to two circles."

"So when you were injured, they had to find a replacement in a hurry."

"Yes. Someone named Sarah." Liss pinned Cal with a look. "And that brings me back to sex. I hear Sarah threatened to charge Victor with harassment. Know anything about it?"

"It wouldn't have held up in court. It was just a case of Victor being Victor. There was no harm in it. Anyway, Ray got her calmed down before she left."

"Ray? What's Ray got to do with anything?"

"He's . . . how shall I put this? He's sweet on Sarah."

The remaining members of *Strathspey* were lodged at Lakeside Cabins. Located a couple of miles outside Fallstown on the shores of Loon Lake, these small housekeeping cabins, each furnished with a wood stove for heat, rented at outrageous rates in the summer. Since it was March, the owners had offered six of them to Liss at bargain-basement prices.

Liss wondered what was going on as she drove past the first five cabins and saw no lights on in any of them. When she came to the sixth, a bit removed from the others and sheltered by spruce trees, she understood. The heavenly aroma of garlic-laced spaghetti sauce wafted out to them, along with the smell of an apple-wood fire.

"Fiona's cooking."

In answer, Sherri's stomach growled.

"She'll have made plenty. Come on."

Liss put off asking questions in favor of eating. The cabin was already crowded—everyone had brought chairs from their own cabins—but the dancers quickly found space for Liss and Sherri to sit on Fiona's bed and supplied them with heavy-duty paper plates loaded down with meatballs, sauce made with mushrooms and onions as well as tomatoes and garlic, and thick slices of store-bought Italian bread.

As she ate, Liss listened to the cheerful chatter around her. Except for Fiona, the others— Jean Ferguson, Anna Buchanan, Laura MacGowan, Serena Guthrie, and Denise Johnson—seemed very young to her, barely into their twenties. They talked about dancing, about clothes, and about television shows or movies they'd seen in hotel rooms all over the country during the tour. No one mentioned Victor.

That was Fiona's doing, Liss supposed. She was hardly ancient—only in her early forties—but she'd fallen early on into the role of mother hen. She was the one who took newcomers under her wing, the one who always seemed to have the knack of keeping morale high, even on the most discouraging days on tour.

Liss hated to destroy the mood, but it was getting late and she still had to drive back to Moosetookalook. She spared a brief thought for Sandy and Zara. She hadn't wanted to abandon them, but she was doing this to help them and they could hardly have come with her. She hoped they'd found something at her house to fix for supper. She'd planned to take them out to eat tonight.

"So, ladies," she began. "Did Detective Tandy come by to talk to all of you?"

This produced a flurry of comment on Gordon's good looks, which Liss tried to ignore. She could sense Sherri's grin even without looking at her friend.

"Yes, but did anyone have anything useful to tell him?" she interrupted. "The sooner he can clear things up, the better, you know."

"What's to tell?" Serena asked. "Victor was the boss. We mostly tried to stay under his radar."

"He was an old grouch," Jean complained. "I didn't think so when I first joined up, but he sure did yell a lot the last couple of months."

A chorus of agreement greeted this observation, making Liss wonder, and not for the first time that day, if something had been wrong with Victor besides his allergy to mushrooms. "Victor changed?" she asked. "Was he having a nervous breakdown or something?"

"Something?" Fiona asked.

"Well, was he taking drugs? I don't mean illegal drugs. At least I don't think I do. Had he been taking some prescription medication that had made him moodier than usual?"

"Not that I know of." But Fiona looked troubled by the thought.

"Maybe someone should search his room," Denise suggested.

"Or ask Emily."

The way Anna said Emily's name made Liss suspect she did not like the other dancer much. "Anyone know where Emily is?"

"The B-and-B," Fiona said.

"Not as of an hour ago."

Out of the corner of her eye, Liss saw Sherri pull out her cell phone and punch in a number. Quietly, while Liss continued to question the dancers about Victor's actions during the last few months and his quarrels with others in the company, Sherri asked for Emily Townsend. A few minutes later, shaking her head at Liss to indicate that Emily was not yet back, she thanked whoever was on the other end of the line and disconnected.

Liss was batting zero on helpful answers as well. If there had been any serious rifts between any of these members of the company and Victor, none of them were admitting it.

"What about the fight between Sandy and Victor in the parking lot?" Sherri asked.

Liss held her breath. Sandy wasn't the one who'd killed Victor. She was certain of it. She couldn't fault Sherri for wanting verification of Ray's story, but neither could she help being glad when no one supplied it.

"What about Stewart and Victor?" Sherri asked.

Everyone agreed Stewart was drinking too much. Everyone thought Victor had it in for him. No one thought Stewart capable of killing anything bigger than a fly, and then only if he was stone-cold sober.

Scone-cold sober, Liss thought before she could stop herself. Her groan was silent, too.

Laura and Jean dished the dirt on Ray and Sarah when Liss asked about them. Apparently it had been a somewhat one-sided romantic attachment, and Ray had been vocal in blaming Victor for Sarah's abrupt departure from the troupe.

"Ray wouldn't go so far as to commit murder," Serena said, and the others all nodded. Liss didn't think so, either.

"He could find work anywhere," Jean added. "Wherever Sarah ended up, he could just go after her. If he really wanted to."

"Unless Victor sent the word out on Sarah. Black-balled her."

"Could he do that?" Sherri asked.

"Maybe. Depends on what he said and who he said it to. Nobody wants to hire a troublemaker."

"What's Sarah's last name?" Sherri asked. Liss had a feeling she was going to run a check on her the next time she was working at the dispatch center at the county jail.

"Bartlett," Jean said. "Sarah Bartlett."

It might be worthwhile, Liss thought, to ask the owners of various hotels and motels in the area if they'd had a Sarah Bartlett registered for the night of the reception.

"I can't see Sarah killing Victor, either," Serena said, as if she'd read Liss's thoughts, "but Emily might have."

"Why?" Liss asked. "I thought they were an item."

"She was sleeping with him, but she said he was an awful old bore in bed. She was hoping he'd get tired of her soon so she could move on to someone more interesting."

"Nice girl," Sherri murmured.

"If he was so boring, why didn't she end it? For that matter, why did she take up with him in the first place?" Liss had a sneaking suspicion she already knew the answers.

"She wanted Zara's part in the show," Serena said. "Figured that was the quickest way to get it."

The other dancers chimed in with words to the same effect.

Liss remembered Victor's words at the reception. He'd all but promised to give Emily the role. Why, then, would Emily want to kill him?

The more questions she asked, the less satisfied she was with the answers. It seemed to her that the other dancers resented Emily, and were taking advantage of the fact that she wasn't around to defend herself to level accusations.

Liss understood the impulse. There was a part of her that wanted Emily to be guilty, too. That would be the perfect solution. She didn't know Emily Townsend. She didn't care what happened to her.

Out of the corner of her eye, Liss saw Sherri glance at her watch. "I've got to get home," her friend said. "I'm on the seven-to-three shift starting tomorrow."

Liss was ready to go, too. She didn't think they would learn any more tonight. She delayed only long enough to say good-bye to Fiona, who'd retreated to the cabin's tiny kitchen area to wash the pots and pans she'd dirtied.

"The spaghetti was wonderful, Fiona. A real feast."

"I thought we all needed some cheering up. You, too." She studied Liss, her fond expression filled with concern. "What happened to Victor wasn't your fault. You're not responsible."

"I know that. In my head. But in my heart . . ."

"Dinna fash yersel, as the Scots say."

"Hard not to. And there seems to be plenty to worry about. Sandy says the shows aren't bringing in as much revenue as they used to. If the company doesn't get back on the road soon—"

"Hey—my problem, okay? I'm the one who's stuck in the role of acting manager, not you. We'll muddle through. We always do."

Liss lowered her voice. "Detective Tandy asked for my input, since I know the people involved."

"And you agreed?" Fiona scrubbed harder at the bottom of the pot, although it looked perfectly clean to Liss.

"How could I not? Victor was *murdered*, Fiona."

"Yes, I can see where you'd have to help all you

can." She put the pan aside and turned to face Liss fully. Her pale blue eyes were troubled. "Do you suspect one of us?"

"Not really, although I don't know what to make of Emily Townsend's disappearance. I've got very mixed feelings about Emily." She shrugged. "I guess it bothers me that I find it so easy to think she might be the killer, just because she wasn't in her room. And because she replaced me in the company. And because I hate that *titter* of hers."

Fiona gave a husky chuckle, the polar opposite of Emily's laugh. "It is a bit much, isn't it? But you mustn't worry about your reaction to Emily. After all, it isn't necessary to like everyone you meet. God knows, I don't! I couldn't stand Victor."

Startled, Liss found herself stuttering. "B-b-but you worked with him for eight years."

"Guess I was just a glutton for punishment," she said with a smile. It faded when she saw Liss's expression. "Don't you think," she asked, "that if I'd wanted to kill Victor I'd have done it years ago?"

"I can't imagine you killing anyone."

"Don't kid yourself. Anyone can be driven to extreme measures, and Victor was certainly getting on everyone's nerves." She glanced toward the main part of the room, but no one was paying any attention to them. Sherri had already gone out to warm up the car. "I wasn't going to say anything, but I think I know what was behind Victor's attitude problems the last six months or so. I'm pretty sure he was borrowing money from the company coffers. Sandy's right, Liss. *Strathspey* is in deep financial trouble, and Victor Owens is the reason why."

Chapter Six

Liss arrived home much later than she'd intended to find Sandy, Zara, and Lumpkin cozily sharing the living room couch and watching a movie on cable. She didn't know what it was, but she recognized a few of the actors' faces. Their names eluded her.

"Well, finally!" Sandy greeted her. "We were thinking of sending out the Saint Bernard."

It had started to snow again, but Liss was used to driving in the white stuff. It hadn't occurred to her that her friends might worry. "I should have called to tell you I was held up. I'm sorry."

"No problem," Zara assured her. "We had a lovely dinner. I cooked." Sandy pantomimed gagging, then yelped as she sent an elbow into his ribs.

Lumpkin, his peaceful nap disrupted, jumped down and stalked from the room, his plume of a tail held high to reflect his disdain for the foolish humans.

"Any luck?" Sandy asked.

"Not much." Liss hated to spoil the mood, but there was no advantage in putting off uncomfortable questions. She settled into the chair opposite the sofa, the perfect vantage point from which to watch his face. "Why didn't you tell me you'd had a quarrel with Victor?"

"Victor didn't quarrel. He sniped." He was grinning as he corrected her.

"This happened in a parking lot. There was a lot of hand waving. No blows were exchanged, but apparently it was a near thing."

Zara reached for the clicker and muted the movie. "You didn't tell me you and Victor argued."

"For the last few months, Victor and I clashed over just about everything. No big deal. Yelling lets off steam." Liss couldn't see his eyes. He had taken Zara's hands in his and spoken directly to her.

"This was in Vermont," Liss said. "Last week."

"Not ringing any bells." And he still wasn't looking at her.

"You shook your fist at him."

"Liss, I'm telling you I don't remember confronting Victor in a parking lot. Maybe I did. Maybe I didn't. If it happened, it wasn't over anything important enough that I remember details."

Far from satisfied, Liss had to be content with that answer. An awkward little silence engulfed the three of them.

"I hope you don't mind," Zara said after a moment, "but when Beth showed up for her lesson, I filled in for you."

Liss squeezed her eyes shut and made a face, annoyed with herself. "I completely forgot she was coming over."

"No problem. She's a sweet kid. Skittish, though." Zara chuckled. "And is she always such a picker-upper?"

Liss knew exactly what her friend meant. Beth Hogencamp was nine years old and extremely shy around strangers. Her nervousness manifested itself, indoors at least, in a compulsion to pick things up and put them down again. Liss usually cleared a space in the middle of the living room for the dance lessons. In the course of an hour, Beth would have handled every picture frame, every knickknack, and every cat toy within reach. She was the same when she visited Moosetookalook Scottish Emporium, where there were even more small items to move about.

"I don't think I'm cut out to be a dance teacher," Liss lamented. "Of course I never did think I was."

"I liked working with her. It was a bit disconcerting, though, to have the cat watching us from the top of the television like some disapproving gargoyle."

"He vanished when Dan came over, though," Sandy put in.

Since Sandy was openly watching her for a reaction, Liss tried to sound nonchalant. "Dan was here? What did he want?"

"To talk to you. He didn't seem surprised when we told him where you'd gone, though."

Good old Moosetookalook grapevine, Liss thought. Having everyone know your business was both the curse and the blessing of living in a small, rural village.

"He stayed for supper," Zara said. "He *liked* my cooking."

Liss's astonishment grew, but she didn't have time to focus on Dan Ruskin's motive. Clearing her friends of suspicion had to come first. "Fiona made spaghetti."

"That's right," Zara said. "She was looking forward to being in a housekeeping cabin so she could cook."

"I talked to everyone except Emily Townsend. Is there any reason I should be suspicious of her because she didn't stay put at the B-and-B?"

Sandy and Zara exchanged glances.

"What?"

Zara spoke. "Emily has her own agenda. She was using Victor as much as he was using her."

"Using him how?"

"To build her résumé. You don't think she intended to stay with *Strathspey* all her life, do you? She wanted my part in the show. Then she'd have moved on."

Liss shook her head. "I thought women had gotten past the need to sleep with their bosses to get ahead. What was she thinking?"

Sandy snorted. "I don't think it's a need so much as a choice. Emily probably looked on cozying up to Victor as a shortcut."

"Someone should really have a talk with that woman about her self-esteem."

"Just because her actions aren't politically correct in this day and age doesn't mean she isn't doing exactly what she wants to do," Zara pointed out.

"Anyway, I wouldn't worry about her." Sandy had snugged an arm around Zara's shoulders and no longer had any trouble meeting Liss's eyes. "She'll turn up. Where's she going to go?"

"She could rent a car and go anywhere."

But Sandy shook his head. "Unless she already had another job lined up before Victor died, she'll stick. In spite of appearances, she's no dummy. She has to know taking off would make her look suspicious. Did she stay around long enough to talk to your cop friend?"

"I think so. I haven't had a chance to compare notes."

"Take my advice and don't worry about Emily. She's the type who always lands on her feet."

"That's because she walks all over everyone else," Zara added.

Liss sighed. "Wouldn't it be nice if Emily did kill him? We could write it off to a lovers' quarrel and that would be that. I wouldn't have to suspect my friends anymore."

She meant Sandy, because of the fight with Victor, but it was Zara who spoke up. "If they arrest me, the rest of the company will be free to go. Emily will have my part with no questions asked."

Liss narrowed her eyes. Zara's expression was once again deeply troubled, her eyes bleak. Even her bright red hair suddenly seemed duller. "You know, if you'd just tell us why you think the police will be interested in you, we might be able to help."

"I can't."

"A clue?"

"I—it's something to do with my family, okay? I'm not going to say any more. It will all come out when they arrest me, but I don't want to talk about it before that."

"Zara—" Sandy tried to tug her closer but she broke away and stood.

"It's late. I'm going up to bed." And with that, she bolted.

Liss and Sandy stared at each other. "Can you get it out of her?"

"Don't you think I've tried?" Sandy let his head fall against the back of the sofa, eyes closed, the picture of discouragement.

"Do you know her family? Can you make any sort of guess what she meant?"

"No."

As if he realized someone needed comfort, Lumpkin reappeared. He took Zara's place on the sofa and insinuated himself under Sandy's right hand, butting his head against it until Sandy began to stroke him.

"No to which?" Liss persisted. "Do you know her family?"

"She doesn't have much family. Just a mother in a nursing home in California. That's all she's ever mentioned to me, anyway."

"Zara is what, twenty-three? How old is her mother?"

Sandy frowned. "I don't know. Young to be in a nursing home, that's for sure."

As one, they looked toward the stairs. Then Liss shook her head. "We both know Zara didn't kill Victor. The police may have to invade her privacy, but we don't need to. Not yet, anyway. Don't pressure her."

Sandy made no promises, just said good night and followed his fiancée up to bed. Liss wandered back into the living room, sank down onto the sofa next to the cat, and stared at the muted television screen. She had no idea what the plot of the movie was, but she watched it anyway. Situation normal, she thought. She didn't know what was going on in her *life*, either.

To add insult to injury, Lumpkin bit her finger when she tried to pet him.

Everyone at Liss's house slept late on Monday morning. No one pounded on the door. No one phoned. By the time Liss got up and put the coffee on, Dan had long since gone to work for his father's construction company and Sherri was well into the seven-to-three shift at the county jail in Fallstown.

"Don't you have to work?" Zara asked when the three of them sat down to toast and coffee at the table in the kitchen.

"The Emporium is always closed on Mondays, to make up for being open on Saturday."

"So you have nothing you have to do with your day?" Sandy asked.

"Not a thing, although I should probably try to reach Gordon Tandy by phone." She regretted sharing that thought as soon as it was out and hastily suggested taking a drive instead. "I'd like to show you some of the sights. There's a ski area not far from here and—"

The ringing of the doorbell cut her off in midsentence. A sense of dread filled her before she got control of her rampaging imagination. *Don't panic before you have to*, she warned herself, and headed for the front door.

This time the figure on the other side was not a tall, muscular state trooper. Liss recognized Fiona's dark red coat with the fur trim and hastily unbolted the door.

"I rented a car," Fiona explained as soon as Liss let her in. It was parked at the curb, a nondescript dark blue sedan.

"We're in the kitchen," Liss said, taking Fiona's coat and hanging it up in the closet.

Lumpkin, who had been sleeping in a sunbeam, lifted his head and opened one eye when Fiona entered the room. She saw him at the same time.

"Oh dear. I didn't realize you had a cat."

Then she sneezed.

Lumpkin tore out of the kitchen as if the hounds of hell were after him.

Fiona sneezed three more times in rapid succession.

"I'll close the door to keep him out," Liss said.

"Won't help." Fiona sneezed again. "There's sure to be cat dander everywhere. It's okay." After another sneeze she rummaged in her purse. "I've got a pill I can take."

Ten minutes later the four of them were back at the kitchen table. Fiona's eyes and nose were red, but she'd finally stopped sneezing. Liss had made more toast and supplied Fiona with tea.

"Stop looking so worried," Fiona said. "Not all allergies are fatal. This one's just inconvenient. You see, I *was* planning to ask if I could move in with you for a few days. That won't work with a cat in residence. You'd have to get rid of him and vacuum everything thoroughly, and I couldn't ask you to do that."

"No, you couldn't," Liss agreed. "But . . . a few days? I thought you were all leaving tomorrow."

"So did I, until I talked to that nice Detective Tandy this morning. I've canceled all the performances we had scheduled this week."

"What?" Sandy looked stricken.

"You can't—" Liss began.

Zara cut her off. "Fiona, you didn't!"

"I can and I did. I am determined to cooperate with the police to the best of my ability. After all, it only makes sense that we do everything we can to get this matter cleared up." She calmly bit into the toast she'd just slathered with raspberry jam.

"Can the company survive that many cancelations?" Liss's appetite had vanished. She exchanged a worried look with Sandy and Zara.

"If it can't, it won't." Fiona didn't seem to care.

"Does this mean you've taken over as manager for the rest of the tour?" Sandy asked her.

"Under duress. And it's not permanent. I'm leaving the company before the next tour starts. I know I haven't mentioned this before—sorry to spring it on you—but I've been planning for some time now to retire. Victor knew."

"What will you do instead?" Liss well remembered how hard it had been for her to adjust to leaving *Strathspey*.

Fiona shrugged. "I expect I'll open a dance school somewhere. I've squirreled away a bit of a nest egg. Enough to get by."

"That's all very well for you," Zara said, sounding

waspish, "but there are twenty-eight other members of *Strathspey*. What do they do if the company folds?"

"It won't if we can find ways to speed up the investigation," Liss said.

"Get this show back on the road?" Fiona quipped.

"Someone must have seen something," Liss insisted. "I just have to find that person."

"Where will you start?" Fiona's amusement had vanished.

"With Emily."

"She's still missing," Fiona told her. "I stopped by at the B-and-B on my way here."

"Then with Janice Eccles, the woman who baked the cocktail scones—the real ones. And with the food service staff at the Student Center. Victor's murderer had to have slipped those adulterated scones into the kitchen. Someone must have noticed him. Or her."

Liss frowned, wondering how the killer had managed to bake them in the first place, and when. The company had arrived by bus only a few hours before the performance began.

"Haven't the police already talked to all of those people?" Sandy asked.

"How would I know?" She realized she'd snapped at him and sent him a quick look of apology along with an explanation: "I haven't heard a peep out of Gordon Tandy."

Instead of backing off, Sandy leaned toward her, elbows on the table. "Look, Liss, maybe you shouldn't get any more involved in this. You ask the wrong person questions and you could get hurt. Dan told us how close—"

She didn't let him finish. "I can take care of myself."

"At least let us ride shotgun."

The image would have amused her if she hadn't been so irritated. "This is not the Wild West. I'm in no danger of being bushwhacked. Now, if you'll excuse me, I have a woman to see about a scone."

The Scone Lady was not at home.

One more setback in a day already overloaded with frustration! Liss returned to her car and sat there with the heater on, trying to decide what to do next.

She glanced at her watch and saw that it was just past two in the afternoon. She'd wasted a good deal of time in Fallstown, trying to track down the people who'd worked in the kitchen Saturday night. Those few she had located either claimed they hadn't noticed anything out of the ordinary or refused to talk to her. She could hardly compel them to answer her questions. She had no official standing in the case.

So—wait and hope Mrs. Eccles returned soon? Head home? Neither choice appealed.

Like Moosetookalook, Waycross Springs had a pretty little town square. Liss was parked in front of Janice Eccles's house and there, just across the snow-covered green, was Tandy's Music and Gifts. Without giving herself the chance to think better of it, Liss was out of the car and walking briskly toward the shop.

A cheerful little bell jangled to announce her entrance. She recognized Russ Tandy behind the sales counter even though she hadn't seen him in years. Russ had more gray in his hair than Gordon did and wore it longer, and he was taller and leaner than his brother, but the resemblance was unmistakable. They had the same dark brown eyes. Good genes obviously ran in the Tandy family.

Liss knew Gordon's grandfather had founded the

business and passed it on to his son, but Russ had run it as long as she could remember. There was some overlap between Moosetookalook Scottish Emporium and Tandy's Music and Gifts in that the Tandys carried a few Scottish-themed items, but the main thrust of the Waycross Springs store was music. Russ not only sold a wide variety of instruments—everything from flutes to tubas—he also taught his customers how to play them.

He glanced at Liss without recognizing her, giving her a professional shopkeeper's smile before he went back to ringing up a sale for a woman in a bright pink parka. Liss took the opportunity to wander the aisles, comparing Russ's merchandise to the items she and her aunt stocked.

A wide selection of CDs took up about a third of the floor space. Another third was devoted to gift items. Those on display had a musical theme. Liss picked up a figurine of a dancing dog playing a drum, amused by the comical expression on its face.

Assorted musical instruments composed the remaining stock and along the back wall, arranged against paneling that showed them off to advantage, were two sets of bagpipes, one on either side of a tall, narrow window. A glance through the glass revealed that Tandy's Music and Gifts overlooked Waycross Stream . . . literally. If the bank hadn't been shored up to keep it from eroding, the entire building would have been in imminent danger of sliding into the water.

To Liss's right, a shelf contained stacked boxes labeled PRACTICE CHANTERS. The remaining section of paneling was the background for a display of awards won at piping competitions by members of the Tandy family—trophies, plaques, and ribbons of all sorts. Russ Tandy's name was well represented, as was that of his daughter, Amanda. Liss remembered her slightly. She'd be in her late teens or early twenties by now.

On the far side were several awards with Gordon's name on them. Not one of them was dated more recently than ten years back. Liss wondered if he still played the bagpipes or if he had given them up altogether after he'd gone to work for the state police. It was not an easy instrument to master, and if a piper did not stay in practice, his skills soon grew rusty.

There was no more grating sound than that of a bagpipe badly played.

When the bell over the door sounded, Liss ignored it. A small charcoal drawing of a piper playing for a dancer had caught her eye. It was beautifully executed and she wondered if the artist was someone local. If so, it might be possible to commission similar pieces for the Emporium.

She jumped at the sound of Gordon Tandy's deep voice. "Small world," he remarked.

He was standing right behind her, back stiff as a soldier at attention, expression carved in granite. She had a feeling he was hiding his reaction to finding her here, but she couldn't begin to guess if the emotion he was being so careful to repress was anger or something else. He looked very . . . official.

Liss cleared her throat, feeling like a kid caught with her hand in the cookie jar. "Isn't it just," she murmured.

Gordon might not have called her, but neither had she tried to reach him. She hadn't told him that she'd talked to the others in the company after he had. She hadn't consulted him about her decision to question the kitchen staff or visit the Scone Lady. It was a good bet he was going to think she'd been meddling . . . and he'd be right.

"So, what brings you to Waycross Springs?" he asked.

"I was about to ask you the same thing." The best defense, she'd once heard, was a good offense. Or was that the other way around?

"I'm here to talk to Mrs. Eccles again."

"What a coincidence. So am I. I just stopped by her house, to thank her for all her hard work providing food for the reception. She wasn't home."

"She was hired to make scones. I'm not sure I understand why that rates a special trip to Waycross Springs."

"First of all, Janice Eccles and I are friends. Second, she made *cocktail* scones." At his blank look, she explained. "A regular scone, at least the way folks around here make them, is usually this big." She held her hands about four inches apart. "The cocktail scones Janice and I came up with for the reception were smaller." She moved her hands so that they were closer by half the distance. "We experimented with some that were bite-size, but those were too hard to make with any kind of filling."

"Might have been the better choice." He held up a hand when she glared at him. "I know. Hindsight is always twenty-twenty."

"Actually I was going to say something about Monday morning quarterbacking, but the point's the same."

He brought the conversation quickly back to business. "So, you're telling me that the scones at the reception were distinctly smaller than regular scones?"

"Yes. I thought you knew that." As they talked, they moved toward the front of the shop and Liss was aware that Russ Tandy was watching them with unconcealed interest.

"I didn't, no." Gordon paused to run his hand over a saxophone on an elbow-high shelf. Liss wondered if he could play that instrument as well as the bagpipe. Probably. He was a Tandy, after all. "Whoever brought the mushroom scones must have known what size to make. They looked just the same on the outside as the others. Who knew they should be smaller, Liss, besides you and Mrs. Eccles?"

Liss opened her mouth and shut it again. She shook her head, but the answer stayed the same. "I mentioned the size in e-mails to friends in *Strathspey*." She dared a glance at his face and winced at the open speculation she saw there. "I even gave them the recipe. I was so pleased with the results, you see. I . . . I was bragging."

"Which friends?" There was a distinct chill in his voice.

Liss didn't want to answer but she knew he could easily find out on his own. "Sandy and Zara. Stewart. Cal. Fiona. Not everyone in *Strathspey* has a laptop but they all have e-mail addresses. And traveling together on the bus the way they do, they naturally talk to each other. I wouldn't be surprised if everybody in the company knew about the cocktail scones."

"Great. Just great."

Liss drew in a deep breath. "I, uh, talked to a few people yesterday. That is, Sherri Willett and I went by the places they're staying . . . to make sure no one needed anything. I . . ." Her words trailed off when she caught sight of Gordon's smirk. "You already knew that!"

"Yup." He took Liss's arm. "Come on. We need to talk and this isn't the place for it." He acknowledged his brother's questioning look with a "later" gesture and a wave, and whisked Liss out the door. "Have you ever been to Glendorra's? No gourmet coffees, just plain old regular."

In the western Maine mountains, as well as in some other areas of the state, "regular" meant that the coffee came already doctored with cream and two heaping sugars. Fifteen minutes later, after a brisk walk, Liss sat opposite Gordon in a small booth. She took a cautious sip of the hot, sweet brew, then set it aside. She was too jittery already.

"So, this is Glendorra's," she said.

She'd heard about the place, but seeing it was something else. The seats were upholstered in bright red leather, cracked and worn in places. The tabletop was Formica. The decor in general didn't look as if it had changed in half a century. There was even an old-fashioned jukebox in one corner. Liss wondered where they found the records—those little 45s—to play on it. No one had manufactured them in ages.

Gordon Tandy was an even greater mystery. She couldn't read him at all, couldn't tell if he was amused by her snooping or ticked off at her.

"I was just trying to help," she said, and could have kicked herself when she heard how apologetic the words sounded.

"Okay, Nancy Drew. Let's hear what you found out." He didn't *sound* angry, but Liss suspected he wasn't much pleased with her.

"Not much," she admitted. "The only really peculiar thing is that Emily Townsend isn't anywhere to be found. Did you talk to her yesterday?"

"The girlfriend? Yeah, I did. She was first on the list after I left your place."

"And?"

"And she was upset, since she'd watched him die. She was in the ladies' room when he ate the scone. She came back in time to see him fall to the floor."

"That's it?"

"That's all I'm prepared to share."

"About Emily? Or at all?"

"What do you want to know?"

"Was there a supply of epinephrine in Victor's room?"

"Yes." A flicker of . . . something crossed his face.

"What?"

"There should have been other prescription drugs there, too. I can't give you details—I shouldn't even be telling you this much—but the autopsy revealed that he had a serious medical condition. If he wasn't being treated for it, then he must have been in considerable pain, but we didn't find so much as an aspirin in his belongings."

Liss was silent for a moment, considering. "I wonder if that's why he was so hard to get along with the last few months."

"Could be."

"But it was the allergy to mushrooms that killed him, right?"

"Pretty much. In addition to the other problem, he was overweight. Doc said his arteries were so clogged up it would take Drano to open them. The allergic reaction sent him into shock and triggered a heart attack. It's a toss-up which actually finished him off."

Liss almost wished he'd stuck to not giving details. She drew in a shuddering breath and asked, "Did Emily know he was ill?"

Gordon declined to answer.

"You're being a tad inconsistent. If you remember, *you* asked *me* for help."

"I didn't ask you to question all the suspects on your own."

"But you want to know if I learned anything, don't you?"

She knew she should tell him about the quarrel between Sandy and Victor, but she wasn't going to. Unfortunately, that meant she couldn't ask if he already knew about it, either. It seemed crystal clear he wasn't inclined to volunteer much in the way of *useful* information.

Liss toyed with the salt and pepper shakers on the table until Gordon caught her hands in his. Startled, she looked up, straight into his dark eyes. There were lighter flecks in the deep brown depths. She stared, fascinated, until he spoke and broke the spell.

"Tell me about Stewart Graham."

"What about him?"

"Alcoholic?" Gordon released her hands and she pulled back, putting as much distance between them as she could within the confines of the intimate, two-person booth.

"Maybe."

"Mad at Victor Owens?"

"I doubt he denied it if you asked him. I also doubt he could have managed to bake scones in the short time between arriving in Fallstown and the start of the show, let alone smuggle them into the Student Center afterward. In fact, I don't see how anyone in the company could have."

Gordon sipped coffee, regarding her intently over the rim of the cup. "What I'm about to tell you goes no further."

After a moment's hesitation, Liss nodded. She took refuge behind her own coffee cup, although it was really too sweet for her taste.

"One of the unoccupied units at Lakeside Cabins was broken into. The oven was used—the owner always leaves the racks out and they were in—and there were pans in the dish drainer."

"That's where the scones were baked?"

"Looks like it. Problem is, so far we haven't found a single fingerprint on the stove or pans, nor was there any trace of mushrooms. Everything was very thoroughly cleaned. We've taken other evidence from the cabin for further testing, but it's not likely to be much use unless we have something to match it to. Fiber or a hair could have come from the person who broke in or from a tourist who stayed there six months ago."

This was a good man sitting across from her, Liss thought. He wanted justice for Victor and he was trying, within the rules he had to live by, to be open with her. He really did want—and value—her input. He was talking to her as a friend, an equal, and she felt compelled to respond in kind.

"Fiona said she talked to you this morning. Does she know about the break-in?"

He shook his head. "I stopped by to see her to ask if she had the victim's medical records. She's filling in for him and had already passed on personnel and financial records, so I figured she'd know where to find them. She did, but they're curiously incomplete. No mention of any recent visits to a doctor. Anyway, Fiona was heading out when I arrived and stayed only long enough to talk to me for a few minutes and hand me Victor's file. She left before the owner hailed me. I gather Fiona rented a car yesterday, right after she agreed to cancel tonight's show."

"Fiona always has been superorganized."

"I'm surprised so many people stayed at the cabins. They're kind of isolated out there."

"Not really. Everyone has a cell phone and I had volunteer drivers lined up to take them anywhere the tour bus didn't. Of course, I didn't think they'd be there more than two nights."

"Stewart Graham have a number for a driver?" Gordon asked.

"No. And I can't see him breaking into a cabin, using a kitchen, or cleaning up every trace of his presence, either. Knowing Stewart, he'd have left a beer bottle, complete with fingerprints, in the trash."

"He has no alibi. He says he was in his room at the motel, having a couple of beers. There were empties in the wastepaper basket. The cleaning crew verified that. Can't prove when he drank them, though."

A waitress interrupted them to ask if they wanted a refill on their coffee, enforcing a momentary lull in the conversation.

"We're all set, Monica," Gordon told her.

"Something else I can get ya?" It was obvious she knew Gordon well. A saucy wink went with the question.

"Just the check."

Looking disappointed but resigned, Monica produced their bill. After a few more flirtatious words with Gordon, she took her coffeepot on to the next booth, but she put a definite wiggle into her walk as she left them.

Gordon concentrated on finishing his coffee. Liss just stared at hers, wondering once again if she should tell Gordon about the quarrel between Sandy and Victor. Instead she asked him what he intended to do next.

"More interviews. We're still talking to the local people who attended the reception—those we know about, anyway. We're looking for a witness who may have seen something out of the ordinary that night."

His words lifted her spirits. For the first time that

day, she felt optimistic about the outcome of the investigation. "The murderer must have been behaving suspiciously. Sneaking into the kitchen. Bringing scones in from somewhere. Someone will have noticed something. I'm sure of it. We'll find Victor's killer. *Strathspey* will survive."

Gordon's response to her sudden enthusiasm was a frown. He glanced at his watch, tossed a few bills on top of the check, and stood. "I've got to go."

"Yes, to talk to Janice Eccles. I'll come with you."

"No, you won't."

"But she—"

One look at the stony expression on his face stopped Liss in midprotest. She felt as if someone had just tossed a dipper of cold water in her face. Straitlaced, by-the-book *Detective* Tandy was back and he clearly did not want help from an amateur.

"Isn't there anything I *can* do to help?" She heard the touch of asperity in her voice and knew he did, too, but he didn't even blink.

"Yes, you can go home and try to stay out of trouble."

Chapter Seven

Sherri was almost at the end of her shift for the day when a woman walked into the small lobby outside the dispatch center. She seemed familiar, but it took Sherri a moment to identify her. Emily Townsend no longer looked sophisticated. Her hair was a tangled mess, she wore no makeup, and she was spooked by the sight of the security camera covering the entrance.

"May I help you?" Sherri asked through the speaker.

Emily started, then peered toward the bullet-resistant glass partition that separated them. She didn't appear to recognize Sherri. "I . . . I'm trying to find the detective. I . . . I don't remember his name."

"Detective Tandy?" Sherri asked, knowing full well that it was.

Emily frowned. "I guess. Is he here?"

"Why don't you have a seat and I'll see if I can locate him?"

Emily perched on the edge of one of the uncomfortable plastic chairs that furnished the jail's "lobby" but she looked as if she might bolt at any moment.

Sherri punched in Tandy's pager number. He could be anywhere and Emily Townsend didn't look inclined to wait very long. She did, however, appear to be about to crack. Sherri's decision was easy to make.

Five minutes later, having gotten one of the other corrections officers on the shift to take over dispatch so she could leave work a bit early, Sherri was buzzed through two security doors and entered the lobby. "Miss Townsend?"

"How did you know my name? I didn't tell you my name!" She was on her feet and heading for the door before Sherri had a chance to explain.

Cursing under her breath, Sherri went in pursuit. She ignored the blast of cold air that hit her the moment she stepped out into the frigid March afternoon—she hadn't had time to put on the coat she carried folded over her arm—because Emily already had a good head start on her. The other woman was running full tilt across the parking lot.

Sherri dropped her coat and sprinted after her. She was in decent shape, but she was not a professional athlete. Emily Townsend was. Fortunately for Sherri, uneven paving dotted with icy spots was a far cry from the typical stage. Emily almost fell, twice, giving Sherri the opportunity to shorten the distance between them. When Emily lost her balance the third time, Sherri leapt, catching the other woman by the sleeve.

Emily turned, arms flailing, and they both went down, Sherri on top. Save for ample breasts, the woman was nothing but skin and bones, and her sharp cry told Sherri that the lack of padding had cost her.

"Hold still!" Sherri struggled to keep a grip on her squirming captive. Her knees throbbed from the impact of striking the ground.

"Let me go! Let me go! I haven't done anything!" One hand, fingers curled into claws, came straight toward Sherri's eyes.

"Then why did you run?" Twisting aside, Sherri managed to grab both of her opponent's thin wrists in one hand. She jerked them above the other woman's head.

Abruptly, Emily went still. She stared up at Sherri with a reproachful look. "You chased me."

"I chased you because you ran. Sheesh! Don't you dare cry."

But it was too late. First Emily's lips quivered. Then big sloppy tears ran down her face, making Sherri feel like the worst kind of bully. To make matters even more embarrassing, she belatedly remembered that they were performing for an audience.

Security cameras didn't just keep an eye on the lobby. They swept the parking lot at regular intervals. Sherri didn't need to look over her shoulder to know that the nearest one was currently pointed straight at her. Aimed, she realized with a sinking sensation in her stomach, directly at her backside.

The slap of boots on tarmac heralded the arrival of other officers. That they were there to "assist" didn't provide Sherri with much consolation. She was in for it now, and it would be a toss-up which part of the ordeal would be worse, explaining to the sheriff why she'd tackled a woman who probably hadn't done anything wrong, or putting up with the ragging of the coworkers who'd witnessed her making a fool of herself.

Liss arrived back in Moosetookalook in a rare temper. If she'd found Sandy and Zara alone at the house, she'd have unloaded on them, confessing her frustration with Gordon Tandy and sharing everything he'd confided to her, even the parts he'd asked her not to repeat.

They were not alone. Beth Hogencamp had come over as soon as the school bus dropped her off. She'd already had another dance lesson from Zara. Now she was seated on Liss's living room sofa, industriously brushing the cat and showing no inclination to leave.

Definitely getting over her shyness, Liss thought.

"He really needed brushing, Liss," Beth said in her most earnest voice. Her big brown eyes pleaded for her to be allowed to continue, to stay longer in the company of real professional dancers.

Liss wondered whether it was Sandy who was the object of her hero worship, or Zara. At Beth's age, she'd bet on the latter. Thank goodness Zara seemed to like kids and was patient with her. She'd be a great teacher if she and Sandy ever decided to go into business with his parents.

"How did it go?" Sandy asked.

"Tell you later." Liss sent a pointed look in Beth's direction. "Anything new here?"

"Nada. It's a good thing Beth came over. Kept Zara from going stir-crazy."

They watched Beth brush Lumpkin. Gobs of fur came away with each stroke—he was a Maine coon cat, a breed well known for its long, luxuriant coat. Beth paused to clean the brush and deposit the wad of hair she removed from it on top of others she'd dropped beside her on the sofa cushion.

"Good grief, Beth! You've got enough there to stuff a pillow!"

At Zara's words, Liss felt her face grow warm. She'd obviously been neglecting Lumpkin's grooming. She'd have to start brushing him more often. Then again, he liked it when she ran the hose of the vacuum cleaner over his fur. Maybe that would make less of a mess.

Lumpkin, meanwhile, had tired of behaving himself and had grabbed the brush in both front paws. Not surprisingly, it went directly into his mouth for an experimental chew.

"You're done," Liss told the cat, rescuing the brush. "Thank you, Beth."

Beth scrambled to her feet, then turned to collect the pile of fur, which she wadded up and stuck in the pocket of her jeans.

Liss started to comment but thought better of it. Beth was nine. At that age, the mind worked in mysterious ways.

When the girl had gone home, however, Liss looked to Zara for an explanation. "What do you suppose she wants with Lumpkin's fur? You don't think she's going to try casting a spell on him, do you?" Beth was a big Harry Potter fan.

Zara chuckled. "I suspect Beth is trying to collect enough to stuff a pillow. Now, tell us what you found out in Waycross Springs."

Once they'd gotten comfortable, Liss in the Canadian rocker in the bay window and Sandy and Zara on the sofa, Liss complied, leaving nothing out. She no longer felt bound by any promises she'd made to Gordon Tandy, not after the way he'd behaved. He'd strung her along, letting her think she was part of his team, and then he'd shut her out completely.

"So that was that," Liss told Sandy and Zara. "Don't call us. We'll call you. My short, illustrious career as a supersleuth sanctioned by the authorities seems to be over."

"Just as well," Sandy said. "We don't want you getting hurt on our account."

Liss shot an exasperated look in his direction. She wasn't sure which was worse, Dan jealous of Sandy or Dan and Sandy ganging up to protect the little woman. She was certain Dan was the one who'd convinced Sandy that it was dangerous for her to get involved in a murder investigation.

It was a little early for a drink, but Liss excused herself to open the bottle of her favorite white wine that was chilling in the refrigerator. A box of dark chocolates with outrageously fattening cream centers would have been better, but she didn't have any in the house.

"Did Detective Tandy say anything about me?" Zara asked, following her into the kitchen.

"He didn't ask about anyone in the company except Stewart, and that was only because Stewart's animosity toward Victor was so obvious."

Sandy joined them and began rummaging in the cabinets. "At least we know now where the scones came from, but I suppose anyone could have broken into that cabin."

"Anyone who had the recipe, knew about the housekeeping cabins, and planned ahead to somehow arrange transportation out there. The timing would have been close. I suppose the next step will be for the police to ask everyone for alibis for the hours between reaching Fallstown and the start of the show."

Sandy and Zara exchanged a glance. She spoke. "We were together."

"Sort of," he corrected her.

Liss didn't like the sound of that. "Meaning?"

She took the package of macaroni and cheese Sandy had found and foraged for a pot. She had hot dogs in the freezer and a bag of salad in the fridge. She wasn't up for preparing anything fancier. They'd have to count on the wine to make the meal more palatable.

"We had a couple of hours to kill." Sandy winced

at his inadvertent word choice, then continued. "We weren't scheduled to meet you until after the show, so we stayed with the bus until it dropped Ray, Paul, and Winona off at the theater. They didn't need our help setting up for the show, and it was too cold to stay on the bus, so we decided to explore the campus. We ended up at the college library. There's a reading room off the lobby. I went in there to see if there was anything interesting in the day's newspapers."

"And I went off on my own."

Zara pressed her fingers to her temples and closed her eyes, presumably to help her better recall how she'd passed the time. Liss filled a saucepan with water for the macaroni.

"I listened to music in the audiovisual center for a while. Then I read a magazine—an old copy of *People*—in the reference room. I didn't see Sandy again until we had to go to the theater and dress for the show."

"Neither of us left the building," Sandy said, "but I don't suppose there's any way to prove that. We didn't do anything to call attention to ourselves. The circulation desk is directly opposite the reading room, but the students working there would have no reason to remember if I was there the whole time or not."

"Same for the girl working the desk in the reference room." Zara frowned. "I think it was a girl. Maybe it was a long-haired boy. I'm afraid I wasn't paying much attention."

"You could hardly be expected to know you'd need an alibi." Liss was about to ask if they knew where any of the others had been, besides the crew, when she saw Sherri's small truck pull into her driveway. The fact that her friend was still wearing the uniform of a Carrabassett County deputy sheriff was not reassuring. Sherri almost always changed into civvies before she headed home. Besides, she should have gone off shift hours ago.

Liss was at the door and had it open before Sherri had a chance to knock. "What's wrong?"

"Nothing. It's good news. I think. Emily Townsend has turned up."

Ten minutes later, Sherri had finished recounting the story of her "capture" of the fugitive. In spite of the seriousness of the situation, Liss was having trouble smothering a laugh.

"Go ahead," Sherri told her. "Yuck it up. The guys at the jail got a major chuckle out of the whole thing."

"Is Emily all right?" Zara asked. "Why was she behaving so oddly?"

"Well, that's the question, isn't it? And 'oddly' is the right word. After running away like that, and in spite of the way I reacted, she decided I was the only one she could trust. Lucky me. I got to transport her to the hospital to be checked out. I wasn't allowed to sit in on her questioning when Gordon Tandy arrived to interview her, but I was with her until then and Emily was rambling the whole time."

"Did she make any sense?" Liss asked. "Rambling" did not suggest it had been a particularly coherent monologue.

"Some of it did. Enough that I think I've pieced together what happened. From the questions the emergency room doctor asked her and a few other comments Emily made, I think she took some medication prescribed for Victor. Apparently, she thought the pills would calm her down. She was pretty shook-up by his death even before she knew it was murder. Whatever she took, it made her paranoid. She convinced herself that Victor's killer was going to come after her next."

"That goes along with what Detective Tandy told me earlier today." For Sherri's benefit, Liss repeated the sketchy facts she had about Victor's medical condition.

"Something that could be painful, huh? That must have been what the pills were for."

Sherri didn't speculate further, but anyone who watched the news on television knew that powerful painkillers were popular on the black market. Liss preferred not to take anything stronger than aspirin herself, but it seemed logical to her that if pain pills could produce a high in some people, they might trigger a different reaction, such as paranoia, in others.

"So you have no idea what was wrong with Victor?" Zara asked.

"Not a clue."

"I wonder why he didn't tell anyone he was sick." Sandy, who had taken over the cooking, drained the macaroni and mixed in the milk, butter, and powdered cheese. Liss popped the hot dogs into the microwave. "I'm surprised no one suspected. If the diagnosis was really bad, that would certainly explain his behavior these last few months. I'd be moody and irritable, too."

"I can almost feel sorry for Victor," Liss said, "but I don't have much sympathy for Emily. In fact, I have to wonder if taking those pills was just a ploy to divert suspicion away from her."

"Where had she been all this time?" Zara asked. "You said she looked awful when she came through the door at the jail."

"She hid out in the Wayfarer, Fallstown's *other* motel. It's a real dive." Sherri glanced at Liss. "There's more, I'm afraid. Remember I said she seemed to be scared of everyone? At one point she seemed to think the entire company had conspired to kill Victor. Then she narrowed it down. She said that Sandy had threatened him. Said he swore to 'stop' Victor 'once and for all.' "

"More paranoia." But a worried frown creased Zara's forehead.

Sandy just looked puzzled. "I honestly don't remember saying that, but I might well have. Victor got me pretty steamed on more than one occasion."

"Including during an argument in a parking lot?" Liss asked. "If Emily repeated that claim to Gordon Tandy, I think you'd better level with us before he comes around again."

Sandy stopped stirring the macaroni and cheese long enough to reach for Zara's hand and squeeze it. "Good intentions will screw you every time. All I was trying to do was avoid repeating what it was that Victor said to make me lose my temper."

"Something about me?" Zara asked.

"Not just you." He pulled her into a hug and met Liss's eyes over the top of her head. "He was bragging about how he'd messed up Sarah's job prospects after she left the company. Then he threatened to do the same to Zara and me if we tried to leave. I told him I'd have thought he'd be glad to see us go. Then he said that what he'd really like was for Zara to be 'nicer' to him and suggested that I should 'share the goodies.' "

"And that's when you lost your temper," Liss said. "Did you threaten to 'stop' him?"

"If I used that word—and I really don't remember exactly what I said in the heat of anger—it wasn't a death threat. Stewart, Ray, and I were already working on a formal complaint to file with the company backers at the end of the tour. I wasn't vowing to kill Victor. I was planning to get him fired."

* * *

The first thing Dan Ruskin did when he got home was look across the town square to Liss's house. Sherri Willett's truck was just pulling out of the driveway. She saw him and waved as she drove away. Margaret Boyd's station wagon, which Liss drove in Margaret's absence, was parked out front. Lights blazed from both the living room and kitchen windows.

Dan didn't bother going into his own house first to check for phone messages and look at the day's mail. Instead he jogged the short distance between his place and Liss's. This evening he even had a legitimate reason for stopping by.

He opened with that: "Are you going to need more volunteer drivers? My sister was one of the ones you originally had lined up and she's already been called out twice. It wasn't a problem over the weekend, but during the week she has other responsibilities."

"You offering to take her place?"

"Ah, no. In case you've forgotten, I have to work."

"So do I. The Emporium will be open tomorrow." She waved him inside. Zara and Sandy were at the kitchen table, just starting on a meal of macaroni and cheese, red hot dogs, and salad. Liss had opened a bottle of wine. "Join us?"

"I'll pass. Go ahead and eat, though, before the food gets cold."

He didn't know if Liss had cooked or Zara had, but either way he knew he'd eat better fixing something for himself. If he ended up asking Liss to marry him, it wouldn't be for her domestic skills.

The thought took him by surprise and for a moment he lost the thread of the conversation.

"Maybe it won't be a problem," Liss said. "Fiona has a rental car now. She can help out. And Sandy and Zara can use the station wagon while I'm at work."

Dan could almost see the wheels turning as Liss pondered logistics. "Everyone's leaving Tuesday, right?"

"I wish I knew. Fiona has canceled several more performances. She's anxious to cooperate with the police so we can get this settled."

While she and the others ate, Liss filled Dan in on the reappearance of Emily Townsend, the break-in at Lakeside Cabins, and the state police detective's thwarting of her plan to question the Scone Lady.

"Sounds like the cops don't need your help anymore."

Liss frowned at him. "You needn't sound so happy about it."

"Hey, just trying to look on the bright side." He'd been worried when Pete told him the state police were going to ask Liss to assist them. What Sandy had said about her plans to question everyone herself hadn't thrilled him, either. Now that it looked as if she'd been cut out of the loop, he couldn't honestly say he regretted that turn of events.

When Liss glared at him, Dan had to suppress a grin. Another minute and she'd come up with a scathing comment designed to put him in his place. He was looking forward to deflecting it, but someone knocked at the front door before she could launch the first barb.

"Now what?" Liss grumbled, tossing her napkin on the table and rising with ill-concealed impatience.

Dan followed her down the hall and into the foyer and was standing beside her when she opened the door to admit a man whose almost military bearing screamed "cop."

"May I come in?"

"I suppose so," Liss said ungraciously. "Gordon Tandy, this is Dan Ruskin, my neighbor."

Dan didn't care for that description, but "boyfriend" was even weaker. He stayed close to Liss and studied the state police detective. Dan had an inch or two on him, but they had similar builds. Tandy was older, although it was hard to tell by how much. And there was something about the way he looked at Liss that Dan did not like.

"Ruskin." Tandy acknowledged the introduction with a nod. He did not offer his hand. "Someone should have talked to you earlier today, about the reception for *Strathspey*."

"Someone did. A uniformed state trooper stopped by the construction site to ask if I saw anything suspicious. I didn't. It was a very short interview."

Another nod. Then Tandy turned his attention to Sandy, who had ventured into the hall. Zara stood behind him, almost hidden except for her hands, both of which were clamped, white-knuckled, around the upper part of his right arm.

"I wonder if I might ask you a few more questions, Kalishnakof."

As soon as they'd disappeared into the library, Zara bit back a little sob. Liss put her arm around the other woman's shoulders.

"What's going on?" Dan asked.

"Sandy had an argument with Victor last week. He threatened him. It didn't mean anything, but I'm afraid Gordon thinks it does."

She'd left any mention of an argument out of her earlier summary. She'd also been calling the state trooper "Detective Tandy," not Gordon. Dan frowned. "Do you know that cop from somewhere?"

"Scottish festivals," Liss said absently, her attention fixed on the closed door to the library. "He and his brother play the bagpipes. Used to, anyway. I wonder what's going on in there."

In heavy silence, they waited. Finally, the library door opened and the two men emerged. No handcuffs were in evidence.

"That's it for now," Tandy said to the group in general. "Sorry to have interrupted your evening."

"I'll walk you out," Liss said.

Dan heard them exchange a few muffled words at the door, but he barely had time to wonder what they were saying before Liss was back. Her bright smile had faded into an expression that combined panic and frustration.

"Damn, damn, damn!" She stamped her foot for good measure. "I thought I could stay out of it. I *wanted* to. But I can't. Not if Gordon Tandy thinks Sandy killed Victor."

"Does he?" Dan asked, shifting his attention to the other man.

Sandy shrugged. "He may. He asked me what I did when we first got to Fallstown. I told him. He didn't look like he believed me. And he didn't bother to verify it with Zara."

"See?" Liss said. "He's made up his mind. *Closed* his mind. That means it's up to us to find someone else without an alibi, someone who had a real reason to want Victor dead."

The determined look on Liss's face was enough to convince Dan that arguing with her would be pointless. Resigned to the only other option—sticking close to her so he could watch her back—he headed for the kitchen to scrounge for leftovers. He had a feeling it was going to be a long night.

Chapter Eight

After foraging in a drawer for a legal pad and a felt-tip pen, Liss carried both over to the sofa, curled her legs beneath her, and rested the pad on her knees. Writing quickly, she listed twenty-nine names. After a moment's thought, she added "Victor Owens" at the bottom. It wouldn't hurt to know where he had been just before the performance.

"Okay. Alibis." Liss wrote each one as she enumerated it. "Stewart says he was alone in his motel room. Fiona was napping in her cabin. That's her usual practice," she added for Dan's benefit. "She likes to be well rested for the performance."

"Zara and I were at the library on campus. Who knows? Maybe someone *will* remember seeing us there. A fair number of students were using the facility, plus the library staff."

"Winona, Ray, and Paul were at the theater, setting up for the show. Winona West is in charge of costumes and props and Paul Roberts is Ray's stage crew."

"So they should be able to vouch for each other," Dan said.

He had settled into one of the easy chairs while Sandy took the other with Zara on his lap. The two men appeared to be getting along well, but Liss couldn't quite forget Dan's outburst on Saturday night. The incident had unsettled her, making her wonder if she knew Dan as well as she thought she did. She wasn't certain why he was still here tonight, either, evidently ready, willing, and able to help investigate a murder. Still, she wasn't about to send him away. As an outsider, he might be able to spot something the rest of them overlooked.

"Liss? Would they all have worked in sight of each other?"

She glanced at Sandy. "Pretty much, but Ray was part of the drive to get Victor fired, right?"

Sandy nodded.

"Because of Sarah?"

He looked uncomfortable, but nodded again.

"Then Ray has to remain a suspect. Sarah Bartlett is a dancer who left the company after a quarrel with Victor," she told Dan. "Ray has romantic feelings for her. If they were working together, that would certainly explain how they got around a tight schedule. She could have provided the scones while he smuggled them into the Student Center kitchen." She hated to think of Ray Adams as a murderer. She'd known him a long time and she liked the guy. But *someone* had killed Victor.

"She'd have been taking quite a risk," Sandy pointed out. "We all know Sarah. Besides, if she baked the scones, why break into one of those cabins to do it? That would have increased her chances of being recognized, what with members of the company staying there."

"She's just one possibility," Liss reminded him, making a mental note to find out exactly which cabin had been used to bake the scones. "Anyone could have broken in."

"How did they get out there to do it?" Zara asked. "Steal a car?"

"Good point." Liss wrote that question on a fresh page.

"Where was the bus parked?" Dan asked. "Could someone have borrowed it to get out to Lakeside Cabins?"

"It was left at the theater," Sandy said. "Again, kind of risky to take it. Crew might have noticed it was gone, plus it would be pretty hard to hide."

Liss tried to envision a map of the cabins and re-alized that they were located in a heavily wooded area. "It would be easy enough to hide a car and not impossible to conceal something as big as a bus. Still, Sandy's right. Why take the risk? The bus sports huge Strathspey Dance Company logos on both sides."

"We can ask around. See if anyone noticed it out on the roads. And who was driving it." Dan wasn't giving up on his notion and Liss briefly considered encouraging him to pursue it so she'd be left to her own devices. Almost immediately, she thought bet-ter of the idea.

"Can you can get off work tomorrow? I could use your help."

"With . . . ?"

"There are some people I want to question again and I'm not stupid enough to do it alone. Sherri's on days at the jail, so—"

"Say no more. I'm at your disposal. Just give me a call at the construction site and I'll meet you wher-ever you say."

"Good. Now, everyone in the company has a cell phone. All we need are the numbers."

Zara had a list of them and as soon as she'd fetched it from the guest room, she, Sandy, and Liss spent the next hour making calls to ask their colleagues where they had been between their arrival in Fallstown and the time they'd reported to the theater to dress for the show. It didn't take long to discover that almost everyone had an alibi.

The five young dancers staying at Lakeside Cabins had been together in Denise's cabin the whole time. They'd had a pizza delivered and had given each other facials. Seven of the male dancers had also stuck together, playing cards in one of the motel rooms. The one married couple in the company, Karen and Jim Nixon, had stayed put in their motel room, too. *Not* playing cards. Charles Danielstone and Jock O'Brien—they weren't a couple, but habitually roomed together on the road to save money—had gone out to get a bite to eat at a fast food place with Roberta Gough and Janet Burns, who occupied the adjoining room at the motel. Cal MacBain and Josie Malone had left the B-and-B as soon as they'd unpacked to take a stroll around town. They'd been together the whole time.

In the end, Liss's list of thirty names had shrunk to six. The only members of the company who did not have anyone to vouch for their whereabouts during all of the crucial hours were Sandy, Zara, Stewart, Emily, Fiona, and Lee Annie, the company songbird. And Victor Owens. No one knew where he had been or what he had done on the last afternoon of his life.

Tuesday morning Dan was scheduled to work at the site of a new house Ruskin Construction was building. He got there early, but his brother, Sam, was ahead of him, drinking coffee out of a thermal mug he'd brought with him from home and studying the blueprints. The smell of chicory drifted toward Dan through the low-hanging fog that had made the drive from Moosetookalook something of a challenge. It was warmer this morning than it had been for weeks, triggering a rapid snowmelt. Another sunny day or two like this one and they'd be smack in the middle of mud season. *Not* the most beautiful time of year in Maine.

"I may have to take off later today," Dan told his brother.

"Why's that?"

"These friends of Liss's . . . she's trying to help them out." He gave Sam a quick recap of the situation.

"Friends like that, who needs enemies?"

"Most of them are okay. One bad apple . . ."

Sam shrugged. "Liss taken to snooping again?"

"You know Liss." They headed for the shell of the house and began nailing sheathing to the frame. Dan held one of the eight-by-four-foot panels of treated plywood while Sam used the nail gun. "At least this time she asked me to watch her back." Even if he had been her second choice after Sherri Willett!

"Seems like she'd have plenty of people to back her up, what with all of those dancers being stuck here."

"Except that one of them is probably a murderer."

"They're all suspects?"

"Pretty much."

"Tell her to butt out. Safer that way."

"Oh, that would go over big. She prides herself on being able to handle anything."

Sam shook his had. "Man, you are so whipped!"

"She's important to me," Dan said quietly.

Something in his tone must have gotten through to Sam, because the smart-ass grin disappeared from his face. "What's really got you scared?"

"You mean besides the fact that I'm afraid she'll

get too close to Victor Owens's killer and end up as victim number two?"

"Yeah." They moved on to the next sheet of plywood.

"I screwed up, Sam. I was jealous of this guy, Sandy—he's staying at her house with his fiancée—and I let Liss see how I felt. She was not flattered. I think she's forgiven me for that, but the last thing I can do now is start issuing orders. If I try too hard to protect her, she'll dump me along with yesterday's trash. I'm not willing to risk that. She's too important to me."

"I sure hope you're not asking me for advice to the lovelorn. I'm no expert on romance." Sam chuckled. "Just ask my wife."

Dan gave a snort.

"You could ask Mary, though. Maybe she can suggest something, being a woman and all."

Oh yeah. That was going to happen. If his brother had thought his inability to deal with Liss was funny, their sister would laugh her ass off. Dan, choosing to use a hammer instead of a nail gun, worked off some of his frustration pounding on the next section of sheathing.

Sam waited until they'd finished the front of the house. "You could ask Liss to marry you. Husbands are allowed to be a little overprotective."

"Don't think I haven't considered it, though I'm not sure Liss would agree with your reasoning." A husband, however, or even a fiancé, could stick a whole lot closer to his woman than a mere "neighbor."

"So, what's holding you back?"

"Abject terror, Sam. I'm afraid she'll say no."

*   *   *

Like Tandy's Music and Gifts, Moosetookalook Scottish Emporium was a family business. Liss's grandfather had started it and for a while her father and her aunt, Margaret Boyd, had run it together. When Liss's parents moved to Arizona, Aunt Margaret had continued the business on her own, until last summer when she'd sold half interest to her niece.

"I love this place." Liss unlocked the door and waved Zara and Sandy inside.

She'd made all sorts of improvements to the business in recent months, adding a Web page and producing a glossy mail-order catalog, but the store itself remained essentially the same. The sales counter was to the left of the door. To the right, beyond rows of shelving displaying all sorts of Scottish-themed gift items, was the "cozy corner" where comfortable chairs had been arranged for the convenience of patrons who wanted to consider before they bought. Several shelves full of books about Scotland, both fiction and nonfiction, also occupied that space.

The rest of the sales floor was taken up with racks of kilts and tartan skirts and display cases holding various Scottish accessories. There was everything from kilt hose and sporrans to *skean dhus*, brooches, and clan crest badges. Along one wall were bagpipes, practice chanters, penny whistles, and drumsticks—the kind with a big ball of fluff at one end, used to play the bass drum in a bagpipe band.

The surfaces of the cabinets, shelves, and tables gleamed, redolent of lemon-scented furniture polish. Every item on display had been meticulously placed to show to advantage. Liss felt her heart swell with pride as she surveyed her domain. She had succeeded in the goals she'd set for herself six months ago when she and Aunt Margaret became partners—she'd brought the Emporium into the twenty-first century and still managed to carry on in the traditional manner. Old customers revisiting the store would find everything just as it always had been, with perhaps a few more items added to the inventory.

"Just show me your pricing system and I'll take it from there," Zara said. "Do you discount to other dealers?"

"Ten percent. I didn't realize you'd worked in retail before."

Zara's face closed up. "It was that or waitressing. I wasn't interested in lugging heavy trays of food around and dodging pinches from customers."

Liss let the subject drop. She spent less than half an hour familiarizing her houseguests with the store's stock. After mentioning a shipment she was expecting that someone would have to sign for, she was out the door. As soon as she picked Dan up, she would be on her way to Fallstown to talk to the rest of the people on her short list. She also intended to look for Sarah Bartlett.

Halfway out to the construction site, her cell phone rang. She pulled over to the side of the road to answer it and was surprised to find the owner of Lonesome Stranger Bed-and-Breakfast on the other end of the line. "Problem, Rosemary?"

"I'm afraid so. All four of my rooms are booked from tomorrow night on—guests coming into town for a wedding. You're going to have to find other accommodations for your people."

"Has Miss Townsend returned to her room?"

"Yes. She's here. Do you want to talk to her?"

"No, that's all right. I'm on my way to Fallstown. I'll see her when I get there. And don't worry, Rosemary. I'll make other arrangements for everyone."

She returned the phone to her purse with a thoughtful expression on her face. It was going to take some work to shuffle everyone around to their—and her own—satisfaction, but this unexpected eviction might turn out to be a blessing in disguise.

Ten minutes later, Liss pulled in at the house the Ruskins were building. "I have another favor to ask," Liss said as soon as Dan opened the passenger-side door.

"What? No 'hello, Dan. That new house is really coming along'?" He slid inside and reached for the seat belt.

"Sorry." She glanced at the building-in-progress through the windshield, but it didn't look like much to her.

"Never mind. What's the favor?"

"You don't have to help, you know. I can go on my own."

"Just drive. What's the second favor?"

"Can you put a few people up at your place?" She explained about Rosemary's incoming guests. "I could probably squeeze more of them in at the motel, but this might be a good opportunity to . . . observe the, uh—"

"Suspects? Jeez, Liss, you just don't know how to let go, do you?"

"If you don't want—"

"I know! Fine. I've got room. You know that. How many and who?"

Dan's place had four bedrooms, if he counted the one in the attic. Liss had good reason to know. She'd grown up in that house. "I thought Stewart." Dan rolled his eyes. "And Ray."

"Why am I not surprised?" he muttered.

"And Cal."

"Who's Cal?"

"Country dances are done by pairs. Cal was my partner for a couple of years and then he danced with Sarah and now he dances with Emily. And before you get any ideas, unlike Sandy, Cal *is* gay."

Dan opened his mouth and shut it again without saying anything.

And that seemed to put paid to conversation for the rest of the drive to Fallstown. Liss made no effort at small talk and neither did Dan.

She drove first to Lakeside Cabins. The building that had been broken into was easy to spot . . . if she followed the twisting driveway until it dead-ended. Yellow crime scene tape made an X across the door.

That unit was the one farthest from the road, almost hidden by two big spruce trees. As Liss visited each of the other cabins to talk to the dancers, she realized that only Fiona's was close enough to see more than the roof of the cabin the killer had used, and Fiona's door faced away from it. Unless she'd been looking out a window, she wouldn't have seen a thing.

It didn't take Liss long to confirm what she'd already suspected would be the case. For two nights, the cabins had been fine, but no one really wanted to be stuck this far from civilization indefinitely.

"Pack up, then," she told everyone. "I'll make arrangements to move you to the motel."

Only to Fiona did she make a different offer, suggesting that the older woman stay in her aunt's apartment above the store. "No cat dander," she promised.

"What a thoughtful suggestion, Liss. Thank you. I'd like that."

"Good. Can you drive a few others up to Moosetookalook with you?"

Fiona frowned. "What others?"

"Well, that depends on who is willing to give up a motel room. I'll call you in an hour." She started to leave, then turned back. "Fiona, you don't happen to know where Sarah Bartlett is, do you?"

Fiona looked startled. "No idea. Why do you ask?"

"Just a passing thought," she lied. "Nothing important."

At the motel she didn't have any trouble coaxing Ray or Stewart into moving to Dan's. Convincing Lee Annie to stay in the extra room at her house, however, was a bit more difficult. Liss had to admit that what she was offering was smaller, and that there wouldn't be much choice when it came to restaurants or shops.

"But it's free," Liss reminded her. "Room *and* board." She thought better of mentioning that she'd probably be the one cooking.

"Okay," Liss said to Dan as they left Lee Annie to pack her things. "Drop me at the B-and-B and go get the five girls from the cabins to move them into these three rooms. Then you can take Stewart and Ray and Lee Annie to Moosetookalook in the station wagon and I'll follow in Fiona's car with the rest of our guests." She pulled out her cell phone to let Fiona know what was going on.

Dan gave her a mocking salute but did as she asked. He even opened the passenger-side door before going around to take the wheel of her aunt's station wagon. He dropped her off at the B-and-B a few minutes later.

Everything now depended upon the cooperation of those currently staying at the Lonesome Stranger Bed-and-Breakfast. If even one of them balked, her scheme would fall apart.

Liss was a little leery of meeting Emily Townsend again, but the tall blonde who joined the others in the B&B's parlor a short time later seemed a different person from the one Liss had met at the reception. Shoulders slumped, face pale and bare of makeup, she regarded Liss through lackluster eyes.

"I'm sorry to have been so much trouble," she whispered.

"It's been a trying time for all of us." Liss resisted the urge to pat the other woman on the shoulder. Emily really did look pathetic.

"What's up, Liss?" Cal wanted to know. "Has something else happened?"

"I'm afraid you have to move out. Your rooms are needed, and since Fiona has committed the whole company to staying on for another few days, I've had to make new arrangements. Josie, are you okay with moving over to the motel and bunking with Denise?"

"Sure, Liss. We get on just fine."

"Great. Cal, you'll be staying with a friend of mine. He has a house in Moosetookalook."

"Is he good looking?"

She stuck her tongue out at him and almost said "He's taken." She stopped herself just in time. She'd have to think about their future as a couple sometime, but not now. Later. *Much* later.

"Stewart and Ray are staying there, too."

"Oh, joy. Oh, rapture."

"Go pack!"

Cal offered Josie his arm and they went upstairs together. Liss turned to Emily and Winona. "I thought, since you two preferred these accommodations to the motel, that you might be more comfortable in an apartment than at the motel. My aunt is away right now, so you'll be staying at her place."

"That's very considerate of you," Winona said. "I do get tired of motel rooms."

"Emily?"

The blonde gave a listless shrug. "Whatever."

"Well, that's settled, then," Liss said brightly. "All

we need to do is ferry everyone to their new digs."
Once again she dug the cell phone out of her purse
to call Fiona.

So far, so good, she thought when she disconnected.
Now all she had to do was figure out which one of
the people she was transporting to Moosetookalook
had killed Victor Owens.

Chapter Nine

Stewart Graham had apparently been intoxicated when he'd agreed to leave Fallstown because now he was on the verge of a panic attack at the thought of staying in a village that didn't have a bar. Dan got him calmed down by assuring him that he could buy beer at either the convenience store or the supermarket and pointing the way to the latter. Odds were he'd spend his entire stint in Moosetookalook in an alcoholic haze. Dan couldn't decide which was going to prove harder to put up with over the next few days, Stewart's drinking or the fact that Ray Adams was a die-hard Yankees fan.

"Can't you talk about something else?" Dan finally asked. "I really don't want to have to punch out your lights."

"Like you could." Ray had made himself comfortable in Dan's living room and was happily surfing through the sports channels.

"We could talk about women instead." He moved a stack of woodworking magazines off a chair and sat down. "You could tell me about Sarah."

Ray's face purpled. His hands curled into fists. For a moment Dan thought the other man was about to come up off the sofa and pound him into the floor. Dan tensed, ready to defend himself.

"You should leave Sarah out of this." Ray's deep, nasal voice sounded even more raspy than usual.

"Whoa! No offense meant. I just heard you were friends with her, that's all. I wondered if you knew where she went when she left the company. Liss wants to get hold of her."

"I should be so lucky."

The sheer anguish on Ray's face convinced Dan that he was telling the truth. "Probably just as well."

Ray's eyes narrowed at the comment. He hit the mute button on the clicker. "What's it to you, Ruskin?"

Dan shrugged. "I expect you've already figured that out. Liss is trying to discover who killed Victor."

"What is she, nuts? Sarah wouldn't—"

"Sarah's just one possibility. She's probably in the clear." Before taking Sandy and Zara over to the Emporium, Liss had called around to every place in the area that rented rooms. No Sarah Bartlett had been registered at any of them, but that might not mean much. Sarah could have used a phony name.

"Sarah wasn't at the reception, y'know?"

"No, but you were."

"So, tell—how did we do it, already?" Anger had morphed into sarcasm.

"Think about it the way a suspicious cop would, Ray. You've got an alibi for the time when the scones must have been baked, but Sarah could have baked them. Then she lies low while you slip them onto the refreshment table for Victor to eat."

Abruptly, Ray started to laugh. "You call that a plan? You *are* nuts!"

"Hey, not my theory." Dan held up both hands, palms out. He had to like the guy. Ray said what he thought.

"So, you want me out of your house? I wouldn't want you should have to harbor a murderer."

"Hell, most of the people Liss invited to stay in Moosetookalook are suspects. I'm more concerned about having to put up with the constant yammering about the damn Yankees."

"Only team worth rooting for since dem bums left Brooklyn."

Dan knew enough about baseball history to recognize the reference to the abrupt departure of the Dodgers from that New York City borough in the late 1950s. "You think so? Then how come so many former Brooklyn fans now root for the Red Sox?"

"Gluttons for punishment?"

"Not hardly. Okay, Ray. Level with me. You got a *reason* Liss shouldn't suspect Sarah?"

"Why should I tell you anything?"

"Because you could be stuck in Moosetookalook for a long time unless someone gets arrested for Victor's murder."

"Stupid name for a town," Ray grumbled. "All right, already. We talk about this once, then that's it."

At Dan's nod of agreement, Ray drew in a deep breath. His hands went into motion at the same time he began to speak, at times gesturing so widely that Dan feared for his lamps.

"Okay. No argument. I blamed Victor when Sarah left. I'd have liked to wring his neck, y'know? But I figured it would hurt him more to lose his job, so me and Stewart and Sandy, we were working on that."

"Why didn't Sarah file a sexual harassment complaint?"

"You think I know? She changed her mind. Probably would have cost an arm and a leg to take the case to court."

"So she just left?"

"Yeah."

"I heard you two were . . . close. You're telling me she took off without a word?"

"All but. What? You're surprised? I'm forty-five years old. Big schnozz. Ugly puss. Going gray. I never had a chance with Sarah." He was starting to get choked up. "Beautiful girl. Redhead, y'know? Young. Graceful. Friendly with everyone, even a guy like me. I should be so lucky as to have her for a friend. I was damned grateful for any crumb she threw my way."

After her previous shift's lively ending—about which Sherri was still getting grief from her fellow law enforcement officers—she was just as happy when Tuesday turned out to be a completely boring day. At three, she showered and changed in the locker room before heading home, and when she left the jail she was thinking about her son and looking forward to having some quality time with him. That prospect took a nosedive when she spotted Gordon Tandy leaning against the hood of her pickup.

"Got a minute?"

"Just about."

"I won't keep you long."

Sherri caught herself wishing it was still as cold as it had been the last few days, but the afternoon sun was warm—almost balmy for March—and it was no hardship to stand outside and talk.

"You know Liss MacCrimmon pretty well?"

"We've seen a lot of each other since she came back to Moosetookalook. We're both from there originally and I was already working part-time in her aunt's shop when she returned."

"What brought her back?"

Sherri was surprised he didn't already know. Then again, maybe he did. Detectives tended to ask questions to which they already had the answers. It helped weed out the lies.

"She injured her knee so badly that she couldn't dance anymore. That pretty much ended her career with *Strathspey*, although now some of the dancers are urging her to consider coming back as manager."

There was a slight but perceptible stiffening of Gordon Tandy's shoulders. "Think she'll take the job?"

"She might. She hasn't said much lately, but I know she really liked the life. They call dancers Gypsies for a reason, I guess."

After a short silence, during which Gordon seemed to be engaging in an internal debate, he reached inside his jacket and pulled out a notebook. "You went to the performance with Liss, right?"

Sherri nodded.

"What time did you meet?"

Interesting, Sherri thought. Had he only just realized that Liss was a possible suspect? "We met at the theater and were together through the performance and at the reception."

"Can you verify where she was before that?"

"I can *tell* you where she was. She worked all day in the shop, and believe me, the neighbors would have noticed if she closed the Emporium long enough to make an earlier run to Fallstown."

"There's an apartment above the store, right? With a kitchen?"

Sherri didn't bother to hide her smile. "If you're thinking Liss baked those mushroom scones, you can forget it. First of all, when Pete and I met up with her at the theater, she didn't have anything on her but an evening bag—much too small to hide baked goods in. But more important—and I have firsthand experience to back this up—Liss MacCrimmon is not a very good cook. She definitely has not mastered the art of making decent scones. Any cocktail scone she baked would have been way too heavy to lift in one hand. Don't forget, I bit into one of the mushroom scones. It tasted terrible, but the pastry was light and flaky, just the way a scone is supposed to be. Liss couldn't have managed that if her life depended on it."

Liss arrived back in Moosetookalook late in the afternoon with Fiona, Emily, Winona, and Cal. To her surprise, Zara had abandoned her temporary job at the Emporium. She and young Beth Hogencamp were across the street in the town square making angels in the snow.

"Go on in." Liss could see Sandy through the shop window. "Sandy can show you where the stairs to the apartment are and you can start moving your stuff in. Cal, I'll be along in a minute to take you to the house where you'll be staying."

As soon as they'd entered the Emporium, she crossed Pine Street. Beth's musical laughter made her smile as she got closer. She could remember making angels in the snow when she was nine.

Zara sprang up, looking guilty. "It's okay. Sandy's minding the store."

"No, it's not okay." Liss grinned at her, then flopped over backward onto the ground.

The wet snow was a shock. It was far from the ideal consistency for making snow angels, but Beth was beside her, giggling, so she made the best of it. Moving cautiously in what was precariously close to slush, she made angel wings with her arms and shifted her legs to form the angel's long robe.

"*Now* it's okay," she told Zara.

Except for the fact that the back of her coat, the seat of her jeans, and her hair were all soaking wet!

Zara gave her a hand up, then pulled Beth to her feet. Moving to the accompaniment of a steady *squish, squish*, they collected more suitcases from Fiona's rental car before trooping inside. The three women had already gone up to Margaret Boyd's apartment, but Cal was in the shop with Sandy.

"Interesting performance," he said. "You look a little damp."

Liss shed her coat and reached behind the sales counter for a roll of paper towels to blot her hair. "A slight miscalculation. For the best snow angels, just the right kind of snow is necessary—different from snowball snow or snowman snow or even snow-fort snow."

"And today you did not have it."

"Sadly, no." She started to pass off the paper towels to Beth and Zara and realized that the entire roll wouldn't be adequate. "Come on upstairs," she told them. "This is a job for terry cloth."

The living space in Margaret Boyd's apartment was limited, but there were two bedrooms, one with twin beds. Emily and Winona had already settled into that one, leaving Fiona on her own in the other. Liss delivered the remaining luggage to its owners, detoured to the linen closet for towels, and returned to the living room, where she'd left Zara and Beth.

"I didn't forget another lesson, did I?" she asked Beth as she helped dry the girl's dark curls.

"I came over because I saw Zara through the window when I got home from school."

"She had excellent timing. I needed a break. I don't think I'm cut out to be a shopkeeper. Don't get me wrong. It's a great store. But being a salesclerk is pretty boring. I mean, you're not exactly swamped with walk-in customers."

"Tell me about it." Liss sighed. These days the mail order and Web site business was responsible for most of the profit. If her aunt hadn't been so against the idea, Liss would have reluctantly considered closing the brick and mortar store and using the space for storage.

The towel now wrapped around her head, her water-resistant ski parka hanging over a heating vent, Beth began to explore the living room. As was her habit, she picked up every object that caught her interest— framed pictures, knickknacks, even the book on hotel management Liss's aunt had left lying on an end table. After closer examination, she returned each to the general vicinity in which she'd found it. Beth continued her inspection of Aunt Margaret's possessions even after Fiona and Winona came in from the bedrooms.

"Emily's lying down," Winona said. "She still hasn't entirely recovered."

"Whatever possessed her to take someone else's medicine?" Liss couldn't imagine anyone being so foolish.

"She was distraught. And Victor apparently told her those pills calmed him down." Fiona lowered her voice. "To tell you the truth, I don't think the girl's too bright."

"She couldn't be if she hooked up with—" Winona broke off as she belatedly realized that Zara, too, had once been romantically involved with the company manager. "Sorry."

"Don't worry about it, but I don't think this is a

suitable topic in the present company." Zara added the last in a whisper, her gaze shifting pointedly to Beth.

"Perhaps the child should leave," Fiona hissed back.

Beth froze with her hand on a hand-carved wooden piper Margaret Boyd had brought back from a trip to Nova Scotia.

"Well," said Liss, a bit too heartily, "Zara and Beth and I will just leave you ladies to settle in. I need to take Cal over to Dan's house and Zara has to help Sandy close the shop. We're all going to Dan's for supper—no cat dander there, Fiona."

"Excellent. And no children, either, I presume?"

Beth had already begun to inch toward the door. Now her face flamed and she bolted. Zara went after her.

"Was that really necessary?" Liss demanded.

Fiona shrugged. "Sorry. The kid was just starting to bug me, that's all." She lifted one hand to her forehead. "I've got a bit of a headache. You'll have to excuse me if I'm out of sorts. It's been a rough few days."

"For all of us." Liss forced a smile, but she hadn't entirely forgiven Fiona for hurting Beth's feelings. "I'll see you in an hour or so. It's the middle house on the right-hand side of the square."

"We'll be there," Fiona promised. "Emily, too."

Still squishing a bit as she walked, Liss collected Cal and escorted him to Dan's house. No one seemed to be around so she showed him to his room, then went in search of Dan. He was not in his bedroom, or in the kitchen. She stepped out onto the back porch and saw that the light was on in the carriage house Liss's parents had used as a garage when they'd owned the house. Dan had converted it into a woodworking shop.

Liss slipped inside and just stood there for a moment, breathing in the soothing scent of cedar paneling and sawdust and enjoying the view. Dan was sanding a piece of wood with a sure, light touch. Lovingly.

She must have made some small sound because he turned and saw her. "Hey."

"Hey, yourself. What's that you're working on?"

"It's going to be a walking stick for my uncle. He's got a touch of gout."

"You usually work on much bigger pieces."

"Yeah, well, it's been a while since I've had a chance to work on *any* of my own projects. Restoring woodwork and furniture for The Spruces is satisfying in its own way, but it isn't quite the same as creating something new from a piece of wood."

"What do you want to be working on?"

"My sister asked me to make her an end table using a slice of a tree trunk from her front yard for the top. Then there's that design you suggested for a book rack that can be used in a chair or in bed. I haven't had a spare moment to work on either."

"I'm sorry. You didn't need a houseful of people on top of all you've got on your plate."

"They're okay. Lee Annie is over at your house. Ray and Stewart went out to explore. Shouldn't take them long. As Ray has already pointed out about a dozen times, there isn't much 'here' here."

"If Stewart is looking for a bar, he's going to be disappointed."

"He's already stocked up on beer at the market. Liss, I had a chance to talk to Ray about Sarah."

She listened intently as he repeated his conversation. "Did you believe him?"

"Yes, I did. That's not to say she didn't kill Victor,

but if she did, I don't think Ray knew anything about it."

"Poor Ray. He's such a nice guy, but I can see why a pretty, young dancer wouldn't give him more than the time of day." She glanced at her watch. "Speaking of which, I'd better go check on Lee Annie. And shower and change." She gave him the short explanation for her bedraggled appearance. "I really appreciate your inviting everyone here for supper. This house has a better layout for entertaining so many people."

"Lucky me."

She gave him a quick kiss on the cheek. "Yes, you are."

A few minutes later, she was back home. On her way to her bedroom she caught a glimpse of Lee Annie in the little one right next to it, the room Liss had originally intended for Sandy. "We're heading over to Dan Ruskin's house in a bit," she called as she passed the door. "We'll be sending out for pizza."

"Whatever."

Lee Annie sounded so downcast that Liss changed course and entered Lee Annie's room instead of her own. "Is something wrong?"

"Only the obvious. It dawned on me on the drive up here that we're not going anywhere until Victor's killer is found. Nothing against your hometown, Liss, but I'm used to city lights. I'll wither and die in a place like this."

"It won't be forever, even if the police don't figure out who murdered Victor. A few days. A week at most." She didn't dare speculate about what that would do to the company's reputation, or to their hopes for future tours.

"I've been racking my brain, trying to think who would want him dead."

Liss came farther into the room and sat down beside Lee Annie on the love seat that opened up into a bed. "Any conclusions?"

"Do you think Stewart could have done it?"

"You tell me. Why would you think so?"

Lee Annie heaved a sigh so deep it made her substantial bosom heave. "I had the room next to his at the motel and the walls are pretty thin. That night, after the reception, after Victor died, I could hear him celebrating."

That had been before they knew it was murder, Liss remembered. "Celebrating how?"

"He was singing." She grimaced. "He's not a very good singer. Can't hold a tune. But the words were clear enough. He was singing 'ding, dong, the witch is dead.' "

Liss blinked, unsure whether to laugh or groan.

"It was bad enough he kept caterwauling at the top of his lungs, but then he dragged out his pipes and started playing 'Scotland the Brave.' Charlie and Jock finally put a stop to that. They took the bagpipe away from him and wouldn't give it back till the next day."

Liss tried to recall her earlier conversation with Lee Annie at the motel and wondered why the other woman hadn't mentioned this then. Probably because she hadn't considered it important. And because Liss hadn't thought to ask her any more about Stewart once Lee Annie told them he'd left the motel. Her questions had centered on what Lee Annie might have seen at the reception and whether she knew of anyone who had a particular grudge against Victor.

"We all cussed him out on a regular basis," Lee Annie had said, as had just about everyone else in the company.

But someone had done more than cuss.

Chapter Ten

By the time Dan opened his door to Sherri Willett on Tuesday night, he was wondering what had possessed him to invite a passel of strangers into his home. Pizza boxes littered his normally neat living room, and the table in the connecting dining room had been turned into a repository for soda and liquor bottles and bowls filled with every junk food known to man. The level of noise had long since passed tolerable. Worse, all the conversations centered on topics he knew nothing about.

So far the members of *Strathspey* had steadfastly avoided talking about Victor's murder, but they seemed only too happy to recount past successes on the road—in mind-numbing detail—and to debate the issue of when and where the tour should resume. To add insult to injury, Liss was so focused on watching Emily Townsend's every move that she'd scarcely said word one to him all evening.

"Wow, Dan," Sherri greeted him. "When did you turn into a party animal?"

He didn't dignify that smart remark with a response, just waved her in and shut the door behind her. It was snowing again, he noticed. He was tempted to grab his coat and go for a walk. It might be cold out there, but at least it would be quiet and peaceful.

"I can't stay," Sherri said, "but I didn't want to try to explain over the phone."

Alerted as much by her demeanor as her words, Dan's drifting thoughts centered. Sherri wouldn't be in Moosetookalook in the evening unless it was important. He glanced at his watch. It was just past eight. She'd have gone home from work, spent time with her son, put him to bed, and come straight here. Whatever was on her mind was serious but not urgent. "You need to talk to Liss?"

She nodded. "Preferably without an audience."

The hallway ran from the front door straight back to the kitchen. Ignoring the doors opening into bedlam, they followed it, but the kitchen was occupied, too. Fiona was going through his cabinets.

"Looking for something?"

She gave a guilty start. "Sorry. Just idle curiosity, I'm afraid. Hello, Sherri. What brings you here?"

"Scheduling problems," Sherri told her. "I work part-time at the Emporium as well as at the jail. Do you suppose you could send Liss out here? I don't want to put a damper on the fun."

"Why would you—? Oh, because you're the one who figured out that Victor was murdered? Don't give that another thought. I'm sure someone would have noticed eventually."

She breezed out of the room, the loose, colorful scarf she wore floating after her. A hint of her jasmine-scented perfume remained.

"Did you just lie to the nice lady?" Dan asked.

"Damn straight. I don't trust any of them."

"Too bad Liss doesn't feel that way."

They exchanged a look that said it all. Liss was too close to these people. She might claim she was trying to figure out which one had killed Victor Owens, but she had a blind spot the size of Cleveland when it came to picking up clues about those she cared for. It wasn't just Sandy and Zara, Dan had realized. She felt protective of the whole damned company.

Liss joined them a few minutes later, looking much more herself than she had earlier. She'd twisted her shoulder-length brown hair into some sort of fancy knot and changed into a dry pair of jeans and a neon-yellow sweater topped with one of her favorite paisley scarves. Definitely the bright spot in Dan's evening, even if she did look worried.

Behind her, in the hall, Fiona was watching, her interest clearly piqued by Sherri's presence.

"This way," Dan said, steering Liss and Sherri into the combination utility room and pantry off the kitchen. Anything to put a little more distance between them and the partying dance troupe. "We can talk in private in here."

"Yes, but can we breathe?"

To ease the crowding, Dan boosted himself onto the top of the clothes washer, giving Liss and Sherri more room in the narrow aisle between the appliances and the shelving.

"You've got trouble, Liss," Sherri said.

"What is it? What's happened? Is Gordon about to arrest someone?"

"Don't panic!" Sherri put a hand on her forearm. "I guess, in a twisted sort of way, I'm probably bringing you *good* news. Gordon Tandy questioned me today, about you. Wanted to know if anyone could vouch for your whereabouts before the performance."

"He's checking *my* alibi?" Liss's voice went up in astonishment.

"Looks that way to me. I thought you should

know. But on the bright side, that means he hasn't yet fixed on any one suspect as being most likely. He's keeping an open mind."

"Maybe a little too open," Liss muttered. "Oh well. You're right, Sherri. It is good that he's still looking at all the possibilities. Can you remember exactly what he asked you?"

Sherri repeated as much of the interrogation as she could recall, but Dan stopped listening when she got to the part about Liss taking over Victor's job as manager of *Strathspey*. Was she really considering leaving Moosetookalook? She hadn't said a word about it to him.

A burst of raucous laughter from the living room reminded all three of them that they were not the only ones in the house. Liss grimaced.

"I'd better get back. This 'gathering of all the suspects together in one place' thing is not working quite the way I imagined it would. I don't have a solution all worked out to reveal in the hope of startling a confession out of someone, and nobody is cooperating by dropping a significant clue in my lap." With a sigh, she pushed through the swinging door.

Dan stayed put, feet dangling off the washing machine. "What's your call on this?" he asked Sherri. "Does Tandy really think Liss is a suspect?"

"Not a chance. He's just eliminating possibilities. The only motive she'd have is if she really did want to take over the dance company."

"You sure she doesn't?"

Sherri Willett was a little bit of a thing. Standing, she was much shorter than he was. From his perch on the washer, he had to look *way* down to meet her eyes.

She glanced up at him. "Funny. Gordon asked almost the same question. He didn't like the idea, either."

"What are you saying?" He slid off the washer and caught Sherri's arms.

"Watch it, bub!"

He released her, holding up both hands in a placating gesture, but his voice was ragged. "Just answer me, damn it! Does Gordon Tandy have a personal interest in Liss?"

"Maybe. I'm just reading body language, Dan. Gordon didn't *say* anything. Well, he wouldn't, would he? Not if Liss *is* a suspect."

"Damn." Sherri had good instincts. If she thought Tandy was attracted to Liss, he probably was. "That's all I need."

She peered up at him, undoubtedly trying to read *his* body language. "I don't think there's anything for you to worry about. Not right now, anyway. As long as Gordon is investigating Victor's murder, he'll steer clear of getting involved with anyone connected to the case."

"So it's good she's a suspect?" He couldn't keep the hint of sarcasm out of his voice.

Hearing it, Sherri grinned. "From your point of view, yeah. And even if Gordon was sure she was in the clear, asking her out would still fall into a gray area. It's always dicey to mix romance with an ongoing investigation."

Not entirely reassured, Dan accepted that there was nothing he could do about the situation, even if Tandy did hit on Liss. Overt shows of jealousy were out and it was probably just as well that fighting for the hand of a lady fair was no longer an appropriate response to another man's poaching. Challenging Gordon to a duel—someone who carried a gun as part of his job—was not a good idea.

"Much as I'd like to stay and party," Sherri said, interrupting a pleasant fantasy in which he punched out Gordon Tandy's lights, "I've got to go. Man, I hate this seven-to-three shift!"

He held the door for her. "Let's not share this conversation with Liss, okay?"

She mimed zipping her lips, then zipped her ski jacket and left by the back door.

Gritting his teeth, Dan headed for the living room. According to Liss's grand plan, he was supposed to be watching his guests for signs of guilt. Ha! All he saw was Stewart Graham drinking too much, and Emily Townsend cowering in a corner. After flipping a mental coin, he sauntered over to her.

"How are you doing, Emily? Feeling a little better?"

"You're Dan, right?" She looked up at him from the depths of an overstuffed chair that seemed to swallow her slight form. The waiflike, Audrey Hepburn look was further emphasized by the skinny black pants and black turtleneck she wore. "I can't seem to hold on to thoughts very well."

Were those tears welling up? "Oh, hey. Don't do that. You're safe now. Everybody makes mistakes sometimes." He had no idea what he was saying, but just the fact that he kept talking seemed to calm her.

She sniffled a little and then, mercifully, seemed to regain control of herself. "You're very kind."

"No problem."

A pained silence ensued. Dan shuffled his feet. He could be in his shop, working on that table Mary wanted. What the hell had he been thinking to—

Abruptly, Emily rallied. "Have you lived here long?"

"Moosetookalook? Or in this house?"

"Both. Either." Cornflower-blue eyes darted from side to side, never meeting Dan's gaze, and she looked as if she might bolt at any moment.

He understood the impulse. Snagging one of the chairs from his dining room set—they'd all been dragged into the living room, though few of the company were sitting—he turned it around so he could straddle it. Then he started rambling. He talked about growing up in rural Maine, about going to school here with Liss and Sherri. He told her how Liss's parents had moved to Arizona.

"They sold this place to a professor at the University of Maine's Fallstown branch, the campus you performed on, but he didn't stay long. When he left, I bought it."

"Isn't it awfully big for just one person?" Emily, calm again, seemed genuinely interested in hearing his answer.

Dan got that question a lot. "I like the space." And the privacy, but he didn't expect to get that back any time soon.

"Are you and Liss . . . that is . . . I don't mean to pry. . . ."

"We've been seeing a lot of each other since she returned."

"Oh." Her brow wrinkled. "What does that mean?"

"Damned if I know."

She laughed. Well, no, it wasn't exactly a laugh. He wasn't sure what to call the sound, but it grated on his nerves. It also attracted the attention of everyone else in the room.

"Ah, a chirp from our chippy." Stewart Graham's phony-sounding British accent was firmly in place.

A few people chuckled. Liss just looked pained. Emily's face turned crimson from high forehead to pointed chin and she fled. Dan followed and was in time to see her enter his tiny downstairs bathroom.

"There aren't any drugs in there, are there?" Stewart asked, coming up beside him.

"No." The only "drugs" Dan kept on hand were aspirin and Pepto-Bismol, both of which were kept in the private bath off his own room. His houseguests shared the second upstairs bathroom, also devoid of over-the-counter remedies. He'd set out a fresh cake of Ivory soap. That was as far as his hospitality went.

"Good," Stewart said. "Then I can safely tell her to take a powder. That girl is a total pill."

When he'd followed through on the threat, shouting his suggestion through the bathroom door, Stewart wandered back toward the ice chest full of beer sitting on Dan's dining room floor. He was chuckling to himself.

Keeping one eye peeled in case Emily came out, Dan also watched the insensitive jerk who'd just insulted her. Dan saw Stewart check for observers, then pretend to grab another beer. What he actually did was keep hold of the same can he'd already drained and pretend it was a fresh one. *Interesting*, Dan thought. Stewart was not drinking as heavily as he wanted everyone to think he was.

What significance that might have completely eluded him.

"The company needs rehearsal space."

Wednesday morning dawned clear and bright. There was a distinct hint of spring in the air. Liss, doing her best to appear bright-eyed and bushy-tailed in spite of being up so late the previous night, flashed a wide smile at Dan. She thought better of batting her eyelashes.

"What am I supposed to do about it?" He sounded out of sorts and she supposed she couldn't blame him. She was accustomed to the eccentricities and petty squabbles of *Strathspey*'s dancers. He was not.

"Provide a place for them to practice. Their last performance was Saturday night."

This garnered nothing but a blank look.

"Same rule as sports, Dan. If the players don't work out regularly, hit the old batting cage or whatever, the whole team suffers. Dancers have to keep in shape, too, and there's only so much they can do individually, especially when all they have is a motel room to work in. I need a space big enough for them to run through the numbers in the show."

"Moosetookalook doesn't even have an assembly hall." For town meetings they usually moved the fire trucks into the street and set up folding chairs in the bays.

"Stewart suggested we empty out your carriage house and use it." She gave him a sweet smile, anticipating his response. They were in his kitchen, which had an unobstructed view of the other building.

"No way in hell. And incidentally, I don't appreciate being serenaded on the bagpipes at three o'clock in the morning."

He turned his back on her to refill his coffee mug from the big pot on the counter. No one else in the house was stirring yet, but he'd been up at least an hour. From her bedroom window, Liss had seen his light go on.

"You did put Stewart in the room my dad soundproofed, right?" He'd done that so he could practice his piping indoors.

Dan glowered at her over the rim of his bright blue ceramic mug. "You mean the bedroom right next to *mine*? Trust me when I say sound-*proof* is a misnomer."

"I did have another thought. About the rehearsal hall?"

"I'm not going to like this one, either, am I?"

"Depends. There are two or three spaces big enough at The Spruces."

"The hotel isn't open yet." He set his coffee mug on the counter with a thump.

She ignored the display of temper. "So? Your father owns it. Owns most of it, anyway." He had a few investors, including her aunt. "He could give permission. I could get everyone to sign waivers saying they won't sue if they are injured on the premises. Come on, Dan. We need to rehearse."

"We?"

"They. *They* need to rehearse. The lobby's big enough if you don't want them in the unfinished portions of the hotel. And isn't there a ballroom upstairs?"

"The ballroom's where we're working now."

The mulish look on his face wasn't encouraging, and she'd already taken advantage of his good nature something shameful, but he was an old softy at heart. She wasn't surprised when he relented.

"Dining room's pretty near finished, and empty. I guess they could use that."

She flung herself at him and gave him a hug. "Oh, thank you. I knew you'd help."

"Wait a second." His arms came around her when she tried to pull away. "There's a price." When he lowered his mouth to hers to exact it, Liss paid up willingly. With interest.

"Are we good?" she murmured when he finally released her. Even her toes were tingling.

"We're good. I'll call Dad and let you know when you can bring in the troops."

"Troupe," she corrected him, and smiled when he winced.

Chapter Eleven

It took several hours to arrange, but early that afternoon Liss led the dancers from *Strathspey,* minus Fiona, who was running late and would drive herself out later, into the newly renovated dining room at The Spruces. Dan trailed along behind, looking unhappy.

From what he'd told Liss, his father had OK'd using the room. He'd even approved turning up the thermostat. Installing a heating system had been one of the first things the Ruskins had done after buying the old hotel, right after rewiring the place. But Joe Ruskin had also ordered his son to stick around and keep an eye on things while the dancers were at The Spruces. Dan would be attending every rehearsal.

"Where's the bar?" Stewart demanded.

Dan gave him such an incredulous look that Liss had trouble stifling a laugh. "That time the pun was unintentional," she whispered. "He means a *practice* bar."

"He wants to practice his drinking?"

Liss punched him in the arm. "Dancers do pliés and stretching exercises using a rail attached to the wall at about waist level. And you *knew* that. I can tell by the twinkle in your eyes."

"Twinkle or not, they'll have to manage without a

bar. I'm not nailing anything up to this paneling. It cost an arm and a leg and a lot of time and effort to restore it to the way it looked in the 1890s."

"No bar," Liss called to Stewart. "And don't go getting handprints on the walls. Make do with floor exercises."

There was general grumbling, but soon they were all bending and stretching and into their individual warm-up routines. Ray appeared in the doorway of the bright, airy room with the recorded music they used for most of the show and the equipment he needed to play it on. There was no sound system in the dining room, but he was an old hand at improvising.

"You should put in speakers, y'know? People like to hear music playing while they eat."

"I'll think about it." Dan sounded distracted.

Liss followed his gaze to the other side of the room. Emily Townsend had stripped down to a leotard and tights, revealing a lithe but shapely body. Her *Strathspey* costume did not show off her bosom to the same advantage as spandex did.

"Earth to Dan."

"Huh?"

"Thank you. I really appreciate that you're letting them use this room. They need to rehearse together on some numbers to stay in peak condition and ensure the quality of performances to come. A dancer can only do so much in the space created by shoving motel furniture back against the wall."

"Not a problem."

"So why are you gritting your teeth?"

"Great place, man!" Jock O'Brien slapped Dan on the back, catching him by surprise. "Are the bedrooms ritzy, too?"

"They'll be comfortable."

Charlie Danielstone was right behind his roommate. "When does the place open?"

"Fourth of July weekend."

"Hey, that's not so far off. You must be almost done fixing the place up, huh? Can we take a look around?"

"There's a lot of construction still going on—"

"Hey, we signed the release." Charlie gave him a cheeky grin.

"Cut it out, guys." Liss introduced them, since Dan had only glimpsed them at the refreshment table at the reception and hadn't had occasion to meet them at the motel.

"So, daily rehearsals as long as we're here?" Jock asked.

"That's the deal," Liss told him, "as long as you behave yourselves."

"Aw, come on. Just a peek at one of the rooms?"

"Not much to see," Dan told him. "They're all empty. Walls and floors and windows are done. Plumbing's in. But there's no furniture. No curtains yet, either."

"What parts of the hotel are you still working on?" Charlie asked.

"Ballroom. Hallways—they need to be carpeted. Kitchen. Laundry room."

"Will you be finished in time?" Liss hadn't thought to ask till now. She'd been too busy with the Emporium to focus on the hotel, and it wasn't Dan's primary project, either. He was far more likely to talk about his plans to one day make a living from the sale of his custom-made furniture.

A blast of music, turned up way too loud, made Liss jump.

"Nice form!" Cal hollered from the other side of the room.

Ray turned down the sound. "Ready when you are," he called to the dancers.

"Fiona's not here yet," Stewart yelled back. "We're short a dancer for the reel."

Jock and Charlie exchanged mischievous glances. Charlie grabbed Liss's hand. "No, we're not!" he shouted, and tugged her toward the middle of the room.

Before Liss fully realized what was happening, her feet had fallen into the familiar steps of a Scottish country dance. The music was "Speed the Plough," a reel that dated back to 1800. When Charlie handed her off to Cal, it felt just like old times.

"Look at her strut her stuff," Sandy teased as they passed each other in the pattern of the dance.

She laughed in sheer delight. And she made it all the way to the end of the piece before, just as the music stopped, her weak knee decided to buckle. If Cal hadn't been standing right beside her, she'd have fallen flat on her face.

"And that's why I'm retired," she muttered, more as a reminder to herself than to inform the others.

"Sorry, Liss." Charlie's crooked grin didn't look particularly contrite, but then he'd never had knee surgery.

"You okay?" Sandy started in her direction but she waved him off.

"I don't think I've done any serious damage." But she would not be so foolish as to try to dance with the pros again. When rehearsal resumed, Liss joined Dan near the door.

He watched her approach with worried eyes. "You're limping."

"No kidding. Come on. No need for either of us to be here."

He sent a doubtful look in Stewart's direction.

"You'll just have to trust them not to damage anything." Liss led him out of the dining room just as the music blared again, though not as loudly as before. After the first few steps, her stride returned to normal. "I've got to get back to the Emporium. I left Lee Annie in charge, since she doesn't have to rehearse with the dancers, but I don't want to take advantage of her good nature. You can go and do whatever you would be doing if they weren't here."

"I'd be at the other construction site, but Dad was right. We can't leave the asylum in the inmates' control. I'll be in the building until they all leave for the day. Every day." He sounded grimly determined.

They had reached the lobby, the first part of the hotel's interior to be renovated. Liss knew that Dan had restored the huge check-in desk himself, as well as the wall full of old-fashioned cubbyholes behind it. When The Spruces reopened, they would once again hold guests' keys and messages.

The remaining space was equally impressive. Pillars divided the lobby and would give the illusion of privacy when sofas and chairs were strategically placed between them. Liss had heard her aunt and Joe Ruskin talk of their plans so many times that she had no difficulty visualizing what the place would look like furnished. There would be plush area rugs atop the gleaming hardwood floors in the seating areas. Ornate brass firedogs would grace the hearth of the big Victorian fireplace with its intricately carved mantel and the even more elaborately decorated mirror above.

It was a labor of love. Liss got that. She understood why Dan and his father were nervous about turning over even a small portion of it to an unruly group like the *Strathspey* dancers. She wanted to reassure him, tell him they were housebroken, but she was pretty sure he wouldn't breathe easily again until they'd left the building.

"Try not to fret," she said instead.

Dan didn't appear to hear her. He was staring out the window. "Your friend the cop just parked next to the bus."

"Sherri?" Liss glanced at her watch. It wasn't even close to three. Sherri should still be at work.

"No, not Sherri. Detective Tandy."

"Oh dear. I suppose he tracked the troupe here."

But when Gordon Tandy came through the door he seemed surprised to find Liss in the lobby, and puzzled by the fact that the bus was parked outside. Liss quickly explained that the dancers were rehearsing.

"Did you want to talk to someone in particular?" she asked.

"Yes, but not one of them." He jerked his head toward Dan. "I need to speak with Ruskin here."

When he didn't say any more, Liss remembered what Sherri had told them the previous night. It dawned on her that Gordon Tandy was still checking up on her. He wanted to ask Dan about her movements on the day of the murder!

"I've got to get back to the store," she said stiffly, and left.

Downtown Moosetookalook was a five-minute drive from The Spruces. Fiona's rental car was still parked in front of the Emporium. Liss couldn't imagine what the holdup was. Fiona was extremely punctual as a rule, especially when it came to rehearsals.

Inside, Liss found Lee Annie Neville happily trying on necklaces and earrings from the shipment that had just come in from Pitlochry, Scotland. They were made using the stems of Scottish heather compressed into blocks and cut into individual pieces. Set with silver and pewter fittings in Celtic designs, the "gems" were surprisingly attractive.

"Back in a minute," she called, tossing her coat in the general direction of the rack beside the door. She took the stairs to her aunt's apartment two at a time.

"Fiona?" She rapped on the door of Aunt Margaret's room and opened it without waiting to be invited in.

Fiona stood by the window, a cell phone to her ear. She held up a finger to indicate Liss should wait a minute and completed her conversation. "Problem?" she asked, sliding the phone into a pocket.

"Only that you're running very late."

"I've got one more call to make, and then I'll head out to the hotel. With Victor gone, I'm the one who has to handle all the arrangements."

"Of course. I'll leave you to it." Liss retreated but stood outside the door a moment longer. Did Fiona mean she was canceling more performances? Liss hoped not.

It was quiet in the apartment, so quiet that she could hear Fiona speaking on the phone. Liss didn't intend to eavesdrop, but when she caught the word "passport" she lingered in the hallway.

Most of the conversation was muffled. She heard a reference to Canada and wondered if Fiona might be trying to get international bookings. There were certainly plenty of people of Scottish descent in Nova Scotia and New Brunswick, and neither province was far from Moosetookalook. Along with Quebec, New Brunswick shared a border with Maine.

Fiona's "Thank you. Good-bye" sent Liss scurrying away. She entered the living room just as Winona came in from the kitchen carrying a cup of tea.

"Liss—join me?" She settled in on the sofa, looking right at home.

Her long black hair, liberally streaked with white, had been braided and then wound in a knot at the back of her head. She wore leggings with a tunic top, both in a burnt umber shade. It was a favorite outfit, chosen for comfort and frequently worn on the road. All that was missing was its usual accessory—a wrist pincushion in the shape of a heart and bristling with straight pins, safety pins of every size, and needles prethreaded in a rainbow of colors.

"I'm good, Winona. And I need to spell Lee Annie. Is there anything you need?"

"Not a thing, sweetie. It's splendid being here instead of in a motel. Even better than the B-and-B."

"Well, good." One thing Liss had always liked about Winona was her ability to look on the bright side of things. It was a knack Fiona had shared until just lately, which made Liss wonder if Winona's cheerful facade might also be wearing a bit thin. "Ah, Winona? Have you thought any more about what I asked you the other day? About members of the company who might have wished Victor ill?"

Winona stared down into the steaming mug of tea between her hands, avoiding Liss's eyes.

"Winona? It doesn't help to hold back. We have to find out who did this terrible thing so we can all move on."

"I just don't like to speak ill of anyone, not even the dead."

"Victor wasn't the nicest guy in the world."

"No. He wasn't. And he was particularly nasty to poor Sarah Bartlett. I was sorry to see her go. I liked her."

"So did Ray, apparently."

Winona smiled. "Yes. Thick as thieves, they were at times, although she was closer, I think, to some of the other girls. I thought for a while he might leave the company, too, after she left. But the last time I saw them together it looked as if they'd disagreed about something. She turned her back on him and stalked off and that was that."

"The last time they were together?" Liss frowned, trying to recall what Dan had told her Ray had said. "Together" didn't strike her as the right word. "Just when was that, Winona?"

The older woman frowned, her snub nose wrinkling. "I'm not sure. Maybe two or three weeks after Emily replaced her. I can't remember where we were. You know how the towns all run together when you're on tour."

"But it was after she left the company?"

"Oh yes. I know I had the uncharitable thought that Sarah was so much more pleasant than Emily Townsend. It would have been nice if she could have come back, but of course that was impossible even before she and Ray fell out. Because of Victor. Sure you wouldn't like a cup of tea, dear?"

"Uh, no. I have to get to work."

Liss headed downstairs, but at no great speed. She was still trying to make sense out of what Winona had said in light of what Ray had told Dan. Hadn't he claimed he'd not seen Sarah again after she left the company? Was Winona mistaken? Or had Ray lied?

"That cop was here," Lee Annie announced when Liss reached the bottom of the stairs and stepped through the door behind the sales counter.

Big surprise. "What did he want?" She was pretty sure she could guess, and that guess depressed her.

"He wanted to know who else worked here and

who spelled you when you wanted to run an errand or something. He already knew about Sherri. Said he'd already talked to her. What's he want, Liss? And why did he head over to the bookstore after he left here?"

"Good question. Will you mind the Emporium for another half hour while I go find out?"

"Depends. Can you give me a discount on this?" She waggled a finger on which she wore one of the heather-filled rings.

"Sure. Take fifty percent off the price that's marked." The jewelry was pretty, but not horribly expensive, even though each "gem" had supposedly been individually shaped and lacquered by skilled craftsmen.

Liss shrugged back into her coat and set off for Angie's Books, the business owned and operated by Beth Hogencamp's mother. Angie spotted Liss crossing the town square and had the door open for her before she reached the porch.

"Funny," she said, "you don't look like a murderer."

"Ha-ha."

"Don't worry. You're off the hook. I told the detective you couldn't have left the Emporium that day without being missed. He already knew that, I think. It was just a formality to ask around."

Like Moosetookalook Scottish Emporium, Angie's Books took up the ground floor of what had once been a one-family home. The Hogencamps lived in the apartment upstairs. Angie sold books of all sorts, new and used, and non-Scottish crafts made by local artisans, including Dan, on consignment. One of his clock-and-picture-frame combinations was prominently displayed. Liss noticed that Angie had replaced the stock photo of a baby with a picture of her own son, a preschooler named Bradley. Since Liss didn't see or hear him tearing around the shop, she assumed he was down for an afternoon nap.

"Sounded to me like he just wanted to make sure you had no chance to transport poisoned scones to Fallstown," Angie said cheerfully. "I swear, I was a little nervous when he first introduced himself, after that business last year. But this one isn't at all like the last state police detective assigned to our area."

"Thank goodness. It isn't exactly comfortable being suspected of murder."

"Again."

"Again," Liss agreed. "Did he ask about anything else? You and Beth were at the reception."

"Yes, but we'd left before that man died." Her smile vanished. "I'm glad we did. Beth doesn't need to be exposed to that sort of thing. Bad enough what she sees on television. But I could tell Detective Tandy that I saw you at the Student Center and that you were right there in plain sight the whole time Beth and I stayed."

"Did Beth enjoy the show? I never thought to ask."

"Oh, she loved it. And she enjoyed meeting some of the dancers afterward. Most of them were very nice to her." A shadow passed over Angie's face, a clear indication that someone at the reception had *not* been so nice.

Liss let it go. There wasn't anything she could do about it if Stewart or Emily or one of the others had been short with the girl. And she had bigger things to worry about at the moment.

Why was Gordon Tandy asking so many questions about her? What had happened to his certainty that the mushroom scones had been baked in that cabin that had been broken into?

She started to inquire into the specifics of Angie's interrogation, but the other woman was staring past her out the display window at Fiona, who was getting into her rental car. Liss glanced back at Angie in time to see a flash of extreme dislike momentarily distort the bookseller's amiable expression.

"*Fiona* was the one who was rude?"

"I didn't hear what she said myself, but I saw Beth approach her—like a fan with a rock star—and I saw my daughter's disillusionment when she was snubbed. Fiona Carlson looked down her nose at Beth and told her to get lost. That's what Beth told me later. She said 'Get lost, kid,' in what Beth called 'a really mean voice.'"

"That doesn't sound like Fiona. We tease her about being the mother hen of the company. She's the one who takes all the younger dancers under her wing."

"That's not the same thing as being good with real children."

"True. I hope Beth didn't let the incident spoil her evening."

"Oh no. She's still talking about the performance, and about her new friend, Zara."

Liss winced. "I'm afraid I'm as bad as Fiona. I completely forgot Beth was coming over for a lesson the other evening."

"You've had a lot on your mind lately." Angie dismissed her oversight with a little wave of one hand. "Beth understands that." Unspoken was the corollary that neither Angie nor Beth understood Fiona's rudeness. Liss didn't, either, but she was willing to give her old friend the benefit of the doubt. Everyone was less than polite sometimes.

"Speaking of your troubles . . ." Angie gestured toward the window.

Liss was afraid to look, and it turned out she had good reason to be wary. Gordon Tandy had just parked in front of the Emporium, in the spot Fiona had vacated. He emerged from his car and, almost as if he could feel her staring at him, turned to look straight at Angie's Books.

Chapter Twelve

They met halfway across the town square.

"Walk with me?" Gordon asked.

"Sure. Why not? If you're sure I'm not going to poison, stab, bludgeon, or otherwise do away with you."

The official stone face hardened further. "I had to rule you out completely. I've done that now." The words were clipped and emotionless.

"I can't tell you how much better that makes me feel. I thought you trusted me already. In case you've forgotten, you asked for my help."

The town square was crisscrossed with walking paths kept well shoveled by maintenance crews based at the municipal building that overlooked one side of it. Their route took them past a monument to the Civil War dead, a flagpole, and a playground with swings, a jungle gym, a merry-go-round, and a slide, eventually ending at a gazebo-style bandstand. Gordon offered her a hand to help navigate the steps and indicated one of the benches. Liss sat.

Gordon Tandy propped one hip against a section of railing and folded his arms across his chest. "When were you planning to let me know that you'd played musical motel rooms with my suspects?"

"No law against providing housing for folks who need it."

"You know what this looks like, don't you? It looks suspiciously like someone's trying to gather all her suspects together in one place. Do you fancy yourself as a modern day Miss Marple?"

Irritated, Liss spoke without thinking. "Perhaps that will make it easier for you to solve the case, Inspector Clouseau."

"Ouch. Low blow!"

Liss searched his face, trying to read his mood. Was that an amused glimmer in his dark eyes? The lighter flecks almost seemed to be dancing.

Liss blinked, laughed a little self-consciously, and decided to risk teasing him. "Would you prefer I called you Sherlock?"

"I'd prefer you stay out of police business, but I suppose it's too late for that." His tone suggested regret rather than annoyance.

"You're the one who asked for my help," she reminded him again. "And then you made it pretty obvious that you suspected my friend Sandy of killing Victor. I thought it would be a good idea to provide you with a few alternatives."

"All right. Cards on the table." He shoved off from the rail to sit beside her on the bench, turning so that their faces were only inches apart. "I do suspect Kalishnakof, but no more than a couple of the others. I do not have a closed mind. If you want to tell me why I should consider one of these folks more closely, I'll be happy to listen to your reasoning."

Gordon's broad shoulders shifted to block her view, but not before Liss had seen Angie come out of her shop. The bookseller was pretending to sweep the porch, but her gaze darted toward the bandstand every few seconds. Lee Annie was almost certainly glued to the window of the Emporium. Liss had the feeling there were eyes watching her from every building that looked out over the town square. It was only a small comfort that none of them would be able to overhear what she and Gordon said to each other.

"Some of the cast and crew now staying here in Moosetookalook had reason to hate Victor Owens," she admitted. "Ray Adams, the stage manager, was in love with Sarah Bartlett, a dancer who left because of Victor's sexual harassment. He has an alibi for the time period before the performance, but if Sarah was working with him . . ."

She waited for Gordon to comment, but he merely nodded. That he didn't pull out his handy-dandy notebook made her suspect he already knew about Sarah.

"Then there's Stewart Graham. He was angry because Victor cut his role in the show and threatened to let him go entirely."

Another nod.

"And Emily . . . well, you must agree Emily Townsend's behavior has been odd. Who knows what Victor did to her? Treated her like dirt, I expect. Maybe she got fed up."

"And then there are your friends Sandy and Zara," Gordon said, "currently engaged to be married. Zara and Victor used to be an item. He was threatening to replace her with Emily."

Liss gritted her teeth, but it was her turn to nod. "You've obviously already thought of everyone I just suggested." The real question was, had he followed up on their motives? Instead she asked, "Any other suspects?"

"Fiona Carlson ended up with Victor's job."

"She doesn't want it. She's planning to retire at the end of the tour."

"Kind of young for that, isn't she?"

"She's a professional athlete. You do the math."

He pondered that for a moment and acknowledged that early retirement made sense.

"I gather I made your suspect list," Liss said. "Is that why you suddenly shut me out when we met in Waycross Springs?"

His lips quirked, almost making it to a smile. "Truth? It never even occurred to me to suspect you until I was talking to Sherri in the parking lot at the jail the other day."

"Then why *did* you pull back? You were acting as if I had something to offer, as if I could help you, and just like that"—she snapped her fingers—"you changed."

"No, Liss. *You* did. Your . . . enthusiasm for the investigation started to worry me. You were excited by the prospect. Excessively so. It made me remember that you're a civilian. I had no right to drag you into a potentially dangerous situation. I'd let my . . . admiration for you blind me to the facts. I shut you out to keep you from getting hurt."

"Oh, for heaven's sake! I wouldn't have—"

"You *did* get hurt the last time you meddled in a murder investigation."

"Fine! Let's everyone protect poor, defenseless, *stupid* Liss! So how did I go from useful source of information to suspect? What was *my* motive supposed to be?"

"The same as Fiona's—Victor's job."

"Oh, please!"

"No interest?"

"I considered it, okay? But not for long." She shifted uneasily on the bench, and then hugged herself. It was chilly sitting there in the shade. "I'm settled here. I like my life the way it is."

"Good."

Liss's eyes narrowed. There was entirely too much satisfaction in his tone.

"Fortunately," Gordon went on, "you're not a suspect any longer. Like I said, I just had to be sure you were in the clear. It's my job to look at everything, even if it means putting personal feelings aside." He reached out to touch her bare wrist, exposed by the gap between the top of her glove and the bottom of her coat sleeve.

Liss felt a distinct tingle when his fingertips grazed her skin. It coursed inward, setting off aftershocks in even more intimate places. His rueful expression told her he was just as aware of the chemistry between them as she was. More so. He'd deliberately provoked the reaction by putting his hand on her.

Frowning, Liss pulled away. He was *flirting* with her. Now that she thought about it, he had been, on and off, all along. And she'd been flirting back.

How had she missed that?

That she was attracted to Gordon Tandy worried Liss. The timing was, to say the least, inconvenient. For one thing, she was supposed to be in a relationship with Dan Ruskin. And even if Dan weren't in the picture, Gordon Tandy was twelve years older than she was. Besides, for all she knew, he could have two or three ex-wives and a half dozen kids.

Her panic subsided as abruptly as it had emerged. No, he did not come with former spouses or with children. She'd have heard about them by now if he did. That was one good thing about gossipy small towns. The bad stuff surfaced quickly.

Gordon studied her, a contemplative look on his face, for a long time before he finally spoke. "Here's the thing, Liss. I'm drawn to you. I have been since we first met. I told myself it was just a fluke. I was trying to ignore how I felt. Then, when you were briefly a suspect, I *couldn't* say anything. Even now, I'm probably crossing a line. But I'd like to spend some time with you when we aren't talking about murder. Will you have dinner with me tonight? At the Sinclair House?"

The Sinclair House was a landmark in Waycross Springs, a turn-of-the-last-century hotel that had somehow kept operating through the hard times. Unlike The Spruces, with which it had much in common, it had found new ways to keep guests flocking to an out-of-the-way location.

Liss stared at her gloved hands as she attempted to examine her feelings. She was still ticked off that Gordon had checked up on her with her neighbors. She understood, on an intellectual level, why he'd had to ask questions about her movements on the day of the murder, but that did not diminish her irritation at being considered capable of killing someone.

She could forgive him for that, she decided. He was just doing his job. He had his responsibilities . . . and she had hers.

If she discounted the tingle . . . sizzle . . . whatever the heck it was—surely an aberration!—she could use him as he'd initially used her, as a source of information. There was no harm in a little mild flirtation, especially if it helped her friends in *Strathspey*.

"Tonight?" she asked, looking at him at last. She sent a bright smile his way. "Why not?"

She told herself she was accepting his invitation so that she could pick his brain about the case and make sure he really was keeping an open mind about his suspects. Not talk about the murder? No way!

"Good." He glanced at his watch. "I have to go now. I'll be back to pick you up at six."

But she shook her head. She needed to be the one in control of the situation. "I'll meet you there at seven."

After her regular shift at the jail on Wednesday, Sherri headed for Moosetookalook Scottish Emporium and her part-time job. She was scheduled to work until closing. She had just gotten out of her pint-size pickup truck when Beth Hogencamp came barreling out of the store and nearly bowled her over.

"Whoa, there, hotshot! What's the rush?" Sherri caught Beth by the shoulders to hold her still—the kid squirmed worse than an eel—but when she saw the tears, Sherri dropped to one knee beside the girl and loosened her grip. "What's the matter, Beth?"

"She's a mean old witch!"

"Who is?"

"Miss Carlson."

"Fiona? What did she do?"

"Zara said I could watch a rehearsal at The Spruces and then *she* said I couldn't. Mom would have let me skip school." Her lower lip began to tremble. That, and the earnestness in her voice, made Sherri's heart ache.

Standing, Sherri took Beth's hand and led her back to the truck, boosting her into the passenger seat. She went around to the driver's side and got in, but she didn't start the engine. With the late-day sun beating down, it was warm enough in the cab to sit and talk for a while.

A few pointed questions elicited the rest of Beth's story. Zara had told her she'd have to ask Fiona if it was okay to watch the troupe rehearse. Beth had obediently trotted up to Margaret Boyd's apartment after school to request permission. She'd been shot down with a blunt "Forget it, kid!" and no explanation.

"Cheer up, Beth," Sherri told her. "You're still taking private lessons from Zara, right?" Liss had told her how the two had bonded. She'd almost sounded envious.

Beth nodded.

"Well, then—"

"Why doesn't she like me?"

"I don't know, Beth. Maybe it's just one of those things. I don't think Fiona Carlson likes Lumpkin, either."

The girl's incredulous look had Sherri fighting not to smile. "How can anyone not love Lumpkin?"

Sherri could come up with several reasons and not even work up a sweat. First among them was Lumpkin's habit of biting people's ankles. "Fiona's allergic to cats. Some people are, you know. The sheriff is. Then again . . ." Her voice trailed off as a long-ago memory surfaced.

"Then again what?"

Sherri grinned. "My great-aunt Susan *claimed* she was allergic to cats. She was my grandfather's brother's wife and my grandmother didn't like her much. She thought the whole 'allergic' thing was just an excuse not to come visit. It wasn't that Gram really wanted Aunt Susan's company, you understand. She just didn't like being lied to. Anyway, one Thanksgiving when the whole family was together at my house—I must have been around your age at the time—Gram decided to test her theory. We didn't have a cat, but our neighbor did, a sweet-natured calico named Calpurnia. Gram borrowed her and put her behind the sofa in her cat carrier before Aunt Susan arrived. Since Aunt Susan didn't know Calpurnia was there, she didn't sniffle or sneeze. Not once."

Beth giggled. "Did your grandmother show her the cat?"

"She intended to, but my mother got suspicious of all the knowing glances Gram and I exchanged. When Aunt Susan left the room, Mom looked behind the sofa, spotted the cat carrier, and made me take Calpurnia back to her owners." Ida Willett had not been amused!

Once Beth headed for her mother's bookstore, in much better spirits than she had been, Sherri entered the Emporium. She found Liss perched on a stool behind the sales counter, attaching tiny price tags to necklaces and sets of earrings. "So, anything new on the murder front?"

Liss kept at her task, which allowed her to avoid meeting Sherri's eyes. "I'm having dinner with Detective Tandy this evening. At the Sinclair House."

Sherri gave a low whistle. "Guess you must have come up squeaky clean in the alibi department."

"Guess so. You understand that I'm only going so I can pick his brain about the case?"

"Uh-huh."

"Really."

"You keep telling yourself that, chum."

"Keep telling herself what?" Dan Ruskin asked as he came through the door.

Sherri glanced at her watch. "You're off early."

"I never started. I had to babysit."

"The company borrowed the dining room at The Spruces for a rehearsal hall," Liss explained for Sherri's benefit, unaware that Beth had already given Sherri a full account of this development. Liss frowned at Dan. "I don't know why you and your father think they need watching every minute. They're all responsible adults."

"Better safe than sorry. So, what are you supposed to keep telling yourself?"

"That she's only going out with Gordon Tandy tonight, to dinner at the Sinclair House, no less, because she wants information on his investigation." Sherri watched Dan's face as she spoke, anticipating his reaction. She wasn't disappointed. It didn't reveal much, but there was a definite flicker of alarm in his light brown eyes and for just a second his whole body went rigid.

"What do you think you'll learn?" he asked. "As a general rule, I don't think cops talk about their active cases."

"But this cop asked for my help. I'm not letting him take that back. And how can I help him if I don't know what he's thinking?" She carried the tray of jewelry from the sales counter to a display case and busied herself arranging the pieces on a length of red velvet.

"I bet I know what he's thinking." Dan spoke too softly for Liss to hear, but Sherri was close enough to catch every word.

"I bet you'd be right," she whispered back.

Liss closed the back of the display case and joined them. "Since you're here, Sherri, I think I'll take off early."

"Fine by me. Go for it."

"Great." She grabbed her jacket and was at the door before either Sherri or Dan could say another word. "See you later."

The shop bell jangled. The door slammed with a thud.

"Damn. She's going to go primp. She wants plenty of time to get ready for her *business meeting* with Gordon Tandy."

"Maybe she just wants to make lists of questions

to ask him. I'm sure she's more interested in pumping him for information than jumping his bones."

"Oh, thanks so much for that image." Dan looked as if he'd just bitten into a sour grape. "Damn it, Sherri, I've botched this up but good. I got jealous of Sandy, who turns out to be a great guy and no threat at all, and now I can't say a word about this dinner with Tandy because she'll think I don't trust her."

"You don't," Sherri pointed out. "Face it, Dan. You *are* jealous. You're also possessive and overprotective." She held up a hand when he opened his mouth to protest. "I'm not saying those are entirely bad things, but try to see the situation from her point of view. She's been a free spirit for years. You can't expect her to change completely in a matter of months."

"I thought she and I were headed somewhere permanent."

"Did you talk to her about that?"

"No."

"Then you're stuck. For now, anyway. Try not to snap at Liss, or at Gordon Tandy, either. Liss won't want anything to do with either of you if you and Gordon start snarling at each other like dogs fighting over a bone." Then Sherri gave him the same advice she'd given Liss: "Just keep telling yourself it's not a date."

Dan's glower was impressive. "The Sinclair House is a pretty damn romantic setting for a business meeting. It would be a hell of a lot easier to convince myself I don't have anything to worry about if they'd have supper at one of the fast food places in Fallstown."

Chapter Thirteen

The Sinclair House had *posh* written all over it. Liss had been to functions there once or twice, but that had been years ago when she'd been a child. She hadn't appreciated the finer touches, like valet parking and the fact that no gentleman was admitted to the dining room without a jacket and tie. She was glad she'd taken the time to twist her hair into a sophisticated style and chosen to wear one of her more feminine outfits, a long tartan skirt and a gauzy white blouse with lots of lace.

They were seated at a cozy table in a window alcove. Their view of the floodlit, snow-covered grounds reminded Liss of a Currier and Ives print. "This is lovely, Gordon."

"So are you."

"For a suspect."

"Former suspect."

"So you say," she teased him. "Maybe this is just a ploy to give me the third degree."

"Trust me when I say that I don't want to spend the evening talking shop, but I do have the answer to a question you asked me earlier today. I know where Sarah Bartlett is."

"Where?"

He shook his head. "You don't need specifics. Suffice it to say that I talked to her on the phone and confirmed that she's nowhere near Maine and could not have been here Saturday night to kill Victor Owens. She's out of the picture, and that pretty much eliminates your stage manager friend as a suspect, as well."

Liss was glad to know Ray was off the hook, but that still left several other friends on it. "Who's your prime suspect?" she asked.

"You know I can't tell you that." His voice was mild, but his eyes had gone as hard as the obsidian she'd decided they sometimes resembled.

With a sigh, Liss gave up. Pleading wouldn't do anything but ruin the evening. She took a sip of the wine Gordon had ordered to go with their meal. He had good taste. And when she looked into his eyes again, the darkness had eased. He'd abandoned all thought of Victor's murder. What she saw there now was warmth . . . and an invitation.

Hastily looking away, Liss fixed her attention on their surroundings. Anything to distract herself from thoughts that were far too confusing.

Like the rest of the Sinclair House, the dining room had been in use for well over a century. There were touches of the Gilded Age everywhere, carefully preserved—a crystal chandelier, flocked wallpaper—while at the same time every modern convenience was provided. Service was fast and efficient.

There weren't many guests at the moment. Perhaps half the seating was occupied, mostly by groups of four, although a stunning redhead sat alone at one table while a couple, obviously newlyweds, billed and cooed at one another.

Was this what The Spruces might become?

Liss turned back to Gordon, a new line of questioning in mind. "Tell me about Waycross Springs."

"What do you want to know?"

"Do you still live here?"

He nodded. "I have a small house about a mile from here."

"So you probably come here to the Sinclair House all the time."

"I wouldn't say that, but the Tandys and the Sinclairs go back a long way. Why are you so interested in the hotel?"

"My aunt invested in The Spruces. You've seen the place. Do you think it has a chance of turning out this well?"

"Not my field of expertise. Is Ruskin—?"

Liss cut him off before he could complete the question. This was not the time to bring her relationship with Dan into the conversation, assuming that was what Gordon had intended to ask about. "I just wonder if this area can support two luxury hotels, even with all the tourists who come for the skiing."

"Don't forget leaf-peeper season and summer. The only time we don't attract tourists is right about now—mud season."

"You don't subscribe to the wisdom that says Maine only has two seasons?"

"That would be 'winter' and 'black fly'?"

They both smiled at the old joke.

An average-looking brunette in a bright fuchsia dress approached their table. "Gordon. How are you?"

"Liss, this is Corrie Sinclair. Corrie, Liss Mac-Crimmon. Corrie and her husband run this place. Lucas's family has owned the hotel for several generations. Liss was wondering what will happen when The Spruces opens," he added. "Will having a similar hotel in Moosetookalook cut into Sinclair House business?"

"I doubt it," Corrie Sinclair said. "There should be plenty to go around, what with both villages being close to good skiing."

"What do you offer that the condos and motels right at the ski areas don't?"

"Luxury accommodations and free transportation," came the prompt answer. "We run vans to Sugarloaf, Saddleback, and Sunday River and also make pickups at both Portland Jetport and Bangor International Airport. And we have our own cross-country trails."

As Corrie enumerated other attractions of the Sinclair House, Liss found herself wishing Dan were with her tonight. Two or three of the things Corrie said sparked ideas that might help ensure the success of The Spruces, particularly what she told them about conferences.

"Small conventions, conferences, and conclaves all love places like this," she explained. "Did you by chance attend our Burns Day Supper in January?"

"I'm not really a big fan of haggis." The annual event, held on the birthday of Scottish poet Robert Burns, followed a set format and featured that Scottish delicacy as the main course. Liss treasured her heritage, but not to the extent of eating something made out of the intestines of a sheep.

"It was . . . interesting," Corrie said with a laugh. "I'd love to host that group every January twenty-fifth but the organizers apparently prefer variety. They won't come back to the same hotel a second year. As soon as The Spruces opens, I expect they'll book the event there."

After a bit more conversation, their meal arrived and Corrie excused herself to join her husband. Liss's jaw dropped when she got a good look at Lucas Sinclair. He was the personification of tall, dark, and handsome, except for the glasses perched on his long, straight nose. The man even had a dimple in his chiseled jaw.

"So," Gordon said, "do you know the Ruskins well?"

"Dan bought the house I grew up in." Liss adjusted her napkin and quickly changed the subject. "What's your next move?"

"I thought we'd finish eating before I made one."

His dry humor made her smile. She picked up her fork and sampled the coquilles St. Jacques she'd ordered. "I meant in the investigation."

He ate a bite of his prime rib and a few mouthfuls of mashed potatoes before he lost the battle to avoid talking about the case. "I have to go to Providence tomorrow to take a look at the apartment Victor Owens kept there."

"What do you expect to find?"

"Nothing." That was all he was prepared to tell her, too.

The rest of the evening passed pleasantly enough, in spite of the ongoing battle for control of the conversation. She wanted to know more about the case. He wanted to know more about her. Every once in a while, the two topics overlapped.

"Did you seriously consider taking over as manager of *Strathspey*?" Gordon asked.

"Yes, but not for long. Have you always wanted to be a cop?"

When Gordon relaxed and unbent far enough to tell her about some of the cases he'd worked on in the past, Liss resolved to stop plaguing him with questions about the current investigation. Besides, it had just occurred to her that if she were to pretend to the members of *Strathspey* that she was still interested in applying for Victor's job, she might be able to get a look at some of the company's records. She set that idea aside to think about later.

Although Gordon insisted that the majority of his work was mind-numbingly routine and boring, his stories held her interest. Time passed quickly and with a sense of surprise, she realized that only the two of them and the wait staff remained in the dining room.

"I should get home. I've got to open the Emporium bright and early tomorrow."

He glanced out at the floodlit landscape. "It's started to spit snow out there. The roads will be slick."

For a moment she thought he might suggest she spend the night at his place. Instead he insisted on following her home to make sure she got there safely. He paid no attention to the objection that he'd then have to drive all the way back to Waycross Springs.

"I'm used to being out on these roads in all kinds of weather. You're not."

Liss thought he was being silly, but found his concern kind of sweet. As she drove slowly from Waycross Springs to Moosetookalook along winding, two-lane back roads—the only kind connecting the two places—she had to admit that she'd thoroughly enjoyed the evening.

Back at her house, Liss was set to say good night at curbside. Gordon had other ideas. He insisted on walking her to her front door. There was an awkward moment on the porch while she fumbled for her keys. He took them from her, unlocked the door, and returned them, keeping hold of the hand he placed them in.

The casual "thanks" she'd been about to utter died before it reached her lips. This close, he was a bit overwhelming. *Pheromones*, she told herself. *Stupid chemical reaction*. But darned if her skin wasn't tingling again, even through two layers of gloves.

He stepped back for a moment, and what she could see of his face in the porch light told her he was experiencing the same reaction she was. Approach/avoidance—wasn't that what the shrinks called it?

Then he kissed her.

Gordon Tandy was a *great* kisser.

Liss needed considerable willpower to ease herself out of his embrace and say good night. She imagined she had a sappy smile on her face when she turned to watch him walk back to his car. It faded fast when she caught sight of Dan Ruskin on the sidewalk. From the glower on his face, he'd witnessed Gordon's fond farewell.

The night air was suddenly jam-packed with testosterone. An image of pit bulls flashed into Liss's mind. To her surprise, even though Gordon's body language was every bit as tense and bristly as Dan's, each of the two men simply growled an acknowledgment of the other's presence. They passed on her sidewalk without coming to blows. No barking. No biting.

"I just came by to make sure you got home safely," Dan said as he reached the porch. He didn't climb the steps—wise of him. "Roads are getting slippery."

"That's why Gordon followed me home."

"Oh?" He packed a lot into the single syllable.

She put just as much of what she was feeling into a look. "It's late, it's been a long day, and I'm going to bed." Turning her back on him, she slipped inside and quietly closed the door behind her. Once again she had to resist the urge to bang her forehead on the wood.

One jealous suitor was annoying. Two verged on the ridiculous.

* * *

Dan's sister, Mary, was the mother of a seven-month-old baby but still managed to have an active life outside the home. She volunteered at the local food bank and as a driver with the Meals-on-Wheels program, taking the baby with her in a car seat. She'd even found time to help Liss out with transportation for the dancers, until that conflicted with a prior commitment. Dan had to plan ahead to catch her at home on Thursday morning.

"What brings you to baby central?" Mary asked when he breezed through her back door.

"What, I can't stop by and say hi to the little rug rat?" He made faces at the baby, currently sitting in a high chair and creating chaos with unidentifiable bits of food.

"Sure you can. Anytime. But I talked to Sam last night and he filled me in on a few things." She looked expectant.

Dan silently cursed his older brother, but the fat was in the fire now. He might as well go for broke. "Turns out I'm the jealous type," he confessed. "Trouble is, that's a real turn-off for Liss."

"So stop being jealous."

"Yeah, right. How?"

"Do you have any *reason* to be jealous?"

"I don't know."

"Ah. So you're just insecure. You don't have enough confidence in your appeal to the opposite sex."

Dan frowned. Where was the sympathy a brother should expect from a sister? Liss found him plenty appealing. Or she had until Gordon Tandy came into the picture.

"What does Liss want?" Mary took note of his blank look and clarified the question. "What are her future plans? Do you have the sense that you're a part of them?" Each question was accompanied by the swipe of a cloth across the baby's food-smeared face. The little guy had been born two months premature, but he was making up for it now. If he kept eating the way he was, his mom would soon have to worry about him turning into a real porker.

"We haven't talked about the future," he said. "She decided to stay here. She bought into her aunt's shop. I figured that gave me time to work up to proposing to her."

"So, you've never mentioned marriage." Mary sighed and shook her head. "That means she has no idea how serious you are about her."

"Sure she does. We've spent a lot of time together the last few months."

"Talking?"

"Some."

"Not enough, obviously. What's your worst fear?"

"That she'll go back on the road." He spoke without thinking but he knew as soon as the words were out that what he'd just said was the truth. It wasn't any person he worried about. It was that recent events might take Liss away from him for good. If she chose her old life, or at least a variant of it, over what she'd done for the last few months, then he was shit out of luck.

Mary hoisted the baby out of the chair and whisked him off to be changed and dressed in clean clothes. By the time she returned to the kitchen, Dan knew what he had to do. He didn't have to sell Liss on marrying him. Not yet, anyway. He just had to convince her to stay in Moosetookalook.

"Do me a favor, Mary?"

She sent a suspicious look in his direction, but nodded.

"Give Liss a call and tell her one of the outfits you volunteer for needs a hand." If she got more involved in the community, she'd have more reason to stick around.

"They always do, but Liss runs a business. She doesn't have a lot of free time. Heck, I'm sure she'd have preferred to play chauffeur for the dancers herself last weekend, but she couldn't get away from the Emporium." She paused for a beat. "Speaking of the dancers, I hear they're still hanging around."

"Oh yeah. Nine of them are staying in Moosetookalook now, three of them at my house."

"Hope you didn't get stuck with Fiona Carlson."

"No, she's in Margaret Boyd's apartment. When did you meet Fiona?"

"She's the one who called me for rides. Saturday *and* Sunday. And she was in a big hurry to get to town both times and very fussy about where she was dropped off, too. You'd think, if it was that important to her to get back downtown right away, that she'd have stayed at the motel instead of out at the cabins."

"She wasn't rude to you, was she?"

"No. Just impatient and preoccupied. And she wasn't too thrilled to share the car with Jason." She grinned down at the baby, who was tugging on a lock of her hair.

Since the aroma drifting Dan's way from Jason's diaper at that moment was not only unpleasant but pungent, his sympathy was with Fiona.

The cozy corner at Moosetookalook Scottish Emporium was perfect for a private conversation, especially on a slow Thursday. Liss supplied coffee and cookies and curled up in her favorite chair, waving Cal MacBain into the one that sat kitty-corner to it. She'd hear the bell if anyone came in, but she was counting on the usual lack of business to allow her an uninterrupted chat with her former dance partner.

"So, Cal, what am I missing?"

"Your career?"

She made a face at him. "Besides that. Things have changed since I left the company. There wasn't so much contention before. Was there?"

"Maybe you just weren't aware of it."

"We all practically live together on the road. How could I have missed it?"

"Rose-colored glasses? Face it, Liss, you're an optimist from the word go. You were totally oblivious to Victor's interest in you until he actually propositioned you."

"That did take me by surprise."

"It shouldn't have."

"But he wasn't mean about it when I turned him down. There were no threats. He changed, Cal. The Victor I knew wouldn't have tried to blackball Sarah or claim he was going to replace Zara with Emily. He was ill, you know. Taking medication."

"So I heard."

"That can cause personality changes, right?"

"Right. Damn fool. He could have told us. Victor was never the most popular person in the company, but we've always been there for each other. We'd have . . . I don't know . . . *supported* him somehow. Nobody wanted him dead, Liss. Nobody."

"But *somebody* killed him." Now who had on rose-colored glasses? "I know about his conflicts with Sandy and Zara, and with Stewart, and with Sarah, and how Ray felt about her. Was there anyone else? Someone who might have hidden his or her resentment a little better?"

"Not that I can think of. There was one thing, though." He stared into space, as if trying to align the facts. "When did Victor find out he was sick? Do you know?"

"I'm not sure, but I got the impression it was shortly after I left the company. Certainly by the time Sarah did."

"Okay. That tracks. But then, just a few weeks ago, it was like there was a new layer of mean tacked on top of the surliness we'd been seeing. Like he found out something else he wasn't happy about."

"More health problems? Maybe the medicine wasn't working right."

"All I know is that he got so he'd stare at people, watching them in case they . . . I don't know—were going to run off or something. He'd come around to each room, claim he was just making sure there were no problems, but it felt like a bed check." Cal gave a short bark of laughter. "Our company manager had turned into a chaperone on a senior trip. It was as if he was *trying* to catch one of us doing something wrong."

"Illegal, do you mean? Damn it, Cal. You were supposed to help me find answers to questions, not raise more of them!"

"Sorry, chickie. I got nothing. Maybe Emily knows more."

Liss grimaced. Emily. The one person she had not talked to about Victor's death. She'd been unable to question her at first because Emily had taken off. Later, Liss had let a mixture of pity and personal dislike get in the way of questioning Victor's most recent lady friend.

"How do you feel about being a shopkeeper for

an hour or so?" she asked Cal. Emily was upstairs in Aunt Margaret's apartment and Fiona and Winona were not. Winona had a tooth that had been bothering her and Fiona had driven her into Fallstown to visit a dentist.

"Go get her, girl," Cal said.

Chapter Fourteen

Liss climbed the stairs slowly, her reluctance to talk to Emily growing with every step. *Get over it*, she told herself. It was childish to resent Emily Townsend because she now danced the part Liss herself had once performed. And it was unfair to the young woman to hold her relationship with Victor against her. After all, as Zara had said, Victor could be charming.

It was, Liss decided, what Serena had said about Emily that stuck in her craw. Had Emily really been intimate with Victor only to advance her career with *Strathspey* at a faster pace? That sounded so "Hollywood Babylon." Surely sensible modern women didn't still try to sleep their way to the top, especially when the "top" wasn't all that high.

That Emily had been bored with Victor was easier to believe. Perhaps she'd entered into the relationship because she'd genuinely liked him and then had found it difficult to disentangle herself. Would that have provided her with a strong enough motive to kill him?

Give her the benefit of the doubt, Liss told herself as she entered the apartment. She was prepared to bend over backward—a trick she could actually manage, even after all these months away from dancing—to be fair to Emily Townsend. But she wanted answers.

"Emily?" she called.

"In here," came a faint, lethargic voice from the guest room.

Liss found her sprawled gracefully on one of the twin beds, her forearm draped over her eyes to keep out the sun. "Are you all right, Emily?"

She answered without changing position. "Don't worry, Liss. I haven't taken any more meds. I learned my lesson there."

Liss sat down on the foot of the bed, forcing Emily to shift her feet. "You really thought those pills of Victor's were tranquilizers?"

"That's what he called them. Well, he called them his 'magic pills' and said they calmed him right down, so I assumed they were Valium or something like that. I didn't know he was sick. He never said a word."

"But you knew about his allergy."

"Oh yes. Everyone did." Shifting her arm, she peeked at Liss from beneath. "What is it you really want to know?"

"How did you get Victor's pills? You weren't sharing a room."

"I had the pill bottle in my purse. It was bulky and he asked me to carry it for him until after the reception."

Liss supposed that made sense. "Did you take Victor's pills before or after Detective Tandy talked to you?"

"After. I wasn't all that upset when I thought his death was just a terrible accident."

"In fact, you were probably relieved."

Offended, Emily sat up. "How can you say that?"

"Did you plan to dump him once he gave you Zara's part in the show?"

The faintest wash of pink colored Emily's cheeks. She scooted away from Liss until the headboard stopped her retreat. Her chin quivered. For a moment, Liss thought she might be about to cry. She pouted instead.

"I wasn't going to break up with Victor. Not right away. He would have taken the role away from me again if I'd done that."

"Do you think he'd have fired you if you broke up with him?"

"Maybe. That's why the split had to be his idea. I figured that once Zara left the company, Victor would hire someone new. Then, being Victor, he'd go after her and leave me alone." With languid grace she rose from the bed and went to the dresser, sitting in front of it to check her hair. She picked up a brush and put it to use, ruthlessly attacking the snarls her short nap had caused.

Not dumb. Conniving. And perhaps a bit naive. "Did Victor try to use his position with the company to coerce you into doing anything you didn't want to do?"

Emily's titter was even more annoying than usual. "You mean kinky sex? Trust me, Victor wasn't nearly as kinky as he thought he was."

Hiding her distaste, Liss did not press for details. She wouldn't be able to stomach them. As Emily continued to primp in front of the mirror, Liss wondered what she'd do now that her sugar daddy was gone. Emily Townsend was not a nice person, but she wasn't Victor's killer. There was no profit for her in his death. In fact, she'd suffered a setback. Whoever replaced Victor, especially if the new manager was a woman, would not be likely to fire Zara and give Emily her part in the show.

"Did you notice anything odd about Victor in the last few weeks before his death?" Liss asked. "Was he worried? More difficult? Was it something he did that made you decide to stay at the B-and-B instead of at the motel with him?"

"No, no, no, and no. I just needed a break."

"Do you know why Victor was so down on Stewart?"

Emily met Liss's eyes in the mirror. "That I can answer. Stewart was too damn clever—and cutting—with all his puns and smart remarks. Victor encouraged him to drink to excess. He was looking for an excuse to fire him." Emily spun round on the stool in front of the vanity, a smug smile on her face. "Want to know a secret? I don't think Stewart actually drinks that much. He pretends to because a drunk can say anything he wants, no matter how nasty, and get away with it. To tell you the truth, I'm surprised it wasn't Stewart who was murdered."

When Gordon Tandy knocked at her door late that evening, Liss eagerly undid the locks. She had been looking forward to talking to him about the bits and pieces of information she'd gathered and she was curious to know what he'd discovered in Victor's apartment.

But the Gordon Tandy who walked into her foyer was not smiling, nor was he alone. A uniformed state trooper followed close at his heels.

"Where's Kalishnakof?"

"Why?" She couldn't read a thing except determination in his set features and cold, dark eyes.

"I'd like a word with him."

That sounded ominous. "He doesn't have to talk to you if he doesn't want to," she blurted. She'd learned that much about the law when she'd been suspected of murder.

Gordon gave her a fulminating look. "That's true, but it's also his decision, not yours."

"He's upstairs. I'll get him."

"*We'll* get him." Gordon caught her arm before she could start up the staircase. "Which room?"

Armed with directions, followed by his colleague, he climbed to the second floor, leaving Liss to stare after them from the bottom step.

She heard their footsteps cross the upstairs hall, then a knock on the guest room door and Zara's gasp when she opened it. It shut again with a solid thunk. Liss considered tiptoeing up and pressing her ear to the wood but decided that probably wasn't a good idea. She'd find out soon enough what was going on.

Less than a minute passed—although it seemed an eternity—before Liss heard the door open and close again. Zara came flying down the stairs. "What's going on, Liss? What do the cops want? Why wouldn't they let me stay?"

"I don't know."

Zara's frightened eyes darted up the stairs. "This isn't good, Liss. I don't know what that detective thinks he knows, but it isn't good. I saw his face—"

A shout from the bedroom cut her off. Then there was more yelling, and a dull thud sounded . . . from outside the house. Seconds later, the uniformed officer pushed past them, heading for the front door.

Although Liss knew at once that a bad situation had just gotten worse, she was slow to put the pieces together. When they finally fell into place, she felt her face drain of color. Then she ran, too, with Zara close behind her. Racing to the back door off the kitchen, she dashed through, pausing only long enough to turn on the outside light but not taking time to put on her boots or her coat.

The room Sandy and Zara shared had a small balcony attached. It was situated directly over Liss's back porch. As Liss started down the two little steps that led to her driveway, Gordon dropped from above, almost landing on top of her.

Zara screamed. Liss managed to hold in all but a muffled gasp, but her heart was pounding as fast as a bass drum keeping double time.

Gordon lost his footing on the muddy strip of lawn between the house and the driveway but clambered up again and was off and running before Liss could do more than gape at him.

Still struggling with disbelief, she turned to stare up at the balcony. The door into the guest room stood open. She'd been right about that thump she'd heard. For some inexplicable reason, Sandy had bolted from the room and leapt over the rail of the balcony, dropping ten feet or so to the ground. What on earth had Gordon said to him to make him that desperate to get away from the police?

"Why would he run?" Zara wailed. "He didn't kill Victor."

"Of course not," Liss automatically agreed.

But running away made him *look* guilty.

Arms wrapped around herself against the chill in the evening air, she slogged toward the front of the house. The uniformed trooper already had Sandy in custody. His hands were cuffed behind him, but that wasn't the worst of it. He was limping. Liss stopped dead and stared. It didn't take much for an awkward landing to do permanent damage. She ought to know!

"He's hurt!" Zara tried to run to Sandy's side, but

Liss held her back. Far from calm herself, she still knew better than to get in the way of an arrest.

Gordon opened the back door of the cruiser parked at the curb. By the time Liss and Zara reached it, Sandy was inside. Liss caught only a glimpse of his face, but that was enough. His features were contorted with pain.

"He's injured," she said to Gordon in an accusatory tone.

"We'll stop at the hospital on the way to the jail."

"Did you come here to arrest him?" Liss demanded. And to think she'd believed Gordon to be fairminded!

"I came to ask questions. Your friend was being so evasive that I suggested he might like to accompany me to another location for the rest of the interview. That's when he decided he didn't want to stick around."

"What are you charging him with?" Liss managed to sound calm, but her fingers had curled into tight fists.

"Assaulting a police officer."

Zara made a little sound of distress and imitated a fountain. Liss just wanted to smack somebody, and it was a toss-up whether her target would be Gordon or Sandy. They were both behaving like idiots.

"Gordon, you can't just—"

"Liss, butt out." Leaving her sputtering indignantly, he climbed into the passenger side of the cruiser. The uniformed officer was already behind the wheel and lost no time getting under way.

Liss stared after the taillights until they disappeared. As if someone had flicked a switch, she became aware that her feet were rapidly turning into blocks of ice. She could hear Zara's teeth chattering.

"Inside," she ordered, appalled to realize that both

her front and back doors had been left wide open. It was a wonder Lumpkin hadn't escaped in all the confusion. She located him in the kitchen, fully occupied with his food dish. "Only sensible one in the group," she muttered. Raised as an indoor cat, he'd probably stuck one paw outside and decided to wait for summer to try exploring the world beyond the house.

After a quick trip to her bedroom to exchange sodden shoes and socks for warm, fluffy slippers, she headed downstairs again. Her hands were still unsteady. She spilled cocoa, slopped water, and nearly dropped a mug, but she craved the soothing effects of hot chocolate and felt the need for something physical to occupy her. Completing the simple task settled her, although it took twice as long as it should have.

The phone started ringing even before she put the water in the microwave. Sandy's arrest had not gone unnoticed by the neighbors. Ray called from Dan's house—Dan himself wasn't at home. He'd been beeped by his brother and gone out, so he'd missed all the excitement. Then Fiona phoned from Aunt Margaret's apartment. Angie was next, followed by Patsy from the coffee shop on the opposite side of the town square. Liss told them all the same thing—she'd talk to them tomorrow, when she knew more herself. Then she unplugged the landline and turned off her cell.

Correctly guessing that Lee Annie would be with Zara, consoling her, Liss filled three mugs with cocoa, put them on a tray, and carried it upstairs. She found both women in the guest room, Zara huddled on the bed, Lee Annie standing by the balcony door and shaking her head in disbelief.

When Liss appeared in the hall doorway, Zara sniffled, hiccuped, and fished for a tissue to wipe her streaming eyes. She accepted the hot chocolate. Liss gave her time for a few sips but she wasn't feeling long on patience. "What happened before you came downstairs?"

"Detective Tandy knocked. I let him and the other cop in. He said he wanted to talk to Sandy alone, but first he needed to ask me a question." She started to tear up again, but got control of herself when Liss fixed her with a basilisk stare. "He had a letter I wrote."

"What letter?"

"I'm not sure."

"How can you not—?"

"He held out a sheet of yellow lined paper, okay? The page was folded so that only the last part showed—my signature. So when he asked me if I'd written that letter, I said I supposed I had. He didn't let me see the whole thing, Liss. Just my name at the bottom. It was my writing, though, and I always write letters on yellow lined pads."

"You should have asked to see the whole thing."

"He didn't give me the chance. He said thank you and told me that would be all. Then he all but shoved me out into the hall."

"What do *you* think was in that particular letter?" Liss perched at the foot of the bed, close enough to see Zara's shuttered expression.

"I don't know," she said evasively. "I write lots of letters."

"Did you ever write any to Victor?"

"Once or twice, back when we were still a couple." She sipped more cocoa, avoiding Liss's eyes.

From behind her, Liss heard Lee Annie shift position in the chair. She thought about asking the singer to leave, but nothing was going to stay secret much longer, not now that Gordon had arrested Sandy.

"Did you write any letters to Victor recently?" she asked Zara.

"No."

"How would that detective have gotten hold of one of her letters, to Victor or anyone else?" Lee Annie asked.

"He was in Providence earlier today, searching Victor's apartment. He probably found the letter there."

Liss hadn't thought it possible for Zara's face to lose any more color, but it did. She shoved the mug of cocoa at Liss, threw herself facedown on the bed, and buried her face in her arms.

"What?"

The other woman just sobbed harder.

"Tell me, Zara! God, you're worse than Emily!" She would have tried to shake an answer out of her if both hands hadn't been full.

"Patience, Liss. She'll have to stop the waterworks sometime." Lee Annie, looking thoughtful, drained her mug of hot chocolate and set the crockery aside. "Maybe you should try to find a lawyer for Sandy."

Guilt swamped Liss as she realized she should have thought of that herself, and long before now, too. She should also have called the hospital in Falls-town, to find out how badly Sandy had hurt his ankle. "Keep an eye on her?" she asked Lee Annie.

"As if she were my own sister."

It didn't take long to make her calls. She only knew one attorney, Edmund Carrier III. As a rule, he didn't handle criminal cases, but he could look quite formidable when he put his mind to it. After she'd exacted his promise to look into Sandy's arrest, she phoned the emergency room, but they wouldn't tell her anything. She'd forgotten about Maine's strict confidentiality law.

Liss returned to the guest room to find that Zara

had recovered her composure. "I think I know what letter it was," she blurted the moment Liss came through the door. "I wrote it more than a year ago, before Victor and I broke up for good. We'd had a spat and he'd said we were finished. I should have let it go, but that was before Sandy and I got close and there were a lot of things I liked about Victor, so I wrote to him to tell him I wanted to get back together with him."

"Foolish girl," Lee Annie murmured.

But Liss understood. She'd known Victor for eight years. He'd rarely been without a lady friend among the dancers and never once had Liss heard he'd harassed or ill-treated any of them until Sarah. She blamed his mysterious illness. Pain and uncertainty could well have accounted for his aberrant behavior.

Zara swiped at the tears once again running freely down her cheeks. "I should never have written that letter. It was stupid of me to want to get back together with Victor. It's not like he was that great a lover or anything, and I knew we didn't have a future together. He wasn't the picket fences and babies type."

Neither was Sandy, but Liss let that pass. She was trying to work out why an old letter had made Gordon suspect Sandy of killing Victor. "Zara, was that letter dated?"

She looked blank. "I don't know. Why?"

"Because if it wasn't, Gordon Tandy must think you wrote it recently, and that Sandy murdered Victor to keep you from going back to him."

Horrified, Zara leapt off the bed. "I'll tell him he's wrong. I'll go right now and—"

"Why should he believe you? Besides, Gordon didn't arrest him for that." Gently, she pushed Zara back down on the bed, keeping her in place with a hand on one thin, trembling shoulder.

Liss wasn't certain exactly what had happened in this room earlier, but she was sure Gordon Tandy hadn't made up the charges. Sandy must have done something stupid even before he jumped over the balcony railing, something it would take someone better versed in the law than she was to straighten out.

Exhaustion hit her like a sledgehammer. Too many questions. Too few answers. Why hadn't Gordon just shown Zara the letter and asked her when she wrote it? Why had he wanted to take Sandy somewhere else to question him? And why had Sandy, in a fit of panic, tried to run? What was he hiding?

"We'll all see things more clearly after a good night's sleep," she said. "I called a lawyer. He'll take care of everything."

Lee Annie, yawning, seemed willing to fall in with her suggestion. Telling them she'd see them in the morning, she headed for bed. Liss was about to follow suit when Zara spoke.

"I thought he'd come to arrest me," she whispered.

Liss turned to stare at her. "Why? What made you think you were a suspect?"

"It doesn't matter now."

"Maybe it does." Checking first to make sure Lee Annie had retreated into her own room, she closed the door. "You want to help Sandy, right?"

"Of course I do. How can you ask? I love him."

And once she'd loved Victor. Unless, Liss thought with unaccustomed cynicism, she'd just been using him, as Emily had. "Why did you think the police would decide you'd killed Victor?"

"Because of the rumors that *Strathspey* is in financial trouble."

"Yes?" This was worse than pulling teeth, Liss thought.

"I trained as a bookkeeper."

"So what? You weren't the one keeping the company books."

"They aren't that hard to get at."

"Still, I don't see—"

"My mother is in prison for embezzling money from the company she worked for! She's an accountant. Oh, Liss, don't you see? I was sure that if the police found out about her, they'd be bound to think the apple doesn't fall far from the tree."

Liss didn't "see" at all. Even if Gordon did know about Zara's mother, he'd have no reason to assume Zara would take money from *Strathspey*, let alone kill Victor to cover it up. Besides, hadn't Fiona told her that it was Victor himself who'd been skimming money from the company coffers?

"If Gordon is focused on Sandy, that means he doesn't believe you stole any money or killed Victor," Liss told her.

"Neither did Sandy!"

"No, neither did Sandy. He isn't a murderer. Or an embezzler." Liss almost smiled at the thought of the latter. Sandy could barely balance a checkbook and was convinced that ATMs had a personal grudge against him. He had so much trouble getting cash from them that whenever he could he had someone else push the buttons.

Liss's amusement vanished when she resumed her contemplation of *Strathspey*'s finances. *Was* there money missing? "What if someone *has* been embezzling from the company?" she mused aloud. "And what if Victor found out?"

That might make sense of what Cal had told her. *A new layer of mean tacked on top of the surliness*, he'd said. And that it had started just a few weeks ago.

Was that when Victor first discovered there was money missing? Or when he figured out who'd taken it?

"Zara? Who could get at the box office receipts?"

"Almost anyone. Victor didn't even keep cash under lock and key. And he mailed in deposits. I can think of two or three ways you could get at the account and make changes. You wouldn't need to forge Victor's signature, either, not if you intercepted the deposit and had access to the company books." She frowned. "I doubt Victor would have noticed for a while if the figures didn't match. He only got statements from the bank every three months."

"He didn't bank online?"

Zara shook her head and prefaced her answer with a short, rueful laugh. "He didn't trust computers."

Chapter Fifteen

Suck it up, Sherri told herself. *Friendship comes first.* The fact that she might lose her job was a secondary consideration.

Yeah, right.

She told herself the risk was small. Deputies served "at the will and pleasure of the sheriff" and the sheriff of Carrabassett County was a reasonable, generally sympathetic soul named Penelope Lassiter. She was second-generation law enforcement but always willing to listen to explanations. On rare occasions, she could even be persuaded to bend the rules. With that in mind, Sherri had traded duties for the day with one of the other corrections officers. She would work inside the jail instead of manning the dispatch center, her usual preference.

"I need a change of pace," she'd lied. A short time later she was locked in with the lowlifes, trying to ignore the pervasive smell of disinfectant and a distinct twinge of claustrophobia.

Not that she'd actually be *with* them. Not most of the time. The majority of the monitoring was done with cameras. The locks on the individual cells were remotely controlled, too. But some eyeballing still had to be done. Cell checks in particular, Sherri's first task of the day.

Later, medium-security prisoners would be released into the cell block to interact with each other and enjoy the meager comforts offered in the central space—a television, the books in the "library," several decks of cards, and a few well-worn board games like checkers and Monopoly. At the beginning of Sherri's seven-to-three shift, the cells were not yet open for the day. As she did a quick visual check of the inmates behind each door—ordinary doors rather than bars, with only a small window for security purposes—she clutched the key that could unlock them so tightly that it left an impression on her palm. She did not use it until she reached the cell in which Sandy Kalishnakof had spent the night. She'd left him till last.

She wasn't doing anything wrong, Sherri reminded herself. She just wanted to have a word with Sandy in private. She rapped lightly on the door, feeling a trifle foolish for observing the courtesy under the circumstances, then turned the key in the lock and let herself in.

Sandy was sitting on his cot, his ankle propped up on a pillow. He looked smaller dressed in a blaze-orange jail uniform and was hollow-eyed from lack of sleep. His pallor was all the more noticeable because of his jet-black hair.

"Hey," she said.

"Sherri." His dark blue eyes fixed on her distinctive brown uniform. "I forgot that you worked here." The words were careful, the tone neutral.

Well, why *should* he trust her? "How's the ankle?"

"Twisted."

She already knew he'd been taken to the hospital for an X-ray and that nothing had been broken. She also knew, from personal experience, that strains and sprains sometimes hurt worse than more serious injuries.

"I've only got a minute but I wanted to make sure you were doing okay."

"Oh, sure. Lap of luxury." He shook his head in disgust as he glanced around the cell. Aside from the bed, made of metal, anchored to the wall, and furnished with a thin mattress and institutional bedding, the only objects in the room were a sink and a toilet, also well secured.

"All the comforts of home," Sherri quipped. "Well, with any luck you won't be here much longer. Liss got you a lawyer. He'll be over to see you later this morning. The way it works, if a prisoner has to go somewhere, even within the secure perimeter—the laundry, the infirmary, or to see his lawyer—he's escorted by a corrections officer. That would be me."

When he didn't respond with more than a bleak look, she pushed an extra ration of confidence into her voice. "Mr. Carrier should be able to get you out."

"Not if bail is set high. I'm not exactly rich, Sherri."

"I expect they'll end up dropping the charges."

"Fat chance," he muttered. "Tandy thinks I killed Victor."

"Well, yes, but that's not why you were arrested."

"Sure it was."

"Sandy, that you're sitting in jail right now is entirely your own fault. If you'd just have gone quietly when Gordon Tandy asked you to come in for questioning—"

"He was going to arrest me!"

"He was not about to do anything of the kind. He hasn't got a case against you." *Yet.* "He wanted to talk to you in neutral territory, away from Liss and Zara.

I suspect he hoped you'd be more forthcoming without them around."

"If that's true, what am I doing in a jail cell?"

"You're here because you shoved Gordon aside when you took off. The charge is assaulting a police officer."

It wouldn't stick, of course. Gordon Tandy had simply taken advantage of the situation to do what he'd wanted in the first place—question Sandy Kalishnakof. Only Sandy, from what Sherri had heard when she'd arrived at work that morning, had clammed up completely after his arrest. He'd refused to say word one about anything. Gordon's attempt to intimidate him had been a total waste of time and the county's money. No, the state police detective, now mildly embarrassed by the whole debacle, would not be pressing charges. He'd wait till Mr. Carrier showed up, though, before dropping them. Sherri suspected he'd also make at least one more attempt to question Sandy.

"Is that why you're standing way over there?"

"What?"

Sandy's chuckle sounded forced, but for the first time there was the hint of a genuine smile on his face. "Afraid I'll assault you, too? Try to escape?"

"You wouldn't get far, and I don't mean just because you've got a bum ankle."

"Don't worry. I'm not feeling suicidal. But I didn't kill Victor, Sherri. You believe me, don't you?"

"Sure I do. But I also think you're holding something back." She glanced at her watch. "I've got to go. I just wanted to let you know that you probably won't be here much longer. I'll be back when the lawyer arrives. You'll meet with him in what they call the contact visiting room. Someone will bring Mr. Carrier in first. Then I'll take you to him and leave you two there. Nobody will listen in because of the lawyer-client confidentiality thing. So do yourself a favor, okay? Don't talk to anyone else till Mr. Carrier gets here, but then level with him. Tell him everything you know—even what you only *think* you know—and take his advice about sharing it with the police. I don't know who or what you're trying to protect by refusing to answer questions, but I'll bet good money Gordon Tandy will get to the bottom of things eventually. Secrets will come out, with your help or without it. You want to make this whole mess go away? Help Tandy do his job."

The invaders were back.

In spite of Sandy Kalishnakof's arrest the previous night, or maybe because of it, the entire *Strathspey* company, even the nondancers, met in the dining room at The Spruces on Friday morning. For the dancers, it would be another rehearsal, and for the third day in a row, Dan would have to stay and babysit.

He hadn't had a chance to talk to Liss about Sandy, but he'd already heard the story from Ray, Stewart, and Cal. And he knew that Liss planned to address the entire company with an update before rehearsal began.

He propped himself against a convenient wall, thumbs hooked in the belt loops of his jeans, and scanned the faces of individuals in the troupe as they waited for Liss to begin. He saw apprehension in some and in others only mild curiosity. Most of them were just impatient to get on with their practice session. The members of *Strathspey*, Dan decided, were remarkably alike in one respect—their lives centered on their work. Everything and everyone else came in a distant second.

"Most of you already know about the latest development," Liss began. "Sandy's in jail in Fallstown, but he hasn't been charged with Victor's murder and I don't think he will be. This is all a misunderstanding because of a letter Zara wrote to Victor more than a year ago. I'm counting on those of you who can provide corroboration to voluntarily go to the police and assure them that Zara and Victor were not planning to reconcile. Without that motive, Sandy had no reason to want Victor dead."

An ominous silence followed this request.

Flushing slightly, Liss continued her little speech. "The other thing I want all of you to know is that I've decided to apply for Victor's job."

Amid scattered applause and whistles, Dan shoved away from the wall with a violence that nearly cracked the plaster. He'd taken several steps toward Liss before he realized what he was doing and put on the brakes. He was less successful at stopping a string of silent curses or the red haze of hurt and anger and sheer indignation. She might have warned him! Did he mean nothing to her?

When Liss had made a few closing remarks and promised further updates on both Sandy's situation and a departure date for the company, her audience splintered. Individuals and small groups spread out around the large room and launched into a wide variety of warm-up exercises.

Dan threaded a path through stretching, bending, and pliéing dancers and dodged one doing a leap to get to Liss. She couldn't be serious about leaving. She wouldn't make such a life-altering decision without at least warning him she was thinking about it. Would she?

He had to contain his impatience when he finally reached her. She was not alone. Lee Annie, who was not needed for rehearsal, had just cornered Liss and Fiona to demand that someone loan her a car.

"Try not to put too much mileage on it," Fiona cautioned, reluctantly turning over the keys to her rental.

"I'll pay for the gas." Lee Annie sounded irritable. "I just have to go off on my own for a bit. Nothing against your quaint little town, Liss."

Liss shrugged off the backhanded compliment and gave Lee Annie driving directions to the nearest good-size mall. When the singer left, Liss flashed the briefest of apologetic smiles at Dan to acknowledge his presence before addressing Fiona.

"I'd like to take a look at the company books before I commit myself," she told the older woman, "although I'm not overly concerned if *Strathspey* is in financial trouble. Moosetookalook Scottish Emporium was in a bad way before I took over and I straightened things out there."

"The police have them, but they're supposed to give them back. I'll get in touch with Detective Tandy and remind him and I'll bring them over to you as soon as he returns them." Impulsively, Fiona embraced Liss. "I couldn't be more delighted. I do not like being the one in charge. Makes me surly!"

"Nothing's settled yet," Liss warned her.

"Just the prospect that someone may take the burden of management off my shoulders makes me feel ten pounds lighter."

"You can't afford to lose ten pounds," Liss teased her.

"Ha! You know what they say."

They quoted together, laughing: "You can never be too rich or too thin!"

When Fiona finally stopped chuckling and began

her warm-up exercises, Dan caught Liss's arm and pulled her away from the others. "We need to talk."

"Not here. Not now."

"Where and when?"

"Dan, I've—"

Abruptly losing patience with her, Dan used the hold he still had on Liss to tow her out of the dining room and into the passage that led to the kitchen. The sudden quiet on the other side of the baize door was startling. "We talk now. What the hell was that announcement in there all about?"

As she jerked free, Liss's eyes flashed blue, then green in the uncertain light of the hallway. "I want to get a look at the books."

"I'm not talking about the books. I'm talking about you applying for Victor's job. Why—?"

"I want to get a look at the books," she repeated.

"Damn it, Liss—"

She stopped the flow of words by placing her fingers on his lips. "I don't want Victor's job. I just said I did so I could get access to the company records. There's a rumor the show is in financial trouble. There may be some embezzling going on."

"Oh." Relief came tempered with renewed fears for her safety. He caught her hand in his. "Do you think it's wise to—?"

"Not now, Dan. Okay? I can only handle one crisis at a time. Two or more will make me nuts."

"Tell me about it!"

She frowned. "You don't mean that literally. I heard the sarcasm. Has something else happened? Something to do with the hotel?"

"Good guess." And she was right. It was the "final straw" theory in action. Add one problem too many and things got crazy. He tried to make light of it, but there was no way it didn't sound outlandish. "We have a ghost in the hotel."

"You're kidding, right?"

He leaned his head back against the wall. "I wish. One of the neighbors spotted lights moving through the second floor of The Spruces last night. Sam and I came out here and looked around, but it's a big place. We didn't find anything. I'm going to search more thoroughly now, in the daylight. Want to help?"

He wasn't surprised when she shook her head.

"It was probably just teenagers looking for a place to neck, but I have to check things out."

"Then it seems you have your mystery to solve and I have mine."

"Missing money, huh?"

"Fiona thinks Victor helped himself from the till. Zara is afraid the police will suspect she did." She waved away his question before he could ask it. "I don't know much yet, but it seems to me that if someone did steal from the company coffers, it could be connected to Victor's murder."

"And applying for Victor's job gives you an excuse to look into it. Does it occur to you that it also might make you a threat to the killer?"

She sighed heavily. "I *have* to do this, Dan. These people are my friends. My family. I spent eight years with some of them. Imagine having the same roommate all the way through college and double it. You don't just abandon someone you've been that close to, even if you may have had a few differences with them along the way."

"Okay. Okay, yeah, I see that." He reached out to run one hand down the length of her arm. "Just be careful. Please? And if you need help—"

She came up on her toes and kissed him on the

lips, cutting off the flow of words. "I'll call you if I need backup," she promised. "I will. Trust me."

"You sure this is what you want?" Sherri asked.

"Positive. Thanks for the lift."

The end of Sherri's shift had coincided with Sandy's release from jail. When he'd asked for a ride to Fallstown Motor Lodge, she could hardly say no. She had been surprised, though, that there was a vacancy. She'd been under the impression that all the rooms were filled . . . with members of *Strathspey*.

"Look, Sandy—"

"No. Thanks, but no. I'm not comfortable going back to Liss's house. Not until I sort out how I feel about Zara."

"I don't get it. Liss says that letter was written more than a year ago." This was not the first time Sherri had mentioned that salient fact.

"No, you *don't* get it." Sandy's face was a mask of misery. "It isn't *when* she wrote the letter that matters. It's that I didn't automatically trust her to have an explanation. I'm the one who failed her, not the other way around. I'm still failing her."

"Sheesh, Sandy! Get over it. If there was ever a time to stick together, this is it. There's still a murderer loose, or had you forgotten?"

"I can't think about this now. I've . . . just . . . thanks for the ride over here, Sherri, but I'd like to be alone now." He all but shoved her out of the room and he did slam the door. She heard the locks engage.

Shaking her head, Sherri gave up and left him to his own devices. At least she could phone Liss and tell her where he was. If Mr. Carrier had already let her know that the charges had been dropped, she'd be wondering why Sandy hadn't returned to her place yet. She'd be worrying about him.

With her hand on the door handle of her truck, Sherri glanced thoughtfully at the motel. Was there another reason Sandy didn't want to return to Moosetookalook? Gordon Tandy sure thought the dancer knew more than he was saying. And maybe, just maybe, with lots of time alone to think, Sandy had figured something out while he was sitting in that jail cell.

Sherri toyed with the idea of going back and confronting him, but she was ready for a little time away from the case herself. He was probably just brooding about Zara anyway. Love! It sure could mess up the thought processes.

Glancing at her watch, Sherri fixed her mind on Adam. It was three thirty on a Friday afternoon. If she hurried, she'd have a whole hour to play with her son before supper.

Chapter Sixteen

By seven Friday evening, Liss gave up on hearing from Sandy. He wasn't going to contact her. He didn't want to talk to her.

Tough. She had a few things to say to him and this was the ideal time. Lee Annie was in the library with the door closed, reading. Zara had gone up to her room right after supper, pleading a headache.

Liss punched in Sandy's cell number but he had turned off his phone. Muttering to herself, she called the office at Fallstown Motor Lodge. She had received reports from both Mr. Carrier and Sherri. She knew where Sandy was staying. She was also well acquainted with the owner of the motel, and she'd recently sent enough business his way that he barely balked when she asked him to keep ringing Sandy's room until he answered. She didn't want voice mail. She wasn't about to leave a message with the desk clerk. She wanted to talk to her "best pal" and she wanted to talk to him now.

It took twelve rings, but he finally picked up the phone.

"Don't hang up!" she ordered.

After a long silence on the other end of the line, she heard a deep sigh. "What do you want, Liss?"

"You. Here."

"I'm not coming back to Moosetookalook."

"Tonight or ever?"

"Don't snarl, kid." He sounded tired. "I need to be on my own for a bit."

"What about your things? What about Zara?"

"I already bought a new toothbrush."

Whoa! That didn't sound good. "Uh, Sandy, what—"

"Look, Liss, I gotta go. I appreciate you getting me a lawyer and all, but I just can't— I don't— Ah, hell. I'll call you later." And he disconnected.

She called him right back. "Don't you dare cut me off again, you jerk. Talk to me. This is no time to hole up and stare at your navel."

What might have been a snigger sounded in her ear. Liss carried the phone over to the Canadian rocker in the bay window and settled in, setting it in motion with one foot.

"I mean it, Sandy. The last thing you need is to be alone. You think too much when you're alone."

"I'm just not ready to see Zara again yet."

"Why not? She loves you, you big doofus." In the silence that followed, Liss started to put two and two together. "Okay, let's try this on for size: Gordon Tandy showed you that letter Zara wrote to Victor. The one with no date on it. And you thought the same thing he did, that Zara wrote it recently. That she was going to dump you for Victor. Idiot!"

"I know it was stupid, but Tandy was so sure . . ."

His voice, full of misery, trailed off into another long silence. Liss was about to speak when he starting talking again.

"I did think she might have decided to dump me in order to keep her job. I didn't think it for long, but

I thought it. The idea never really made sense, but that just makes it worse . . . that I believed it was possible, even for a second. I lost faith in her. I'm supposed to love her, to trust her without question. I failed her, Liss."

"Oh, for heaven's sake! You're not a saint, Sandy. So you had a moment's doubt. So what?" Too agitated to sit still, she left the chair and stood at the window, looking out at Dan's house. Everybody had lapses, didn't they?

"How can I face her?"

"How can you not? You love her. She loves you. Get on the damn bus tomorrow when it heads up here for rehearsal. First chance you get, confess your great 'sin' and ask her forgiveness. She's not going to dump you, Sandy. I repeat: she *loves* you. Everything will work out just fine, but you have to talk to each other."

This time she hung up on him.

Men! What on earth had Sandy been thinking to go to the motel instead of coming straight back here when he got out of jail, especially with a bum ankle? Was he keeping it elevated? Putting ice on it? Sherri had said he was supposed to use a cane for the next few days.

A car passed by, momentarily blinding her with its headlights. Liss blinked. Come to think of it, how had Sandy managed to get a room at the motel? They should all have been taken. She'd booked every room in the place herself.

Frowning, Liss contemplated motels, hotels, B-and-Bs, and cabins. What with one thing and another, she was becoming very familiar with what was available for lodging in the area. After a few more minutes of careful consideration, she reached for the phone once more and made two calls. Then she grabbed her coat and an umbrella—it had started raining an hour earlier—and headed for Dan's house.

"Good news," she told him when he opened the carriage house door to her knock.

"You know who killed Victor?"

"Not yet, but I have solved *your* mystery."

Dan felt like a character in a Scooby Doo cartoon. Followed by Liss and Pete, the latter in full uniform and armed, he crept along a shadowy corridor at The Spruces. The only light came from the narrow beam of the flashlight he carried. Outside a storm raged. Wind howled. Rain pounded against the windowpanes. Eerie drafts had the hair on the back of his neck standing straight up.

The previous evening, he and Sam had driven to the hotel in separate trucks to investigate reports of lights moving on the second floor. Neither that search nor the one he'd made earlier today had yielded any evidence that the hotel had been broken into. If teenagers had been using one of the rooms, they'd been extraordinarily neat.

This time they approached with stealth. They'd parked some distance away and walked to the front entrance. They were searching for intruders in semidarkness, switching on lights only after they'd already entered a room and closed the door behind them. He wondered what the neighbors would think of that.

Lightning flashed, making Dan jump. He heard a muffled squeak from Liss. Great. That would be all they'd need, to have the power knocked out by the storm. The hotel had its own generator, but Dan wasn't about to fire it up just to hunt for . . . what—ghosts or squatters? He liked the second choice better.

Liss touched his arm. When he turned to look at her she pointed to her nose and made sniffing motions. The smell was faint, but recognizable. Someone had been cooking in one of the rooms. Frying something with garlic in it.

Still fanciful in the darkness, his thoughts leapt from Scooby Doo to the Scoobies. Liss as Buffy, the Vampire Slayer? Highly unlikely, he thought with a grin, though she did have that female empowerment thing down pat.

They rounded a bend in the hallway and spotted what they'd been looking for. A thin strip of light showed faintly beneath one of the doors ahead. A suite. One of the more expensive ones. The intruders had good taste.

As they'd agreed back at Dan's house, they let Pete go in first. After all, Liss couldn't be a hundred percent sure she knew the identity of the squatters. When the time came, though, Dan took the precaution of catching her by the waist to make sure she stayed back. She squirmed out of his grasp and burst into the room only seconds behind Pete. By the time Dan went through the door, the deputy had two men lined up against the wall and was patting them down.

Liss was doing what looked suspiciously like a victory dance.

When Pete told his captives to turn around, Dan saw that her guess had been correct. The hotel's unofficial guests were Charlie Danielstone and Jock O'Brien.

Danielstone looked worried . . . until he recognized Liss. "Busted," he said, grinning at her.

Pete managed not to laugh as he started reciting charges: "Trespassing. Breaking and entering. Theft of services. You—"

"Hey!" Jock O'Brien objected. "We didn't have to break in. We were already here."

"Let me guess," Liss said. "You wanted to save the price of a couple of nights in the motel?"

"Well, yeah." Jock gave her a look that said that much must be obvious. "Why pay for something we could get for free? You were pretty generous about offering some people a place to stay, Liss. We figured you'd have extended the courtesy to us, too . . . if you'd thought of it."

"It's not her courtesy, it's mine." They were so earnest, so cocky in their assumed innocence, that Dan was also having trouble keeping a straight face. He had to give them credit for ingenuity. He just didn't want to do it out loud.

"Oh, come on, man. You've got this whole big hotel just sitting empty. We didn't hurt anything."

"I notice you chose to camp out in one of the luxury suites. Shall we say two fifty a night? That's a discount rate, you understand, because you're friends with Liss."

Danielstone went pale. O'Brien's jaw dropped.

"You're not open yet!" Charlie Danielstone objected when he got over the shock. "No services. We had to cook our own supper." He gestured at the hot plate on the floor near an electrical outlet.

"No furniture," O'Brien chimed in. "Nice carpet, but hard."

"You're breaking my heart," Dan told them.

"If you want to get off the hook," Liss said, "we want a full confession. How come Dan and his brother didn't find you guys here last night when they searched?"

"Have you looked at this place? There's like a gazillion rooms. And lots of good hiding places."

O'Brien backed up his buddy. "We had to improvise last night. We got lucky. They couldn't search every nook and cranny. They didn't find our stuff and we kept moving, always a little ahead of them. But today we had time to work out a plan. If we'd seen headlights or heard you coming, we'd have been able to scatter ourselves and all our possessions in five minutes flat. You'd never have known we were here."

"How *did* you know we were here?" Charlie asked.

"Neighbors saw lights."

"No, I mean how did you know it was us?" He pointed an accusing finger at Liss. "You weren't surprised to find us here."

"Sandy was able to move into a room at the motel— long story—and that made me wonder who'd left. It wasn't too hard to find out. The manager's a friend of mine. Then I called Paul and asked him where he'd been dropping you two off the last two days." Paul Roberts, sole member of Ray's stage crew, doubled as the company's bus driver. "He said he hadn't. That you'd told him you'd made your own arrangements. Add the reports of someone here late at night and it was elementary, my dear Charlie."

As one, they stood up straight and clapped their hands together, a sort of mock salute to her achievement. Liss grinned and, bouncing on the balls of her feet, bowed to them in acknowledgment.

Apparently, modesty was beyond Liss's capabilities. She was tickled to have solved this one small mystery. She *had* been clever about it. Dan had to admit that much.

"Do you want to press charges?" Pete asked.

"No, but I want these two out of here."

"First thing in the morning," Jock O'Brien promised, "but you'll have to find us somewhere else to stay."

"Not a problem," Liss told him. "As of rehearsal tomorrow, I'm pretty sure your old room at Fallstown Motor Lodge will be available."

Liss awoke on Saturday morning to find Lumpkin's tail in her face. She pushed him away and tried to get back to sleep. Bouncing cheerfully out of bed was beyond her. Sure, she'd solved one small mystery, but she didn't have a clue who had killed Victor, nor did she have any idea how to proceed next.

With a groan, she rolled over and buried her head under the pillow. It didn't help. She couldn't escape the unpalatable truth: there was no way the investigation of Victor's death would turn out well, not when someone she knew was bound to be his murderer.

Liss sighed deeply as her thoughts took a side path. She'd given her word to both Dan and Sherri that she would be careful. She'd fully intended to avoid being alone with any of the "suspects" when she questioned them, but she hadn't done a very good job of sticking to her promise. It was too hard to remember, let alone accept, that her efforts to solve the crime might put her in jeopardy from one of her old friends.

Then again, they might not *be* her friends much longer, not if she continued to alienate them by asking intrusive questions.

Liss tossed the pillow across the room and sat up. Tempting as it was to contemplate abandoning her investigation and letting Gordon Tandy find the killer, she knew she couldn't do that, nor could she spend the entire day in bed.

She hesitated one last time when she remembered

that it was the Ides of March, an unlucky day by anyone's reckoning. It wasn't as if the Emporium would be awash with customers. She *could* sleep in . . . except that she couldn't *sleep*. She threw her legs over the side and stood. If she was just going to lie in bed and worry, she might as well get up.

She found Zara already in the kitchen and more wired than Liss was.

"Can I borrow your station wagon?"

Liss sent a quelling look over her shoulder as she reached for the coffeepot.

"You have to work, right? That means you don't need it." Zara could barely sit still.

Liss wondered if it was too late to crawl back into bed and pull the covers over her head. "Give me a minute," she begged, all but inhaling the first life-giving gulp of the coffee and scalding her tongue in the process.

Zara toyed with the salt and pepper shakers. She realigned place mats that were already perfectly straight. When she tried to wipe away the wet ring Liss's mug had just left, Liss gave up the struggle to ignore her.

"What is *wrong* with you this morning?"

"Not a thing. I feel great. Can I borrow the car?"

"Sheesh! You sound like a teenager with a hot date." The penny dropped. "Oh, good grief! That's it, isn't it? You want to go to Fallstown to see Sandy."

"I've decided to forgive him for his momentary lapse of faith." A grin spread slowly over Zara's face. "Trust me when I say that the make-up sex is going to be great!"

"That is such a bad idea."

"Why?"

"The guy asked for time alone. You can't invade

his privacy." At Zara's crestfallen look, Liss relented. "Besides, if you let him grovel first, the make-up sex will be even better."

Brightening, Zara allowed that she might be right. "But that means I'll have *hours* to wait," she lamented. The next practice session at The Spruces wasn't until one o'clock, and even though Sandy wouldn't be able to dance with a bum ankle, Zara would be expected to participate in the rehearsal.

"What you need is a distraction. Come to think of it, we could both do with something to take our minds off things."

Lee Annie timed her entrance perfectly. Five minutes later, she'd agreed to mind the store again . . . if Liss would make her a gift of another piece of heather jewelry.

"Done." That settled, Liss went to the phone and punched in the number for Angie's Books. "Can Beth come out and play?" she asked when Angie answered.

Zara's face lit up. "What a good idea."

Once it was arranged that Beth would come over for a lesson, Liss relaxed over a second cup of coffee, then changed into practice clothes. She'd been neglecting physical therapy for her knee since she'd had guests in the house and was determined to make up for the lapse. She came back downstairs to find that Beth had arrived and she and Zara had moved all the furniture in the living room. There was now a bare space large enough for all three of them to do floor exercises.

A dancer's warm-up routine and post-knee-surgery physical-therapy exercises had much in common, but when Zara and Beth stood to use the back of the sofa as a bar, Liss removed a pair of adjustable ankle weights from the drawer of an end table. She was supposed to do the leg lifts every day. If she skipped more than a few sessions, she'd have to drop down to a lower weight. The equipment she used could be adjusted in one-pound increments, but she'd worked too hard to reach the five-pound level in the first place to allow herself to backslide now.

At the sound of Velcro separating, Lumpkin magically appeared. Liss shoved him away and fastened the first weight to her right ankle. He was back before she had the other one in place.

"What's his problem?" Zara asked, lifting her head from her knee as she stretched her leg out along the makeshift bar.

"He likes Velcro." As if to prove her point, Lumpkin tried to grab the end of the flap with his teeth. "Cut that out!"

"He likes to chew on things," Beth chimed in. "Once, before Liss lived here, he tried to eat a shoe. The tongue had all these little teeth marks on it and some of the leather was missing."

"Why doesn't that surprise me?" Liss jerked Lumpkin's prize away from him, avoiding his claws when he tried to get it back. "He gnawed right through one section of my first set of weights. His teeth punctured the one-pound bag of sand inside. Talk about a mess!"

Liss stretched out on her back and began to do leg lifts. Her knee was strong now, *almost* normal. She stared at the ceiling and willed her mind to go blank as she fell into the routine. Sometimes a good workout helped her think more clearly. She sincerely hoped that would be the case today.

Slowly, she lowered the leg with the bad knee and lifted the other. Five pounds felt much lighter on this side . . . until Lumpkin wrapped both front paws around her foot and tugged. She yelped when her heel landed on the carpet with a bruising thud.

"That's it!" She reached for Lumpkin—she'd swear he was smirking at her—grabbing him just as he tried to take off. A moment later, he was safely confined in the library and she was back on the floor, ignoring Beth's giggles and Zara's outright laughter as she resumed the exercise.

The phone rang just as they finished warming up. Drenched in sweat but feeling limber and flexible enough to twist herself into a knot if she wanted to, Liss swiped damp hair out of her eyes. She glanced through the window as she reached for the receiver. Last night's rain was long gone, but a gusty wind had set the flag in the town square flapping and the sky was an ominous gray. And a state police cruiser was just pulling away from the curb in front of the Emporium.

She snatched at the phone. "What's wrong?"

On the other end of the line, Fiona chuckled. "Not a thing. I just got the ledgers back. Do you still want to see them?"

Liss's heart slowed to its normal speed. "Yes, I would, but can you bring them over here? We're halfway through a workout."

If she'd still been dancing for a living, her concern would have made more sense, but Fiona understood that she was trying to avoid a chill. The body was an instrument, and weather affected how it would play. You didn't work up a sweat and then go out in a windstorm.

"I'd be happy to," Fiona agreed, "if you promise to lock up that cat and vacuum first. I don't feel like doping myself up on antihistamines."

"Give me ten minutes."

Half the task was done already. As soon as she hung up, Liss fished the vacuum cleaner out of the closet to take care of the rest. "I doubt that will get rid of every speck of cat hair and dander," she said to Zara and Beth, "but Fiona won't be staying very long."

"Anything we can do to help?" Zara asked.

"Go on with your practice session." As long as she kept moving, Liss knew that her muscles would stay warm. She could finish the rest of her physical therapy routine after Fiona left.

Zara put on a tape of "Monymusk," a suitable tune for practicing the Highland Fling. "Why is Fiona coming over?" she asked as Beth ran through the steps Zara had taught her.

"The police have finally returned the company's ledgers. I'm going to take a look at them. See if there *is* money missing. Fiona thinks there is, and that *Victor* took it."

Zara looked thoughtful. "If he did, he may have kept two sets of books to hide it. This set may look perfectly legit."

"Not what I want to hear!" Liss finished vacuuming while Zara worked with Beth, this time without the music.

"Bow, rise on the balls of your feet and take your arms to first position. Good. Now disassemble on the left foot and execute the shedding movement with the right foot—one, two, three, four. Good. Now beginning with the spring—right foot—instead of the disassemble, repeat bar one with the other foot—five, six, seven, eight. Good."

Fiona breezed in looking windblown and a trifle breathless. "Is the weather always this unpredictable in March?"

"Yup, but wait a minute and it'll change."

Liss accepted the ledgers from Fiona and placed

them on a convenient table. "The cat's locked in the library and I just vacuumed. I think you're safe if you want to stay for a cup of coffee."

Fiona looked nervously around for Lumpkin. Her gaze fell on Beth and she frowned. "Thanks, but no. I need to get going."

"At least sit for a minute." Liss indicated the sofa, which had been turned around so that it faced the pocket doors that led to the hall and foyer and away from the area in which Beth had been practicing. "Did the police tell you anything?"

Reluctantly, Fiona slipped out of her coat and sat. Zara joined them, leaning over the back of the sofa, as interested as Liss was to hear Fiona's answer.

"He didn't drop a single hint about what's going on," Fiona complained. "Just handed over the ledgers and left again. It wasn't even that nice Detective Tandy. He sent a uniformed officer I'd never seen before."

"Well, no news is good news, I guess. They had to let Sandy go."

Fiona looked surprised, but if she secretly thought he'd killed Victor she didn't say so. Not with Zara standing right there. "I brought you this, too," she said instead, digging a memory stick out of the pocket of her skirt. "Personnel files for the company. If you're going to take over, you'll want to have a look at them. In case you want to make changes."

"I'd like to keep everyone right where they are, you included." Liss took the small electronic storage device and tucked it into her own pocket.

"Sorry, Liss. Not a chance. End of this tour and I'm gone."

"When do we go back on the road?" Zara asked.

"I . . . I'm not sure. I hoped staying on here would result in answers, but now I wonder if the police will ever discover who killed Victor. I don't believe they know any more now than they did when they started. Sometimes I think it would have been better for everyone, Liss, if your friend had left well enough alone. Then everyone would still think Victor had died by accident."

"Simpler, maybe, but not better. Fiona, I—"

Without warning, Fiona sneezed.

At the explosive sound, Lumpkin leapt straight into the air, landing on the back of the sofa, fur bristling. When Fiona turned, they were face-to-face. Her expression contorted horribly and almost at once she sneezed again.

That sent Lumpkin into total panic. He ran straight over Liss, who was sitting next to Fiona on the sofa. Zara tried to get out of his way, but he hit her legs at calf-level with enough force to send her sprawling. Her flailing arm hit the table with the ledgers.

Zara knew how to fall. She went limp, minimizing the damage when she landed but not the shock of being bowled over by a fifteen-pound feline. The heavy books tumbled down on top of her.

Liss recovered first. She gave Fiona a box of tissues and offered Zara, who was staring at the ceiling with a dazed expression, a hand up. Then she looked around for Beth. The girl stood in the middle of the open space, her big brown eyes open even wider than usual and a distinctly guilty look on her face.

"I guess I don't have to ask who let the cat out," Liss muttered.

Her words galvanized Beth. "I didn't mean for anyone to get hurt," she wailed, flinging herself at Zara.

Bemused, Zara hugged the girl. "What just happened?"

"Where's the damn cat?" Fiona barely got the question out before she convulsed in another fit of sneezing.

"Upstairs. Probably hiding under a bed." Liss had caught a glimpse of his bushy tail as he'd rounded the newel post.

Still sneezing, Fiona staggered to her feet, grabbed her coat from the rack where Liss had draped it, and fumbled for the door. A moment later, a blast of cold air marked her passing.

Quiet descended, broken only by Beth's sniffles.

"Stop that and come here." Liss waited until the girl had left the safety of Zara's embrace and was standing in front of her. "Why did you let Lumpkin out when you know Fiona is allergic to cats?"

"It was just an experiment." Beth blew her nose on the tissue Liss thrust at her. "Sherri said sometimes people say they're allergic but they really aren't. I thought Fiona just didn't like cats. That she made up the allergy stuff. I'm sorry I put Lumpkin behind the sofa."

Liss studied her, thinking hard. She didn't know all that much about children, but she didn't think she should let this kind of behavior pass unpunished. Forgive and forget was a dangerous way to go when Beth's actions might have caused real harm. "Zara could have struck her head when she fell, or broken an arm or a leg. Apologize to her, not to me."

Beth did, with obvious sincerity.

"You owe Fiona an apology, too." At Beth's stricken look, Liss relented slightly. Perhaps it would be best to keep the two of them apart just now. "You will write her a letter explaining what you did and why and why it was wrong, but you'll have to deliver it in person."

Beth looked mutinous but agreed.

"Good. Why don't you go home and get started on it now? Take your time. Make it a very good letter. You don't have to take it to her until, say, tomorrow."

After Beth left, Liss and Zara pushed the furniture back where it belonged and picked up the ledgers. "As a distraction," Zara said, "that was a doozy, but I think, if you haven't anything else in mind, that I'd just as soon sit here quietly and go through the accounts until it's time for rehearsal."

Chapter Seventeen

For once, Liss was glad there were no customers in Moosetookalook Scottish Emporium. Now that the dancers had all gone to rehearsal at The Spruces, she could finally take a look at the memory stick containing their personnel files. Liss assumed what she had was a copy of the original documents kept by the board of directors, but she wasn't sure what to expect when she plugged the "key" into her laptop and waited for the menu to surface.

She felt a little guilty about snooping into confidential files on *Strathspey* employees, but she told herself it wasn't any worse than asking pointed questions. Besides, the police had undoubtedly gone through another copy of these files already, just as they'd gone over the company's books.

Was it only wishful thinking that these electronic files might be more helpful? Zara had examined the financial records and almost immediately reached two conclusions. One, Victor had invented his own bookkeeping system. That was going to make things considerably more complicated. Two, and perhaps more importantly, she would need to see the company's bank statements in order to make comparisons.

There had been one thing even Liss could spot: income had dropped drastically over the course of the last six months. This couldn't be explained by increased wages paid to members of *Strathspey*. The payroll records—a separate ledger—were all in perfect order. No one had gotten a raise in the last three years. In fact, Emily was being paid considerably less than Liss had earned.

Resisting the temptation to read Emily's file first, Liss called up Zara Lowery's. As she'd already admitted to Liss, she had a background in accounting. Somewhere along the line she'd been advised, Liss supposed, to train for a "practical" career. Many creative people were pushed to do likewise, on the theory that a career in the arts wasn't likely to put bread on the table. It looked as if Zara had worked in a bank until Victor "discovered" her at a Scottish dance competition and signed her up for *Strathspey*. Until then, dancing had just been a hobby. She found nothing else of interest under Zara's name, certainly no hint that Victor had suspected her of embezzlement.

Liss took a look at her own personnel file next, finding it in a folder marked FORMER EMPLOYEES. She barely remembered what she'd written when she'd filled out her application to join the company eight years earlier. It looked pretty standard to her—high school, her associate's degree in business, the awards she'd won for dancing. She winced at the photograph she'd submitted—she looked very young and very innocent.

Next she skipped to the yearly evaluations. Victor's comments were brief and to the point. He had meticulously listed all her nondancing contributions to the company. He'd been downright generous in giving her credit for designing *Strathspey*'s Web page, and for other work in the area of public relations. Her career-ending accident, however, had been summed up in a brief paragraph that ended with "Resigned. Replaced."

The sound of footsteps on the stairs behind her had Liss quickly closing the laptop. Fiona and Zara were the only ones who knew she had a copy of the records and she wanted to keep it that way. She fixed a smile on her face as Lee Annie swanned through the door.

"I'm going for a drive," she announced.

"I thought Fiona had the car."

"I have a rental car of my own now."

Liss wondered when she'd managed to arrange that but didn't suppose it mattered. She'd just as soon have Lee Annie out of the way while she went through the rest of the personnel files. "Is Winona still upstairs?"

Lee Annie nodded. "She's reading. She said she'll probably take a nice long nap a little later. She didn't sleep very well last night. Gotta go. Bye."

Curious, Liss watched her through the window. Lee Annie got into a bright red sports car and took off with a roar, even squealing her tires a little as she rounded the corner.

She'd better watch out, Liss thought. The police station was just across the square.

Back at the laptop, Liss took a look at Lee Annie's personnel record. Well, well, she thought. Yet another person who'd been to business college. Had she studied basic accounting there?

If that old mystery-novel cliché that the least likely suspect would turn out to be the killer were true, then Lee Annie Neville would be a shoo-in for the role. Liss considered what she knew of the other woman. Lee Annie was older than she was. If, only eight years after graduating, Liss had forgotten most

of what she'd learned about bookkeeping, then Lee
Annie's skills weren't current, either. Then again, Liss
had given herself a crash course in the subject when
she'd taken over the Emporium's finances, bringing
herself up to date on the latest software and refreshing her basic math skills. Lee Annie might have
done the same.

A headache had begun to pound at the back of
Liss's skull. She wasn't even certain that bookkeeping
skills would have been necessary in order to steal
from Victor Owens. He'd been exceedingly careless
about keeping track of the company's money. She
still hadn't found a record of how much should have
been in the company coffers.

Shutting down Lee Annie's personnel file, she called
up the next one. For the most part her colleagues'
records made dull reading. She learned very little that
she didn't already know. One or two of the dancers—
Serena and Cal—were older than she'd supposed.
Paul, their one-man stage crew under Ray, had once
studied to be a minister.

Fiona had taken charge of the company before,
shortly after Liss's departure. Liss wondered if that
had been when Victor first found out he was ill. Had
his absence from the company provided the opportunity for someone to start stealing? Fiona would
have been less familiar with the financial end of
things, though not, it seemed to Liss, any more easily duped.

Emily's record came in for particular scrutiny, but
Liss could find nothing in her background that raised
any flags. That Emily was talented, ambitious, and out
for herself, Liss already knew. The dancer had grown
up in Chicago and done both dancing and acting
there. In the photo *she'd* submitted with her applica-

tion, she'd struck a glamorous pose that looked anything *but* innocent!

Finally, Liss had only one file left to read, one in the FORMER EMPLOYEES folder with her own. Nothing in Sarah Bartlett's background seemed out of the ordinary, except that Victor had made a note to the effect that she had a twin sister named Susan. The cynical thought that he'd probably been hoping for a twosome crossed Liss's mind.

She scrolled down the page, stopping when she came to Sarah's picture. She studied the head shot for a long time, trying to decide why Sarah, a stunning redhead, looked so familiar. With a little fiddling, she figured out how to enlarge the photograph and the memory she'd been reaching for clicked into place—the woman dining alone at the Sinclair House. That had been Sarah Bartlett.

Liss fumbled for the phone on the other end of the counter, then realized she didn't know what number to call. She had to hunt for the telephone directory, but once she had the Yellow Pages open to hotels, it was easy enough to locate the ad for the Sinclair House.

"Do you have a Sarah Bartlett registered there?" Liss asked when a cheerful, very young-sounding male voice answered the phone. College student, she guessed, working his way through school.

"Yes, ma'am," he said. "Shall I ring her room?"

"No! I mean, no, thank you. Is Mrs. Sinclair there? Corrie Sinclair?"

"Yes, ma'am." The voice sounded a bit more cautious. "I'll connect you."

Corrie came on the line a moment later, having already been briefed by her employee. "This is Mrs. Sinclair. To whom am I speaking?"

"Corrie, this is Liss MacCrimmon. Gordon Tandy introduced us the other night."

"Oh, of course I remember you, Liss. How can I help you?"

"I know this is an odd request, but you have a guest staying there—Sarah Bartlett. She used to be a member of the dance company I once belonged to and I . . . well, I need to know how long she's been there."

"Does this have something to do with the murder investigation Gordon is working on?"

"I'm afraid so."

She could hear Corrie's hesitation even over the phone, but apparently Liss's connection to Gordon carried some weight. "I'll check the computer," Corrie said. After a few faint clicking noises, she reported that Sarah had arrived on the same day Ray Adams moved into Dan's house.

Thanking her, Liss hung up. Now what? It could be just a coincidence, but Liss didn't buy that explanation. *Be a good citizen*, she told herself. More to the point, *Be smart*. She punched in the number Gordon had given her when he'd first asked for her help.

She was frowning when she hung up. She'd expected to reach state police headquarters. Or perhaps Gordon's voice mail. Or maybe a pager. Instead she'd gotten one of those annoying cell phone company messages that told her the customer was unavailable. That could mean anything. He might have turned off his cell phone because he was in court, or he could be in one of the county's many "dead" zones, where a cell phone signal simply could not reach.

Wherever Gordon was, Liss wasn't about to wait around for him to become available again. What if the desk clerk was the chatty type? He might tell Sarah someone had been asking for her.

Liss glanced at her watch. Sherri was still at work. Dan was stuck at the hotel—he was taking his "babysitting" duties even more seriously after catching Charlie and Jock trespassing. *If Winona's still awake*, Liss bargained with herself, *and she's willing to mind the store, I'll just take a quick run over to Waycross Springs and see if Sarah will talk to me.*

She was on her way ten minutes later.

Liss pulled in under the porte cochere at the Sinclair House and turned her keys over to the valet. On impulse, she asked the young man—obviously yet another college student—if he knew Miss Bartlett.

"The redhead with the classic Corvette? How could I miss her?"

Liss didn't know much about cars, but his words struck a chord. "Isn't that a sports car?"

"Yeah. Cherry red. I was some surprised she let anyone else drive it, but the last time her friend was here, she let her take off with it for the night."

"Let me guess—another redhead?"

"Yeah. Not so much of a looker, but she's got a real pretty voice."

As the valet drove off in her aunt's station wagon, Liss fished the cell phone out of her purse and tried Gordon's number again. It was still out of service. "Damn it, Gordon! Where are you?"

She asked the same question of Corrie Sinclair a few minutes later.

"I've no idea where he is, but unless something new came up with one of the cases he's working on, he was hoping to take a little time off this weekend."

For some reason, Liss had envisioned Gordon working round the clock until Victor's killer was caught. Talk about unrealistic! He'd taken a break to escort her to dinner, hadn't he? And obviously he would be involved in other ongoing investigations, too. He'd pretty much have to be, since he was the only state police detective officially assigned to Carrabassett County.

"Is there anything I can do to help?" Corrie asked.

"Okay, here's the thing," Liss said, and spilled what she knew, and what she suspected, about Sarah Bartlett.

"That doesn't sound like enough to warrant calling in the police. Let's try this instead." Corrie reached into a drawer for a passkey . . . and a canister of pepper spray.

A few minutes later, with Corrie for backup, Liss rapped on the door of one of the hotel's most expensive rooms. Whatever else was going on, Sarah Bartlett was not hurting for money.

"May we come in?" Liss asked when the redhead answered the door.

Lee Annie appeared in the opening behind Sarah, a deer-in-the-headlights look in her eyes. "Liss! What . . . ? How . . . ? Did you *follow* me?"

"Never even occurred to me." With Corrie close behind her, Liss pushed past the two redheads and entered the living room of their suite.

"Then why are you here?"

"That's the same question I was going to ask you."

"Oh, for heaven's sake!" Sarah planted herself at Lee Annie's side and slid one arm around the other woman's waist. Then she gently kissed Lee Annie's cheek. "She's my girlfriend. Do you have a problem with that?"

"Only if the two of you conspired together to embezzle money from *Strathspey* and kill Victor Owens."

Sarah's response, a slow blink, provided counterpoint to Lee Annie's squawk of denial. With admirable self-possession, Sarah weighed the situation and suggested they all sit down, have a good stiff drink, and put their cards on the table.

Although Liss was already half convinced she was barking up the wrong tree, she took Sarah up on her invitation—for the talking, not the drinking—and started by asking the dancer where she had been the previous Saturday.

"St. Louis," came the prompt reply, "with a touring company of *Chicago*."

"And you just up and left your job when you heard about Victor?"

"Not quite. I have a twin sister who is also a dancer. Susan is filling in for me. Pretending to *be* me, actually. She's good for another week or so. Then she has to get back to her other job. She's a children's book illustrator."

"Is she the one Detective Tandy talked to?"

Sarah nodded and took a sip of the champagne she'd already poured before Liss and Corrie's arrival.

"Can you prove it was you and not your sister who performed the night Victor was killed?"

She shrugged. "If I have to."

Liss could detect no nervousness in the other woman's manner. In fact, she seemed mildly amused by Liss's suspicions. "Okay. Let's say I believe you. When did you arrive in Fallstown?"

"Monday. I was planning to stay with Lee Annie in her motel room, even though doing so meant I had to be careful no one else saw me, but then you came along and put the kibosh on that plan."

"Why didn't you want to be seen?"

"I was trying to keep my private life private."

"Ray doesn't know about us," Lee Annie said, sotto voce. "He'd be hurt if he found out she preferred me all along. We were just trying to spare his feelings."

Liss suspected that knowing the truth might make Ray's case of unrequited love more bearable, but it wasn't up to her to enlighten him. Nor was this particular love triangle any of her business . . . as long as it didn't have anything to do with Victor's murder.

"You traded up from the Fallstown Motor Lodge," she observed. "Pretty ritzy digs on a Gypsy's salary." Liss had never even considered booking the members of *Strathspey* into the Sinclair House. It was way too expensive, not to mention a long commute to either Fallstown or Moosetookalook.

Corrie Sinclair, who had all but faded into the woodwork, came alert at Liss's comment, probably wondering if Sarah's credit was good. Ignoring the hotel owner, Liss kept her attention fixed on Sarah.

"How *can* you afford all this?" She waved a hand to encompass the tower suite with its private balcony and fireplace and fully stocked bar.

"Victor Owens." When Liss goggled at her, Sarah laughed. "You heard that he threatened to fire me if I didn't put out? Yes, I thought you had. And that I threatened to bring charges of sexual harassment against him? The upshot was that he wanted the matter hushed up. He paid me off. I call it my 'out-of-court settlement.' *Way* out of court, if you know what I mean, and no lawyers involved."

"Where did he get the money?"

"Don't know. Don't care. I do, however, intend to spend every cent of it having fun. Hence this suite. I'll go back to working for a living when the money runs out."

"And when will that be?"

"At the rate I'm going? No more than another week."

"She's a free spirit." The look on Lee Annie's face combined love with hero worship. "Money doesn't mean a thing to her."

Liss believed her. After a few more questions, to clarify the timing of certain events, Liss left the lovebirds to their tryst. Armed with Corrie Sinclair's easy-to-follow directions, she went next to what Gordon Tandy had described as his "little house."

He hadn't been kidding. The place was tiny, a one-story cape on a postage-stamp-size lot. Gordon was just getting out of a dark green pickup truck when Liss pulled up in front. The look he gave her was wary in the extreme. Not surprising, she supposed. The last time she'd seen him, he'd been arresting her best pal.

"I've been trying to get hold of you all afternoon," she said.

"I've been back in the boonies. Out of cell range."

"Business or pleasure?"

"What do you want, Liss?"

"I've found out a few things that you should know."

He stared at her for a long moment, his expression enigmatic. Then he gestured toward the house. "You'd better come in."

The interior was warm and welcoming, decorated with comfort in mind but color coordinated and tasteful. Liss wondered if there had been a serious girlfriend, maybe even a fiancée in the picture at the time he'd purchased it. She didn't think it wise to ask.

He settled her at the kitchen table, plugged in the coffeepot, and grabbed a lined tablet. "Talk."

She surveyed the room, taking in the bright yellow cabinets and the country scenes on the wallpaper.

"What?"

"Just checking for rubber hoses."

She was rewarded with a flash of temper. "For God's sake, Liss!"

"Sorry." *Not!* "Gordon, you *did* ask for my help."

"And you're never going to let me forget it," he muttered. "I also warned you not to meddle."

"I tried to reach you." She attempted to look virtuous, but the glare she got in response warned her she'd better stop teasing the wolf. "I did try the number you gave me. Twice. Then I went to talk to Sarah Bartlett at the Sinclair House."

"Sarah—? No, wait. First tell me you didn't go alone."

"I didn't go alone." Since he was clearly waiting for a name, she supplied it. He cursed. "There wasn't any danger."

"You didn't know that going in."

"Okay, I might have made a mistake, but will you please just listen to what I found out? It may be important."

He gestured for her to continue, too angry, she suspected, to trust himself to speak.

She filled him in on her search of the records and her conversation with Sarah and Lee Annie, then grabbed the pad on which he'd been taking notes and tore out a blank page. While she wrote, he poured two mugs of coffee and set one down in front of her.

"Here's the order in which I think events must have occurred." She read what she'd written aloud. "First, Victor is ill, but may or may not be getting treatment yet. He's moody, irascible, acting out of character. For one thing, he propositions Sarah. She threatens to sue, which he realizes could cost him his job. He knows he's ill, or he finds out right about then, and he knows he needs the job, and the medical insurance. He offers to pay her off. He takes the money out of the company funds, and that's when he realizes that someone else has already dipped a hand into the till. He figures out who it was. He threatens to turn that person in if he or she doesn't put the money back, plus enough to cover what Victor took. Rather than risk exposure, the embezzler kills Victor and tries to make it look like an accident."

"Nice theory." Gordon took a long swallow of the coffee. "Pretty close to one we considered ourselves. Problem is, there's no proof."

"Is there money missing?"

Still reluctant to share more than he had to with her, he gave a curt nod.

"How much?"

"How much does Sarah say she was paid?"

When Liss told him, he looked thoughtful.

"Well?"

"We've still got people working on the books, and the bank records the board of directors supplied, but it looks like there should have been a lot more money in the *Strathspey* accounts, especially this late in a tour. As much as ten times what Victor paid Sarah."

Liss gave a low whistle of astonishment. "How could Victor not miss that much?" Then she answered her own question. "He was ill. It had to have started after he got sick. He had his own crazy bookkeeping system, but it passed muster for eight years. He couldn't have been doing too much wrong."

"Drink up, Liss. Then go home. This is police business."

"In other words, butt out." She sighed and reached for the coffee. She might just have to follow that advice. She was fresh out of bright ideas.

Chapter Eighteen

"Fiona?" Liss called as she let herself into Aunt Margaret's kitchen by way of the back door to the apartment.

It was the first time she'd used that entrance in some time, since it could only be reached by climbing a flight of outside stairs. They were snow-covered and slippery in winter. They weren't any prize today, what with the rain pouring down again. Mud season was in full swing.

"Fiona? Emily? Winona? Anybody home?"

"In here," came Fiona's muffled voice, and Liss followed the sound to the bedroom. "Hello, Liss. Winona is with Ray, making a check of all the equipment and costumes and props."

"I did see the bus parked in front of Dan's house." Liss felt dumb for not realizing what that meant. "And Emily?"

"I think she's trying to turn over a new leaf. She volunteered to help Winona. So, what brings you calling?"

Fiona was packing, as Liss supposed many of the members of *Strathspey* were. They'd finally decided to move on. First thing tomorrow, Monday, they'd be on the road, making the eight-hour drive to Clifton Park, New York, for a performance that evening.

"I'm at loose ends," Liss admitted. "It's Sunday, so the Emporium is closed. Sandy and Zara are so busy billing and cooing at each other that they barely know I exist, and Lee Annie . . ." She hesitated, not sure how much to tell Fiona.

"It's all right. She phoned me. She's leaving the company at the end of the tour, just as I am. You're going to have your work cut out for you, Liss, finding replacements."

"Uh, about that. Fiona, I lied to you. I don't want Victor's job. I won't be applying for it. That was just a ploy to get a look at the company records. I thought I might find something that would help me figure out who killed him."

"I see." A flash of annoyance crossed her face. "Did you?"

"No." Restless, Liss wandered the bedroom as Fiona continued to sort and fold the clothing she'd just laundered using Aunt Margaret's washer and dryer. The desk beside the window was littered with paperwork, everything from the company's schedule for the rest of the month to the rental contract for the car Fiona had been driving. She'd have to return it today, Liss supposed, glancing idly at the date at the top. She'd rented the car on March 8 and this was the sixteenth so she probably owed the rental company a pretty penny.

"I don't suppose I could convince you to change your mind?" Fiona said, emerging from the closet.

"Not a chance. *You* could stay on as manager."

"Get stuck with the job, you mean? No, thanks."

"They need you, Fiona."

"Well, I don't need them." She had started to say

more when they were interrupted by a knock at the back door. "Now what?"

"Shall we go see?" The last thing Liss wanted was to quarrel with one of her old friends. "And while we're in the kitchen, I'll make us a nice cup of tea."

"Good idea," Fiona said. "I baked bread this morning. I'll slice it and we'll have some toast and jam to go with it."

Beth Hogencamp stood on the small landing outside the back door. She was a picture of reluctance, head bowed, eyes on the ground, shifting her weight from foot to foot as she waited for someone to answer her knock. In one hand she clutched an envelope.

She looked up when Liss opened the door and seemed surprised to see her. Her gaze darted to Fiona, then back to Liss. "I wrote the letter," she announced.

For a moment, Liss couldn't think what on earth the girl meant.

"What are you doing here?" Fiona looked up from the bread board, serrated knife in hand, scowling when she caught sight of Beth. "Haven't you caused enough trouble?"

"I came to apologize!" Beth sounded defiant.

Startled, Liss stepped back and let her in. What had happened to that shy little girl? Or was this just bravado? It took courage to admit to being wrong, to confess to bad behavior. Liss knew that from personal experience.

Fiona snatched the envelope Beth held out to her, ripped it open, and read the letter inside. Then she swore ripely.

"Fiona! Language!"

"I'm sure she's heard worse in the schoolyard. God, I hate children!"

"Then why on earth are you planning to teach them?"

As soon as Liss asked that question, it was as if something clicked in her brain. Pieces fell into place. Glaring inconsistencies stood out as if written in neon.

Fiona was lying about her plan to open a dance school. Her obvious dislike of young people made that plain. She'd *said* she was going to teach dancing because it was a logical thing for a retired dancer to do, and retired dancers, unless they were independently wealthy, still needed to make a living.

Fiona had a "nest egg." She'd said so. And now Liss was pretty sure she knew where that money had come from.

Fiona had not been taking a nap on the afternoon of the day Victor died.

Something Dan had said days earlier came back to Liss in a rush. His sister, Mary, had made *two* trips to the cabins to ferry someone in the company into Fallstown proper. That had been Fiona. Both times. Because Liss had given Fiona Mary's phone number herself. A specific volunteer had been assigned to each member of *Strathspey* staying at the cabins.

As Liss's thoughts tumbled, one after another, into a line that pointed straight to Fiona, a sense of despair settled over her. The other woman's guilt suddenly seemed so obvious. Why had it taken her so long to notice all the clues?

Fiona's cabin had been in sight of the one that had been broken into. Had she used the other unit to bake the scones or had that been a red herring? More likely, Liss thought, she'd prepared them in her own oven, covering up the evidence by making spaghetti—with mushrooms in the sauce—the next day.

But it was the date on the rental contract for the

car that cinched Liss's certainty. March 8 was the day of the performance, the day of Victor's murder. Fiona had picked up the car on Saturday, not Sunday, giving her the mobility to carry out her scheme as well as a place to hide the mushroom-filled scones until she was ready to smuggle them into the kitchen at the Student Center.

Shock left Liss reeling. She couldn't stop herself from staring at Fiona, nor could she disguise the revulsion she felt.

Fiona's eyes narrowed. "You never could hide what you were thinking."

"Beth, get out of here!"

"I don't think so." Fiona caught hold of the girl with one hand and grabbed the knife she'd been using to slice bread with the other. Before Liss could blink, the serrated blade was digging into Beth's throat.

"Fiona, you don't want to do this."

"Do you expect me to go docilely off to jail? I did kill Victor, you know. But you've already figured that out, haven't you?"

"Fiona, you'll only make things worse if you—"

"Shut up." The knife pierced Beth's neck, drawing blood. The red seemed very bright against her pale skin and the yellow rain slicker she wore. Beth's big brown eyes, wide with fear, silently pleaded with Liss to save her.

"Okay. Okay. You're right, Fiona. I guessed what really happened. But if you let Beth go and get in your rental car, I promise I won't call the cops. I'll make sure you have plenty of time to get away before I even hint that you're missing."

"You don't lie worth a damn, either, Liss. And you'll do what I tell you to do. For starters, hoist yourself up on that stool with your back to me and put your hands on your head. Keep your eyes straight ahead. Don't move. Don't even think about moving or I'll slit the kid's throat."

Liss obeyed, but Fiona hadn't said anything about not talking. "You thought Victor's death would be ruled an accident," she ventured, "but once the police suspected murder, you knew you might have to flee at a moment's notice." She'd head for the Canadian border, Liss realized, remembering the phone call she'd overheard. Superorganized, Fiona had a contingency plan in place. "You were prepared to run, but surely you never intended to take a hostage?"

"Shut up!"

Behind her, Liss heard Fiona give a series of commands to Beth: "Open that drawer. Take out that roll of duct tape and tear off two strips, each about three inches long. Now two more, each about eight inches long."

Liss winced at the sound of ripping tape but she tried to tell herself that this was good. Fiona was going to tie them up and leave them in the apartment. Someone would come eventually. Emily and Winona would return within the next few hours. Nobody would get hurt.

When Fiona ordered Liss to lower her hands and hold her wrists together behind her back, she obeyed, though she couldn't contain a grimace when someone, probably Beth, wrapped them with the duct tape. When Beth moved in front of her to apply one of the smaller pieces to her mouth, Liss saw that Fiona had already used the other one. The girl's eyes were wide and terrified above the strip of gray. Her hands trembled as she pressed Liss's gag into place.

Liss sent her what she hoped was an encouraging look, but she wasn't at all sure the effort had been successful. How could it be when she was just as scared and shaky as her young neighbor?

Fiona jerked Beth out of Liss's line of sight, barking an order: "Don't move or turn around."

More sounds told Liss that Fiona was taping Beth's hands. Then she heard footsteps leaving the kitchen—Fiona and Beth going to the bedroom for Fiona's suitcase, already conveniently packed. Liss considered making a run for it, but she couldn't abandon Beth. She stayed put. After a moment, they returned.

"Stand up," Fiona ordered.

Liss obeyed. She expected to feel duct tape being wrapped around her ankles, preparatory to leaving her behind. Instead, Fiona tossed one of her own coats, a navy blue poncho, over Liss's head, effectively hiding her bound hands.

Liss froze, unable for a moment to grasp what was happening. When she did, she spun around and was dismayed but unsurprised to find that Beth, tears streaming down a face leeched of color, was carrying Fiona's suitcase. Her hands had been taped in front of her.

Fiona, who had donned a coat, wrapped a scarf around her head turban-style and put on dark glasses, once more calmly pressed the blade of her knife to Beth's throat.

Liss went cold with dread. It was not the same knife Fiona had used before. She'd upgraded, exchanging the serrated blade for a butcher knife, one of the ones Liss's aunt kept well sharpened.

"Listen carefully, Liss. We are going to go downstairs and get in my car. I'm not willing to take the chance that you'll be found too soon, so you two are coming with me. When I get close to the border, if you've been very, very good, I'll let you out of the car. Do you understand me?"

Liss nodded. What choice did she have? Irrationally as Fiona was behaving, Liss couldn't take the chance that she would injure, or even kill, Beth Hogencamp.

Fiona flipped the hood of the poncho over Liss's head, partially concealing the duct tape over her mouth. She did the same with the hood of Beth's rain slicker. It was still pouring out, raining so hard that Liss doubted any of her neighbors would realize that Fiona was leaving with two prisoners.

They went down the outside steps single file, Liss first. Fiona followed close behind, one hand gripping Beth's arm and the other holding the knife.

"Get in," Fiona ordered, opening the back door.

Liss had never realized how difficult it was to balance while climbing into a car. With her hands fastened behind her, she had no way to steady herself when her weak knee buckled. She ended up in an awkward sprawl across the seat. Fiona shoved Beth in after Liss and slammed the door, obviously unconcerned about seat belts. A moment later, she was behind the wheel and had started the engine.

Dan Ruskin stood at his living room window staring out at the rain-swept street. He'd just watched three people get into the dark blue Dodge Stratus Fiona had rented and drive away. There was something peculiar about what he'd seen, but he was having trouble putting his finger on what it was.

"Was that Fiona in the turban?" Stewart wandered through from the direction of the kitchen, a freshly opened can of beer in one hand.

"Yeah."

"Odd."

"What is?"

"That's her rental car, right?" At Dan's nod, he

looked momentarily bemused. "Why would she have rented a car on Saturday?"

"It's Sunday, Stewart."

"Not today. Last Sunday. That's the earliest she *should* have rented it."

"Let me get this straight—you saw Fiona driving that car *before* Victor Owens died?"

"Isn't that what I just said? It was well before we knew we'd be stuck in this godforsaken backwater for more than a week. That's what I meant when I said it was odd. Of course, I didn't realize at the time that the woman driving that car was Fiona, but I do remember the turban. I wondered then why she seemed familiar, but I did not pursue the matter. I had other things on my mind."

Translated, that meant he'd been looking for a place to buy beer. "Are you sure?"

Stewart gave him a haughty look and his accent got even more plummy. "My dear fellow, I am not drunk all the time. I know what I saw." He took a long swallow of Keystone Light before he wandered off again.

No, he wasn't, Dan thought. And with shattering abruptness, he knew what it was that had bothered him about what he'd just seen. Both of Fiona's passengers had gotten into the back of the car.

"Hell!" Dan grabbed for his coat with one hand and fumbled for the keys in his pocket with the other. Something was wrong. He wasn't entirely sure what it was, but he wasn't taking any chances. He was going after Fiona.

The *Strathspey* bus was blocking his driveway.

"Move that thing!" he yelled, scrambling into the driver's seat of his pickup truck.

"What's wrong?" Cal shouted.

"Do as the man says," Stewart bellowed at him. Apparently the penny had dropped for him, too. He'd returned to the living room in time to follow Dan outside. Just as the bus started moving, Stewart climbed aboard.

With what seemed to Dan to be excruciating slowness, the lumbering vehicle backed out of his way. He gunned his engine and, tires squealing, set out in pursuit of Fiona's rental car.

He tore around the corner of Birch and Main just as Sherri signaled her turn onto Birch. Dan caught only a glimpse of her face in passing, through the rain, through the windshield, but it was enough to tell him that she'd recognized him and guessed something was up. She leaned on her horn, but he wasn't about to stop to explain himself. A sense of urgency rode him, all the more pressing for being so ill-defined.

He'd seen Fiona leave Margaret Boyd's apartment with two other people. He was convinced one of them was Liss. He had no idea why he was so certain of that. He just was. He was equally positive that she was in danger. It was odd to put two passengers in the backseat and none in the front. It was even odder to shove one of them into that backseat. It hadn't really registered with him till now, but Fiona had pushed whoever had been wearing that yellow slicker. Hard. Then she'd slammed the door shut after her.

Fiona had the car a day before she should have. Mary had said she'd taken her into Fallstown on both Saturday and Sunday, but that hadn't meant anything to Dan before. Now it did.

A jury might have trouble jumping from "Fiona lied about the car" to "Fiona killed Victor," but Dan didn't. Logic be damned. Liss was in danger. *That* he was sure of.

He drove faster, scanning the road ahead for any sign of a dark blue car. Where would Fiona go? If he was right, if she had murdered Victor, if she was a fugitive fleeing justice, with hostages . . .

Taking hostages made no sense.

Then again, neither had killing Victor.

When she'd left Moosetookalook, Fiona had been driving north. If she wasn't thinking too clearly, there was one obvious place for her to go. After all, Carrabassett County shared a border with Canada. Why she thought she'd get across, or be able to avoid extradition if she did, Dan didn't know, but that had to be where she was headed.

It would take her almost two hours to reach the border crossing. Dan grabbed the cell phone mounted on his dash and punched in 911.

The rain was getting worse, slowing Fiona's high-speed escape, but she still managed to hit every pot-hole in the county. In the backseat of the rental car, Liss and Beth had little control over which way they bounced. It was like being tumbled around inside a clothes dryer, Liss thought. She'd have bruises on her bruises by the time this ride ended.

The first few times Fiona heard them thrashing about behind her, she had glanced over her shoulder to make sure they weren't up to something. Now she just drove, ignoring their plight. Even before Liss managed to prop herself sideways on the seat, Fiona had lost all interest in her prisoners. Controlling the car on the slick, winding, narrow road required all her concentration.

Liss closed her eyes and did some concentrating herself. Although it had been years since she'd tried this trick, and her knee wasn't in the best shape, she still had the basic requirements—long arms and a small butt.

The poncho was a hindrance. She had to wriggle and squirm to get that out of her way first. Then she had to fold herself nearly in half until, bit by bit, she could ease her hands forward and slide them beneath her backside. Thank goodness Beth had left her a little slack when she'd bound her wrists.

She rested a moment, praying she hadn't just made things worse. If she got tangled up in this position, she wouldn't be able to maneuver at all.

Checking to make sure Fiona was still preoccupied with her driving, Liss slid off her boots, then slowly tipped backward, lifting both legs and tucking her knees under her chin. Twisting herself into a pretzel had been a lot easier before knee surgery. Muscles screamed at her to stop as she worked her toes through the circle formed by her bound hands. For a terrifying moment, everything stuck. She couldn't move forward or backward. Then, accompanied by an ominous popping sound, her feet slipped through and her hands, although still bound, emerged in front of her.

Liss sprawled on the seat, sweating profusely. The poncho had worked its way up over her face. She waited until her heart rate steadied to shrug it back into place. Then, after a quick glance at Fiona, to be sure the other woman hadn't noticed anything amiss, Liss went to work on the duct tape covering her mouth. She didn't dare rip it off for fear that the sound would alert Fiona. Instead, inch by painful inch, she tugged it loose.

Beth, wedged into the opposite corner of the backseat, watched Liss with an awed expression in her dark eyes. After a moment, she started picking at her own duct-tape gag, wincing each time a section released its grip on her skin.

The downpour they were driving through helped hide their efforts. More than once, the rain thudding down on the roof of the car masked a small sound of pain, and the wet road conditions continued to command Fiona's full attention.

As soon as Beth freed her mouth, she opened it to speak. Liss's warning shake of the head stopped her. Even a whisper might reach Fiona's ears, in spite of the storm. Deprived of the means to explain what she was up to, Beth wriggled around on the seat until she could reach the right-side pocket of her jeans. She tried to wedge her hands into it but, bound together as they were, her wrists couldn't twist far enough.

Puzzled, Liss watched the girl's efforts while she finished removing her own gag. After she'd verified that they were unobserved—Fiona was watching the road and not her prisoners—she scooted toward Beth. She had a better angle of attack, although the maneuver was still awkward. It required several minutes of fumbling before she succeeded in tugging a Ziplock bag out of Beth's pocket. At first she had no idea what it contained. Then, slowly, comprehension dawned.

Fiona hit another pothole, nearly dumping Liss onto the floor, but she was smiling when she righted herself. She hadn't lost her grip on the Ziplock bag.

Patience, she warned herself. She mustn't do anything while the car was moving. The risk was too great that Beth would be hurt, or even killed. So they'd wait.

Fiona had said she'd let them out near the border. Maybe she would, but Liss wasn't going to count on it. What were two more murders when she'd already committed one? They needed an advantage, and the element of surprise, and Beth had just given her the key to both.

Biding her time, she slid her feet back into her boots and started working on the duct tape that bound Beth's hands. Once she'd freed the girl—which she quickly realized was not going to be as easy as getting rid of the gags—Beth could return the favor.

She was still working on the tape when the rain abruptly ceased. The sun peeked out from behind the clouds, revealing a misty landscape. Liss didn't recognize their surroundings. She had no idea how much farther they'd have to drive to reach the border.

It seemed as if they'd been in this car forever, but she supposed as little as half an hour might have passed. She was just thinking that it could be a long while yet before she had the chance to take action, when a fully loaded pulp truck came roaring around a bend in the road.

Startled, Fiona jerked the wheel too far to the right, ending up on the shoulder. She tried to steer the car back onto the pavement once the truck had gone past, but the ground was too soft. Her tires sank into mud and the vehicle fishtailed. She hit the brakes—harder than she should have—and the next thing Liss knew, they were facing the way they'd come.

She squeezed her eyes shut, expecting at any moment to crash into a tree, but after a sickening drop as the rear tires went down an embankment, the car came to a stop without hitting anything.

Fiona swore loudly and inventively, but she did not waste long venting her frustration. She scrambled out of the driver's seat—a tricky proposition when the front of the car was sticking up in the air—and jerked open the back door.

"You're going to have to get out and push," she said, grabbing hold of Liss.

Fighting a wave of pain and nausea when she put weight on her bad knee—the consequence of that loud pop, she presumed—Liss staggered to the side of the road. The poncho covered her to midthigh. Fiona couldn't tell that her hands were no longer bound behind her and she didn't seem to notice that both of her prisoners had rid themselves of the duct tape that had once covered their mouths.

It was time to follow the plan. She had to incapacitate Fiona so she and Beth could take off running. She told herself that her knee would hold up. It would have to.

While Fiona was occupied with hauling Beth out of the car, Liss worked open the Ziplock on the plastic bag. She flexed her leg, and was relieved to discover that it didn't hurt as much as it had at first. Then she waited. Beth, her hands held close to her rain slicker so Fiona couldn't see the trailing end of duct tape, managed to put a little distance between herself and her captor. There would never be a better opportunity.

"Run, Beth!" Liss shouted, and rushed Fiona.

Fiona turned, the knife clutched in her hand. Liss dodged to one side, at the same time thrusting the clump of cat fur she'd removed from Beth's Ziplock bag directly into Fiona's face.

The result was all she'd hoped for. Fiona started to sneeze and couldn't stop. Her eyes teared, blinding her. Liss followed up with another thrust. Who would have imagined that a wad of Lumpkin's fur, saved from a brushing to stuff a kid's pillow, would make such an effective weapon? This time, Fiona dropped the knife.

Beth, watching from the edge of the trees that lined

the road, came running back. She retrieved the knife and sliced through the duct tape that bound Liss's wrists. After another pass with the cat fur, Liss returned the favor.

Fiona, eyes red, nose running, was still sneezing uncontrollably when Dan's truck pulled up behind the rental car.

Sherri's pickup was right behind him.

Followed by the company bus.

And Sandy and Zara in Aunt Margaret's station wagon.

Stewart bounded out of the bus, rope in hand, and had Fiona trussed up like a Christmas turkey before she had time to recover from the allergy attack. Grinning, he bent down to examine the clumps of cat fur that now lay scattered on the ground.

Liss expected a bad pun. Instead, he pronounced Fiona's fate "poetic justice" and hauled his prisoner to her feet just as Gordon Tandy arrived in the county sheriff's cruiser driven by Pete Campbell.

Gordon surveyed the scene, his usual stony expression absent as he took in the extraordinary number of people milling about. For once he seemed at a loss for words.

Liss was not. "How did you all get here?" she asked, directing her question to Sherri.

"Everyone followed Dan."

"None of us knew where we were going," Ray chimed in, "but we knew something was up."

"I saw her leave with you," Dan said. "Took me a little while to figure out exactly what I'd seen, but with Stewart's help, I realized Fiona had to be the one who killed Victor."

Amid gasps and exclamations from members of *Strathspey*, Gordon's gaze briefly zeroed in on Liss. She thought she saw a flash of relief in his dark eyes, but it was quickly masked. "Do you have proof?" he asked Dan.

"You can arrest Fiona for kidnapping," Liss said. "That should give you time to prove she also murdered Victor."

He nodded. "Shouldn't take long. As it happens, we've already got a pretty good case against her. We've been following the money trail. In fact, I was on my way to Moosetookalook to ask Ms. Carlson a few questions when Ruskin called for help."

Liss glanced at Dan, a question in her eyes.

He shrugged. "I didn't know I'd have the cavalry at my back. Figured I'd better call in the big guns."

Sandy, leaning against the side of the bus, cane in the crook of his arm, said in a cheerful voice: "Capture the villain, rescue the fair lady—all in a day's work."

"Beth and I rescued ourselves," Liss reminded him.

Zara had taken charge of the girl. She was applying first aid cream to the small nick the knife had made in Beth's neck and to the places where the duct tape had left red marks on her skin.

Gordon lifted a hand to touch a similar mark on Liss's cheek. "I thought I warned you not to meddle."

"I didn't. Honestly, I didn't do anything but go next door to tell Fiona I wasn't really interested in Victor's job. But one thing led to another and all of a sudden I realized that she was the one who'd killed him." Liss dropped her gaze, hating to admit the next part. "It took me by surprise, and she just . . . knew. She saw my face, and she knew I knew, and she lost it."

"You shouldn't be allowed out without a leash," Dan muttered.

"I heard that."

"I meant you to."

Gordon met Dan's gaze over Liss's head. "See that she gets back home, will you? I need to take charge of the prisoner."

Although Liss was tempted to tell them she'd rather take the bus, she meekly let herself be led to Dan's truck. Just at that moment, it didn't feel so bad to have two overprotective males looking after her.

The *Strathspey* bus left on schedule Monday morning with twenty-nine people onboard. With remarkable efficiency, Zara had stepped into the void. As the new acting manager, she'd persuaded Lee Annie not to leave the company just yet. That she'd hired Sarah to take Fiona's place had a good deal to do with Lee Annie's change of heart. Ray had been surprised but not devastated to learn that they were a couple.

Liss stood outside in the warm March sun, waving and calling farewells to her friends. Beth was next to her, doing likewise. Angie, once she'd recovered from the shock of hearing about her daughter's narrow escape, had not had the heart to deny Beth's request to say good-bye to Zara.

When the bus had gone, Liss felt bereft. She barely noticed when Angie left to take Beth, only a little tardy, to school.

Was it too late to change her mind? To go with them?

Of course it was!

Shaking her head at her own foolishness, Liss went back inside the house. She was only limping a little.

Lumpkin was waiting for her in the foyer.

"Obviously, I couldn't abandon you." She scooped

him up, all fifteen pounds of homegrown Maine coon cat, and buried her face in his fur. "I owe you big time, you hairy monster, you."

He tolerated the display of affection.

"Don't you worry about me leaving," she told him. "Moosetookalook is home now. In fact, I have a few new ideas for the Emporium, thanks to that visit I made to Waycross Springs, and a couple more that Dan should consider for The Spruces, too."

She thought about Dan, and about Gordon, as she carried the cat out to the kitchen, setting him down on the floor so she could rummage in a cupboard for the container of cat treats. Gordon Tandy had left her with the distinct impression that he would be calling on her again, and not in a professional capacity.

"Well, why not?" she asked aloud. "I've decided to settle down and stay put, but that doesn't mean I have to rush into a commitment to any one man. In fact, I think I like the idea of having two attentive males in my life!"

Lumpkin butted her so hard that she had to take a step to keep her balance. Purring loudly, he began to rub himself against her legs.

"Obviously, I misspoke," Liss told him as she handed over the cat treat. "I meant to say *three* attentive males."

*'Tis the season to be jolly, but in Moose-
tookalook, Maine, Christmas cheer is in short supply
due to a snowless winter that's keeping skiers and
shoppers at a distance. Fortunately, Liss MacCrimmon of the Scottish Emporium has a plan . . .*

Liss's brainstorm focuses on Tiny Teddies, the new
hot toy of the season. Every store across the country
is out of stock—except a few wee establishments in
good ol' Moosetookalook. It's easy enough to drum
up approval for the idea of luring consumers to town
and keeping them there with a stockingful of New
England holiday charm. Liss's real challenge lies in
contending with bickering businesspeople and—once
America learns of Moosetookalook's Tiny Teddy
cache—doggedly determined shopaholics.

The first sign of something amiss occurs when the
last Tiny Teddy is summarily executed: shot through
the heart in the display window of greedy toy store
owner Gavin Thorne. But the Teddy's demise is just
a precursor toe the eerily similar murder of Gavin
himself . . .

The two men in Liss's life want her far from the
case, but she can't help feeling guilty for starting the
fur frenzy that seems to have led to Gavin's death. Besides, how can she ignore the lengthy list of suspects,
not the least of whom include Gavin's vindictive ex-
wife, an unscrupulous selectman, a ski shop owner
with an axe to grind, and a rabid toy collector packing heat in her purse?

Now, with the Twelve (or, in Scots terms, the Daft)
Days of Christmas rapidly approaching, Liss has a
plate full of things worse than haggis to contend with,

starting with a stockroom packed with poultry (don't ask), and ending with a killer who'd like to see Liss's goose well and fully cooked . .

**Please turn the page for an exciting sneak peek of
A WEE CHRISTMAS HOMICIDE
coming in October 2009!**

Chapter One

Banners reading HAVE A JOYOUS YULETIDE, MERRY NOLLAIG BEAG, and HAPPY HOGMANAY decorated the interior of Moosetookalook Scottish Emporium. A box of Yule candles sat next to Liss MacCrimmon's day-by-day calendar on the sales counter. It was open to the current page—Tuesday, the ninth of December.

As Liss wielded a feather duster and rearranged stock, a snippet of an old Christmas carol lodged in her mind and stuck there. *Christmas was coming. The geese were getting fat.* Or at least Liss supposed they were, not being acquainted with any personally. But with sales virtually nonexistent, she had a scant supply of pennies to put in *the poor man's hat.*

Or was it the *old* man's hat?

Liss never could remember the exact lyrics. She wasn't much of a singer, either. Alone in the shop, she contented herself with humming the melody aloud. Even that small musical effort was off-key, but not far enough to silence her.

A glance through the plate-glass display window at the front of the store revealed the same bare, unappealing landscape she'd seen every other time she'd looked. Skeletal branches reached up into an impossibly blue sky, starkly silhouetted against that cloudless backdrop. On the ground, patches of dead, yellow-brown grass alternated with piles of rotting leaves, pummeled by hard rains into shapeless, colorless lumps of vegetation. The vivid hues that had brought tourists flocking to Maine in the fall were only a distant memory.

Bright morning sun made the scene even more depressing. Still no snow. How could it *not* snow in Maine in December?

"Think snow," Liss muttered to herself. "I ought to put *that* on a banner."

People had a right to see the white stuff on the ground by now. Skiers expected to be able to take their first outing of the season during Christmas vacation, if not before. Even more important, the residents of Carrabassett County needed tourists to show up and spend money on lift tickets, lodging, food, and gifts. Without that regular influx of business, everybody suffered, especially the tiny town of Moosetookalook.

With a sigh, Liss turned away from the window. Wishing wouldn't make it snow, not even if she had Aladdin's lamp and a genie at her beck and call. What a pity that neither magic nor science could accurately predict the weather, let alone control it.

After retying the bright red scarf holding her long, dark brown hair away from her face, Liss busied herself straightening the display next to a sign that read KILT-HOSE STUFFERS. To Liss's mind kilt hose—or knee socks, as those not into Scottish-American heritage in a big way would call them—made ideal Christmas stockings. She'd gathered together an eclectic assortment of items that might be tucked into the toe or made to cascade enticingly over the top. There were pennywhistles and small figurines of pipers, refrigerator magnets and campaign buttons bearing pseudo-

Scottish sayings and puns, and the cutest little stuffed bears Liss had ever seen, all dressed up in kilts and plaids and wearing minuscule Balmoral caps. Liss had dubbed the four-inch high toys "Wee Scottish Bears" in the online catalogue she'd set up for the store.

The display table in order, Liss turned next to the tall shelves that held a variety of Scottish imports, everything from tins of Black Bun, the traditional Twelfth Night cake made with fruit, almonds, spices, and whiskey—*lots* of whiskey—to canned haggis. She had no trouble dusting the upper reaches. She stood five-foot-nine in her stocking feet.

Fourteen shopping days till Christmas, Liss thought as she worked. There was time yet to make a profit. If she started opening on Sundays, then it would be sixteen shopping days. She already planned to extend the shop's hours by adding the two Mondays before Christmas. The rest of the year she took that day off to compensate for working Saturdays. Would it be worth the effort, and the expense, to staff the store *seven* days a week?

The loss of her part-time sales clerk, Sherri Willett, had made scheduling more difficult. At the moment, Liss was not only half owner of the Emporium, but the store's only employee. To leave the shop for any reason, she had to lock up and put the CLOSED sign in the window.

Still, the extra hours might pay off. There was always the chance of a stray shopper wandering in. Liss sighed again. She should give it a shot. After all, she'd already calculated expenses down to the last decimal point. It wouldn't cost all that much more to keep the heat at sixty-eight degrees for those extra days.

The raucous jangle of the sleigh bells she'd attached to the door had Liss smiling in anticipation. A customer at last!

Her spirits plummeted when she recognized Gavin Thorne. Like Liss, he owned a store that faced Moosetookalook's town square. Several months earlier he'd bought the building that had once housed Alden's Small Appliance Repair and opened The Toy Box.

"Don't you look the fine Scottish lassie!" Thorne had a big, booming voice and a smile that showed a great many large white teeth. Both were in marked contrast to a milquetoast appearance.

Liss glanced down at the white peasant blouse and tartan miniskirt she'd selected from the store's stock that morning and was suddenly glad she'd put on wooly dancer's tights beneath the skirt. She did not know Gavin Thorne well, but the last thing she needed was for *another* man to take an interest in her. Juggling the two she already had was hard enough!

"You know the store policy," she quipped. "Model what we sell."

"When am I finally going to meet this aunt of yours?" he asked as he made his way slowly through the shop. He paused to look at several of the displays, including the one of kilt-hose stuffers.

"She's arriving on the nineteenth."

A sudden thought had Liss taking a closer look at Thorne. She saw a lumpy individual with hair the color of dry grass and eyes hidden behind small, round-framed glasses. Liss wasn't sure how old the toy store owner was, but he was surely closer to Aunt Margaret's age—fifty-nine—than her own twenty-eight years. Could Thorne have a *personal* reason for asking about her aunt?

He approached the sales counter with one of the "Wee Scottish Bears" in hand. "These selling well for you?"

"They do okay," Liss fibbed.

She'd sold only one, to Sherri as a present for her young son. She'd expected to sell another to Angie Hogencamp, who owned the bookstore on the other side of the town square and had a small collection of designer teddy bears that her children were not allowed to touch, but Angie had taken one look at the stuffed toys and given a disdainful sniff.

"Maybe they'd do better at my place." Thorne's watery blue eyes looked straight at Liss, but only for an instant. The speed with which his gaze skittered away from hers set off an alarm of air-raid-siren intensity. "I could take them off your hands if you're willing to sell them to me at dealer discount."

Liss's suspicion that he was trying to pull a fast one hardened into a certainty. The standard discount businesses gave one another didn't leave much room for resale profit. The little bears were cute, but their suggested retail price was only $9.99.

"I don't want to mess up the display." Liss waited, curious to hear what he'd say next.

Thorne fiddled with the bear, smoothing one broad thumb over its tiny kilt and tugging at the itty-bitty hat to make sure it was securely attached. He inspected the minuscule manufacturer's tag, which identified the company that had produced and distributed the toy.

"I don't suppose you have any more of these in your stockroom?" He glanced toward the closed door to the area where Liss processed mail orders and unpacked deliveries. "Some you haven't put out yet."

"A few." In fact, Liss had been so taken with their Scottish regalia that she'd bought an entire case—an even hundred of the little bears.

"Well. Well, that's good then." All sorts of nervous twitches suddenly manifested themselves, from the traditional shuffling of feet and playing with rings to an odd little gesture unique to Thorne—he rubbed his knuckles back and forth over the underside of his chin. "I don't suppose—?"

"No." Liss injected every bit of firmness she could manage into her voice. "The way I see it, you hardly need one more toy in a store that already offers hundreds of selections, whereas these little guys fit in perfectly with the other items the Emporium sells." Liss leaned across the sales counter until she was almost nose to nose with the shorter man. She plucked the stuffed bear out of Thorne's hand and tried to recapture his gaze. "What's this *really* about?"

"Nothing. Not a thing. Just making conversation. Well, gotta go now. Bye." Backpedaling, literally and figuratively, the toy seller beat a hasty retreat.

Something landed on the Emporium's hardwood floor with a soft plop just as the door slammed behind Gavin Thorne. As soon as the sleigh bells had stopped their racket, Liss came out from behind the counter to investigate.

He had dropped a folded section of a newspaper. It had been sticking out of the pocket of his jacket, Liss realized, and had been knocked free when he bumped into the door frame in his rush to get away. She picked it up, glancing at the date. When she saw it was from the previous weekend's Boston paper, she started to toss it into the trash. A headline caught her eye as it fell, and she quickly snatched it out again.

TINY TEDDIES IN SHORT SUPPLY.

Heart rate speeding up as she read, Liss skimmed the article. Then she took a good hard look at the small bear she still held in her other hand.

Liss carried the newspaper to the section of the store her aunt had dubbed the cozy corner. It was furnished with two easy chairs and a coffee table. She settled into the more comfortable of the chairs, curling her legs beneath her. Then she slowly reread every word of the story. There was no mistake. "Tiny Teddies," the proper name for her "Wee Scottish Bears," were the hot gift item this Christmas . . . and they were sold out in much of the U.S. The reporter who'd written the article believed there were no longer any to be had in the six New England states.

"Holy cow," Liss whispered. If this was for real, she was sitting on a gold mine.

Across the town square from Moosetookalook Scottish Emporium, an imposing red brick building housed the town office, the public library, the fire department, and the police station. Sherri Willett, wearing a stiffly starched blue uniform that sported a shiny new badge above the breast pocket, was the sole occupant of the three small rooms that comprised the latter.

Once she'd caught up on all the outstanding paperwork, she had nothing in particular to do. In fact, she'd been ordered to do nothing unless someone actually asked her for help. Jeff Thibodeau, who'd been promoted to chief of police just before Sherri was hired, had explained that the town budget didn't extend to extra gas money. They were not to use their one patrol car to go out looking for trouble.

Never good at twiddling her thumbs, Sherri wandered into the reception area. The police department had never employed a receptionist. Three full-time officers and a handful of part-timers handled everything. The door straight ahead of her led, by way of a short hall, to the town office and the bays for the fire trucks. Another, to her right, opened directly onto the parking lot at the rear of the building.

Sherri straightened a row of uncomfortable-looking plastic chairs, then wondered why she'd bothered.

There was no other furniture in this outer room. No plants. No magazines. Just a scuffed-up tile floor and a cobweb hanging undisturbed in one corner of the ceiling.

Retreating back into the office, recognizable as such only because it contained two battered army-surplus-style desks and an equally antiquated metal file cabinet, Sherri headed for the coffeepot. The glass was so streaked and spotted that it was difficult to tell what color the contents were, but what landed in Sherri's cup had the consistency of sludge. She shuddered when she inspected the grounds.

Carrying the whole mess to the communal kitchen down the hall, she scrubbed the coffeepot and basket, then returned to the P.D. to collect all the mugs and cups scattered about and toss them into the suds. She hoped she wasn't setting a bad precedent. She might be Moosetookalook's only female police officer, but neither making coffee nor cleaning house was part of her job description.

She'd made that very clear to her coworkers when she'd started her last job and there had never been any trouble. Until recently, she'd been a corrections officer, dispatcher, and deputy—the three jobs were all one in rural Carrabassett County. She'd worked at the county jail, appointed by and responsible to the sheriff.

Sometimes she regretted leaving the sheriff's office for the police department, but not when she opened her pay envelope. The town fathers of Moosetookalook might be frugal, but they were nowhere near as miserly as the county commissioners.

While a fresh pot of coffee brewed, Sherri resumed rambling. She stopped on the brink of entering the tiny holding cell in the P.D.'s closet-size third room. It probably *had* been a closet at one time, since it could only be reached through the office.

"What were you planning to do?" she muttered to herself. "Dust?"

Reversing course, she flung herself into the over-size chair behind one of the two desks in the larger room. The seat, which bore the permanent imprint of Jeff Thibodeau's posterior, seemed to swallow her whole.

This was not what she'd expected. Oh, sure, she'd always known police work was 99 percent boredom and 1 percent sheer panic, but—

The shrill ring of the phone at her elbow startled her so badly that she let out a small squeak of alarm. Embarrassed, she cleared her throat as she reached for the receiver and put all the authority she could muster into her voice.

"Moosetookalook Police Department. Officer Willett speaking."

Ten minutes later, Sherri strolled into Moose-tookalook Scottish Emporium. Although Liss hadn't made a lick of sense on the phone, Sherri was relatively certain there was no crime in progress at the shop. Curiosity, rather than concern for her friend's safety, had convinced her to forward all incoming calls to the P.D. to her cell phone and venture out on "foot patrol."

It took another ten minutes for Liss to bring Sherri up to speed. She recounted Gavin Thorne's visit and its outcome, stopping now and again to answer Sherri's questions.

"So you *do* have more of these Tiny Teddies?"

"Almost a hundred of them. And Marcia bought some too."

"Why?"

"I liked the little kilts. I figured I'd corner the market on kilted teddy bears. I never expected—"

"No, I mean why does Marcia have Tiny Teddies? She runs a consignment shop. Second Time Around stocks mostly clothing."

"She bought hers for decoration. They're dressed like Santa's elves. From what I can gather—I did some checking on the Internet—the company that makes Tiny Teddies only manufactures a limited number wearing any particular costume. That makes all the varieties more collectible."

Sherri nodded. Now that she thought about it, she'd noticed that the Tiny Teddies in the display window of The Toy Box, Gavin Thorne's store, all wore different outfits. "So Tiny Teddies come in many varieties, in all sorts of get-ups. They're considered collectibles by adults as well as being toys for kids. And if you really have cornered the market on teddies in kilts, you can name your own price. But if this is such a hot item, why haven't buyers already found your supply? You put the bears in the online catalog at the Emporium's Web site, right?"

"Yes, but I didn't call them Tiny Teddies."

"So update the description."

"I've had a better idea." Liss's changeable blue-green eyes gleamed with barely suppressed excitement. "We make the buyers come here. This could be just what Moosetookalook needs. There isn't much time, but we do still have more than two weeks until Christmas. I've been making lists."

"Of course you have." Liss always made lists.

"First I have to talk to Marcia. Then to Gavin Thorne. And then we need to bring the whole town in on this." Liss turned the OPEN sign to CLOSED, grabbed her bright green coat off the rack by the door and led the way back outside.

A blast of cold air hit Sherri as soon as they left the Emporium. She looked hopefully at the sky, but there wasn't a cloud in sight.

They hurried past Stu's Ski Shop with its life-size skier on the roof of the porch and dashed across the intersection of Pine and Birch Streets. Marcia and her husband had bought the corner house a few years back. In common with most of the old Victorians that surrounded the town square, the downstairs portion had been converted for use as a business while the upstairs rooms had been turned into an apartment. Marcia lived there alone now. Almost a year ago, apparently in the throes of a midlife crisis, Cabot Katz had decamped. Sherri had no idea where he'd gone, but several months later, Marcia had dropped the name Katz and gone back to being Marcia Milliken.

A small bell above the door tinkled merrily and more melodiously than the one at the Emporium. Once inside the consignment shop, Liss waited a moment, then called out a greeting: "Anybody home?"

"Hang on a sec!" The sound of a disembodied voice was followed by a flush. Sherri and Liss exchanged a rueful grin. When you owned a small shop there was rarely anyone available to cover for you when you needed to use the facilities.

Marcia emerged through a door behind the small desk she used as a sales counter. She was a tall, angular woman in her forties with a pale complexion and wheat-colored hair. Unlike Liss, she did not wear her store's stock. She was comfortably dressed in well-worn jeans and a cable-knit sweater. She needed the latter. Marcia kept the temperature in her building at a frugal sixty-two degrees.

"Liss. Sherri. Hi. What brings you out on this nippy morning?"

"Have you seen this?" Liss thrust the newspaper at her.

Marcia's eyes widened as she read. "Those dumb little bears? Get out of here!"

"How many do you have?"

"Two dozen. I didn't buy them to sell. I'm using them for Christmas decorations."

Liss started to explain her plan but Marcia didn't let her get very far.

"eBay."

"What?"

"Online auction. That's the best way to sell them. Put the bears up one at a time. Set a nice high minimum bid for each one."

If this were a cartoon, Sherri thought, the artist would draw dollar signs in place of Marcia's eyes.

Liss looked horrified. "You can't do that!"

"Why not?"

"Because we have a chance to do something good for this whole town. Gavin Thorne has some of these Tiny Teddies, too. We need to go talk to him. If we work together, I know we can pull this off."

Marcia looked doubtful. "Are you sure you want to deal with Thorne? I can't say as I like him much. I stopped by to welcome him to town when he first opened The Toy Box and he gave me such a chilly reception that I haven't been back since."

"He's recently divorced," Sherri put in. "That tends to make folks sour." She gave herself a mental kick when she realized Marcia might take that comment personally, but the consignment shop owner simply nodded in agreement.

"He and his wife had a toy store in Fallstown," Marcia said. "The wife got the building. Thorne got the contents."

Sherri tried to think if she'd heard anything else about Gavin Thorne, but the local grapevine had been remarkably quiet on the subject.

"He did join the Moosetookalook Small Business Association," Liss said, "but he hasn't been to any meetings." Quickly and concisely, she filled Marcia in on Thorne's visit to the Emporium.

"He tried to con you and you still want to work with him?" Marcia's outrage showed plainly on her long, thin face.

The show of temper surprised Sherri. Until now, Marcia had never struck her as one of those people with a short fuse. Then again, she didn't know the woman well. Marcia was a relative newcomer to Moosetookalook. She hadn't grown up in the village, as Sherri and Liss had.

"It couldn't hurt to talk to Thorne," Liss insisted. "For one thing , he's the closest thing we have to a local expert on toys."

A short time later, Marcia in tow, Sherri and Liss retraced their steps past Stu's Ski shop and the Emporium. They passed Liss's house—one of only two surrounding the square that was still used exclusively as a residence—and turned onto Ash Street. The Toy Box was located in the center of that short block, between the post office and Preston's Mortuary.

Thorne's shop had no bell over the entrance. The door closed, however, with a resounding thunk that echoed in every corner of the small store.

"With you in a minute," Thorne bellowed from behind a sales counter built so high that a child would have to reach above his head to pay for a purchase. It was also an awkward height for Sherri, whose friends universally described her as a petite blonde. It hit the taller Liss squarely at bosom-level.

The minute stretched into several. Sherri and Marcia wandered off to inspect the shop's offerings, leaving Liss to inch closer to its surly proprietor.

Keeping her six-year-old son's belief in Santa Claus in mind, Sherri browsed. Thorne had a great selection of action figures and shelves filled with board games and jigsaw puzzles, but the store seemed a trifle thin on miniature trucks and cars. Video games took up another significant section of shelving. So did toys for very young children. In a far corner she came upon two Tiny Teddies, one dressed as a ballerina, the other as a clown.

Marcia joined her there. "There are ten more on a table on the other side of the shop. All different."

As one, they headed for the front of the store, arriving just in time to see Liss go up on her toes to prop her elbows on the polished wooden surface of the sales counter in order to thrust her face into Thorne's peripheral vision. He gave a start and looked up from his computer screen with a glower.

"We need to talk," Liss said. When he stood, she stepped back and held out the newspaper.

Thorne leaned over the sales counter, his expression still thunderous. The floor on his side was a good foot higher than the area where Liss stood, so that he loomed over her. Nobody, not Liss or Marcia and Sherri, who had formed ranks behind Liss, was impressed.

Thorne did a double take at the sight of Sherri's uniform. "You planning to arrest me?"

His sneer faded when she just stared at him, her gaze level and no hint of a smile on her face. Holding her head at that awkward angle was giving her a kink in her neck—another black mark against the surly toy seller.

"Come out of there!" Liss snapped the command in a no-nonsense voice.

Thorne blinked hard behind his Harry Potter glasses and obeyed, descending the two little steps from the office area. He led them to a small seating area at the back corner of the store. Small was the operative word, since the chairs were designed for children. While Thorne leaned against the wall, Marcia dropped into a beanbag chair, joking that she'd probably need a forklift to get her up again. Sherri was small enough to ease into one of the child-size rockers but she still had to stretch her legs out in front of her to avoid a collision between knees and chest. Following Thorne's example, Liss opted to remain on her feet.

"How many Tiny Teddies you have?" she asked him.

"Two crates. Mixed."

"Two *hundred?*"

Sherri felt a slow grin spread across her face.

"It looks as though the three of us may have the only supply of Tiny Teddies in New England. There are people everywhere who want them. If we work together, we all increase our profits." Liss rubbed her fingers together in the universal gesture for money.

"What do you have in mind?" Thorne's aggression had vanished. He looked harmless again, even amiable, a short, middle-aged man with a sagging midsection and weak eyesight.

"We make the customers come to us. That way the whole town benefits."

Thorne looked skeptical, but he kept listening.

Liss took out the lists she'd tucked into her coat pocket and ticked off each point in turn. "One: get hold of the rest of the members of the Moosetookalook Small Business Association and tell them what's going on. Two: attend the board of selectmen's next meeting, which just happens to be scheduled for tonight. Both groups are a potential source of seed money. The selectmen know business has been slow, even with the boost Moosetookalook got when the hotel reopened last summer. So, when we ask for assistance to get the word out about our supply of Tiny Teddies—the financial wherewithal to run ads—I think they'll go along with our request."

"Newspaper, television, or radio?" Thorne asked.

"All three if we can swing it. The thing is, we want to do more than just attract customers to our own stores. We want to encourage shoppers to stick around long enough to spend money at all the local businesses. It's short notice, but I think I can pull together a Christmas pageant—I've been thinking of it as The Twelve Shopping Days of Christmas." She gave a self-conscious little laugh. "Maybe we could be a tad more subtle than that, so any suggestions for alternate names are welcome."

Sherri repressed a snort of laughter. Subtlety was not Liss's strong suit, but Sherri had to give her friend credit for ingenuity. As Liss expanded on her idea—twelve days of special ceremonies, one for each stanza in the Christmas carol, culminating in a pageant on the last day that included them all—she could see how the events might encourage tourists to come to town.

"I can find the ten ladies to dance and the eleven pipers," Liss said, "but I may need some help recruiting leaping lords and milkmaids. And drummers. We'll need twelve of them."

"Try the high school," Sherri suggested. "Convince one of the teachers to offer extra credit to those who participate."

"When will you hold the final pageant?" Thorne asked. Whatever his earlier reservations, he sounded as if he'd now come around to Liss's way of thinking. Although he still propped up the back wall of his shop, his stance had changed from studied indifference to rapt attention.

"If we call Saturday the first day of Christmas, then the twelfth day will fall on Christmas Eve." Liss frowned. "That's wrong, of course. Twelfth Night is actually *after* Christmas, but since celebrations in the U. S. center on the twenty-fifth of December, we'll just have to take a little poetic license. I—"

"Christmas Eve is too late," Thorne cut in. "You need to schedule things so that the final pageant falls on the weekend *before* Christmas."

Liss's face fell as she mentally subtracted days. "That would mean we'd have to have to hold the first day's ceremony tomorrow!"

"Partridge in a pear tree, right?" Marcia asked.

At Liss's nod, Marcia gave a dismissive shrug.

"No big deal if people miss that one. Or the next six, either." She ticked them off on her fingers. "Two doves, three hens, four calling birds, five gold rings, six swans, and seven geese. All poultry except for the rings, Liss—and boring! Until you start counting people, there won't be anything interesting to see."

"Okay. Okay, you're right. But on the twelfth day we can make a terrific spectacle out of all of them." Her enthusiasm only momentarily dimmed, she rummaged in another pocket for a pencil and started making notes on the back of one of her lists. "We'll put a pear tree up in the town square next to the municipal Christmas tree. I know a taxidermist who can supply a stuffed partridge. Jump ahead to—"

"Jump ahead to customers arriving in droves to

spend money," Thorne interrupted, "and to the prices
we're going to charge. People will pay a heck of a
lot more than ten bucks for these babies now."

Liss looked as if she wanted to object, but held
her tongue when she saw Marcia's eyes light up.

After Thorne and Marcia had agreed to attend the
selectmen's meeting that evening with her, Liss and
Sherri left the two of them engrossed in a discussion
of the best wording for their ads.

"Time to get back to the P.D.," Sherri said. "You
won't need my help dealing with the MSBA. You've
already got an in with the top man." Dan Ruskin,
newly elected as president by the other small businesspeople in town, was one of the two men Liss had
been dating since she'd returned to Moosetookalook
seventeen months earlier.

Sherri started to cross the square, then paused to
look back over her shoulder. "By the way—thanks,
Liss."

"For?"

"Salvaging my morning. I was bored to tears." She
grinned. "And if this plan of yours actually works, it
will also be thanks for all the overtime I'm going to
earn working crowd control."